silent altitudes

Valentina looked at her for a moment. "Why me? I don't understand."

"Say yes, and one day you will," Katherine said, "but if not, you'll be on your own once you graduate from this school. The choice is yours."

tried to generate the field in one place, the power requirement would be infinite because there would be no boundary. A good way to picture it would be like trying to fill a glass of water without the glass. One of my research assistants completed her doctoral work on the interaction of the field with the earth's varied surfaces. Her model will allow us to account for the properties of the terrain and topography so that the field is propagated completely and charged uniformly."

"What is this going to cost?" someone in the crowd asked.

"What could go wrong?" another shouted.

"Well," Milford said, "not much. Going wrong, I mean. I don't know the cost."

The audience looked up as part of the fabric covering of the stage pavilion tore from its frame and flapped in the breeze. The secretary-general leaned toward the microphones and put an arm around Milford's shoulder as the sheet of white canvas blew behind them. "Thank you all for your questions, and thank you again, Dr. Pennychuck. I think we need to wrap this up. There is much work to be done, and I have no doubt we'll be hearing more from you soon."

The two men shook hands and posed for the photographers for several minutes before stepping down from the platform to go their separate ways and mingle with the audience. Milford smiled when he spotted a young woman working her way through the crowd toward him.

"You did great! Congratulations!" Dr. Laura Pottersmith gave Milford a quick hug. Laura was in her mid-thirties, slender, with blonde hair, blue eyes, and a cheerful smile.

"Laura"—Milford beamed—"I didn't know you were planning to be here. That was awful. I couldn't concentrate. I don't think anyone even listened to what I had to say."

"No." Laura shook her head. "The wind was a distraction, but I think you explained the plan well. I had a feeling they were going to pick your proposal."

"Our proposal," he said. "I would still be working on the theory today if you hadn't made such a crucial contribution." Milford pushed his fingers across his eyebrows and then sighed. "Laura, my nerves are frazzled. It's so good to see a familiar face. I'm glad you're here."

"Dr. Pennychuck," a woman called as she approached.

Milford's nerves resumed their uncomfortable buzzing. "Oh. Hello, Katherine."

Katherine Morgreed shook his hand. "I must congratulate you. Obviously, I'm pleased they chose your proposal."

"Thank you. Um, Katherine, this is Dr. Laura Pottersmith, my former research assistant. Laura, this is Katherine Morgreed, head of Morgreed Industries."

"I see," Katherine said, offering a brief handshake and a cursory glance in Laura's direction. "I have dinner reservations. Perhaps you'd like to join me. You can bring your friend."

"Laura?" Milford hoped she would accept. He didn't relish the prospect of dining alone with Katherine. She'd never made for pleasant company.

Laura shrugged. "Sure. Craig took the girls camping for the weekend, but I don't want to impose."

"Not at all," Milford said, right as someone screamed from the stage area. The entire pavilion collapsed, and the remaining connections of the fabric cover ripped, allowing it to blow away.

"Whoa," Milford said. "Was anyone still on the stage?"

"Probably not," Katherine said. "I can't say for sure."

CHAPTER 3

Dr. Laura Pottersmith stood on the summit of Mount Washington, breathing in the cool alpine air and admiring the view. She was glad to step out of the visitor center, a long concrete-and-glass building operated by New Hampshire State Parks, with the Mount Washington Observatory housed in the western portion. She waved to a staff member checking the weather instruments on the observatory tower. Her phone rang.

"Hello?"

There was no answer.

"Hello?" Laura checked the display, realizing too late who was calling.

"Mom!" Two sweaty bodies pressed into her from behind and hugged her.

"Summer, Autumn," Laura said, turning to face her daughters. They were identical twins, twenty years old, and growing up too fast, as far as she was concerned. "Didn't I ask you not to do that again? You're going to give me a heart attack."

"Sorry," Autumn said, "but it's fun, and you keep falling for it."

Laura sighed. "I know. But please, no more . . . So how was your hike?"

"Good. We came up the Ammonoosuc Ravine Trail again. It was busy this morning."

"And we ran into some friends from Dartmouth at the hut," Summer said, "but they were only going to Mount Monroe. A few of them said to say hi if we saw you. They were in your geology class last semester."

"Oh, that's nice."

Summer took off her backpack and stretched her arms and shoulders. "Can we go inside? I'm hungry."

"Sure," Laura said. It was nearly lunchtime, and the smell of food from the cafeteria was enticing.

They entered the main lounge. "Let's grab that empty table by the windows," Autumn said.

Laura led them through the maze of tourists attired in shorts and sandals who had ascended the mountain via the Auto Road or Cog Railway, privately owned routes to the summit that attracted visitors from all over the world. She dodged the sharp point of a trekking pole swung by a careless hiker donning his pack. He was one of many sweaty climbers fighting for position in the cafeteria line and crowding the tables with their gear. Laura considered the balance of respect and animosity between the two groups as she reached the table.

Summer set her bag on a chair and looked out over the White Mountains. "The visibility is great today. I haven't seen it this clear for a while."

they couldn't stop the outrage when a meeting transcript was leaked in which several less disruptive layout plans were rejected because of their impact on the properties of the wealthy.

Katherine Morgreed, head of the primary system contractor, Morgreed Industries, was quoted saying, "I don't give a (redacted) about some temple in some (redacted) backwards country. We're not building anything within fifty miles of my vacation home in Sedona." That was the same home, the media quickly pointed out, that had been built on land with protected cacti that "somehow" disappeared after her initial building permit application was denied. And that was the same Katherine Morgreed who'd had one of her corporate lawyers appointed head of the EPA through her political connections. Then that head of the EPA, Barry Calavari, had appointed Morgreed's pick to the role of Pennychuck System director. And that director, Dr. Valentina Severnaya, was the woman Milford had worked with for the last four years and would now need to call on a Sunday afternoon about this new problem on his computer screen.

He picked up his desk phone and hit the first number on speed dial. He didn't like calling Dr. Severnaya. She was all business, and maybe it was due to cultural differences that he didn't understand, but that didn't seem like a sufficient explanation for the way she made him feel. He always got the impression that she'd stab him in the back without the slightest hesitation if it suited her purposes. She wasn't even half his age, and he could only wonder how someone so young could be so cold.

"What is it, Dr. Pennychuck?" Valentina answered.

That was the other thing that made Milford uncomfortable. It was more than the accent. The way she spoke spanned an unsettling range from seductive to threatening without ever being clearly on either end. It was bad enough on the phone but far worse in person. Valentina was a knockout beauty and took full advantage of it. Milford had seen and experienced how she manipulated men and intimidated other women. He was sure something was up between her and Barry, the head of the EPA, because it was more than evident that she had him wrapped around her little finger.

"Dr. Severnaya," Milford said, "sorry to bother you, but it's important."

"It better be."

"I finished my new process model, and the results are troubling."

"How so?"

"Well, it could be nothing to worry about, but I'm seeing a slight possibility of the reaction drawing carbon particulates into new greenhouse gases under certain conditions. That's the opposite of what we need it to do."

"Explain."

"I'm guessing here, but it could have something to do with the new refrigerants that were mandated last year or the high carbon levels. You know as well as I that the IPCC has been turning a blind eye to increased pollution. Everyone assumes we'll just reverse it with the system, but we might be beyond capacity."

"How certain are you of this problem?"

"Not at all. I just saw it this afternoon. Maybe we should delay start-up until we look into this further."

"That would be premature, but I'll discuss it with Barry. In the meantime, why don't you keep working on it and we'll see how it looks later this week."

"Fair enough," Milford said, though he was interrupted by the dial tone. She did that every time they spoke on the phone, and it never failed to annoy him.

SUNDAY, JUNE 29, 3:35 P.M. ET
Private Martial Arts Studio—Arlington, Virginia
Elevation: 272 feet

Later that afternoon, Dr. Valentina Severnaya stood on the blue rubber mat of a boxing ring in a dimly lit basement near her home in Arlington, Virginia. She'd been strongly encouraged to join the clandestine Soviet-era training gym shortly after moving to the DC suburbs to assume her position at the EPA. The facility was old but well equipped, and she never had to wait for other patrons. She wasn't sure whether there even were other patrons.

Valentina's personal trainer appeared from the shadows outside the ring. He was older than her by perhaps a decade, and his massive body displayed the scars of a violent past. They never spoke of such things, but Valentina assumed the burly Russian had been in the special forces or some similarly combative occupation.

"This week we have a boxer from Murmansk," the trainer said in a thick accent as he pushed a younger man through the ropes. "He is serving thirty years for armed robbery. Age twenty-five years. Weight eighty kilos."

Valentina brought her bare fists up and studied the muscular young man. Each steady breath she drew was permeated with the familiar odors of sweat, disinfectant, and damp cinder blocks. The smell was unpleasant but strangely comforting in a way that cleared her mind of everything but the task at hand in the small square arena. She watched as the boxer approached. She always let the other fighters come to her, never giving them the slightest inkling of her speed or style. She ducked to avoid a right jab to the head and slipped past the boxer, then turned to face him again.

No one knew much about Valentina's early life. She'd been an orphan in Russia, but she excelled at her studies and received a private sponsorship to attend the Northern (Arctic) Federal University in Arkhangelsk, a cold and isolated city in the north of the country on the White Sea.

The boxer came at her, faked a left jab, then followed with a right uppercut. She dodged both and moved around him again.

After completing her doctorate, she was assigned to a position at a leading climate studies think tank in Moscow, from which she'd been recruited for the EPA role at Katherine Morgreed's direction.

The boxer stepped forward with his head low, taking a little more time to think before trying a right to Valentina's midsection. She spun to the side and dodged past him.

Valentina had come up to speed on the Pennychuck plan and become familiar with the professor's models and research. She also worked closely with Morgreed, often changing contracts and specifications in ways that benefited Katherine's corporation. If she needed something from EPA director Barry Calavari, she knew how to convince him. Katherine provided her with details of the inside stock trading Barry had been doing since working in the legal department, and if blackmail wasn't sufficient to get what she needed, she had other ways.

The boxer was determined this time. Valentina could see it in his eyes. He came at her faster, but before he could throw a punch,

Valentina edged to the side and swung a kick at his knee. It wasn't hard enough to break anything—she didn't possess that kind of strength—but it hurt, and it startled him into looking down right as she spun and sent the heel of her other foot into his face. As the boxer leaned backward and put his hands up to his broken nose, Valentina punched him hard in the throat and followed with a knee to the groin. He doubled over and stumbled backwards, gasping for air.

Valentina had no close friends. In her situation, there were people that she could use and people that couldn't offer her anything. The latter were of little consequence. All that mattered was completing the project, and there was almost nothing she wouldn't do to see it through.

The boxer's face was turning purple as he struggled to breathe. Valentina landed a kick to his solar plexus that crumpled him to a seated position against the ropes, followed by a crushing blow to the head that put him on the mat. As she turned and walked back to her corner, the trainer reached into the ring and checked for a pulse.

Valentina reached into her gym bag and took out her phone. She placed a call to Barry and waited through several rings while she heard nothing but silence behind her. The boxer would be smuggled back to the prison in Siberia where they'd fill out the paperwork concerning his supposed death at the hands of another inmate. It was an efficient system.

"Hello?" Barry answered.

"It's me."

"Oh, Valentina. What's up?"

"I'm out for a jog, but we need to talk."

"Listen. I'm sorry about the other night. I didn't mean to grab your wrist so hard, but my wife was right in the next room. Can you please be more discreet? Your behavior was inappropriate, and I think she suspects something, but I hope I didn't hurt you, did I?"

Valentina watched as the trainer pulled her opponent's body out of the ring and dropped it to the concrete floor with a thud. She inspected her wrist, turning and flexing it while she recalled Barry grasping at her hand in panic as it wandered past the bounds of propriety. Had he hurt it? She almost laughed at the thought, given it was her right hand, the same one she'd just used with lethal force.

"Valentina? Are you still there? Are you all right?"

"I think you might have twisted it. It's been really sore."

"Oh, man, I'm so sorry."

"But that's not why I'm calling."

"Oh?"

"No."

"Then what is it?"

"Barry, you know how I've mentioned several times that Dr. Pennychuck may be showing signs of dementia?"

"Yes, you've been concerned about that for a while."

"Unfortunately I think it's progressing rapidly. He called me this afternoon and said he'd found a solution to the climate problem. He thinks we can inflate the CO_2 molecules with helium and send them into outer space. He also asked if the construction on the system had started yet."

"Really?"

"Yes, I was shocked. I was talking to him yesterday, and he seemed quite lucid. I think it comes and goes."

"What should we do?"

"I'll keep an eye on him and perhaps get him to see a doctor. In the meantime, it would be best if you remove his access to the system control program."

"Wow, I never would have thought . . . But you know him better than I do. If you think it's for the best."

"I do. We can't take any risks right now."

"I agree. But I feel really bad about your wrist. Are you free tonight? What can I—"

Valentina ended the call. Barry would be fretting for the rest of the evening, wondering whether she were mad at him, which would keep his mind off thinking too much about the situation with Dr. Pennychuck. She didn't need Barry to think. She needed him to do the things that would bring unwanted questions if she did them herself.

"Have a lovely evening, 'Mrs. Smith,'" the trainer said, holding the ropes apart for Valentina to climb out.

"And you as well, 'Mr. Smith.'" She handed him an envelope containing payment in cash. The format of their exchange hadn't varied for a long time, and she had every intention of keeping it that way.

Valentina stopped in the locker room to change into her jogging outfit and connected her earpiece to a different cell phone before heading outside for a run. She increased her pace over several miles until she was sprinting flat out and her lungs burned. When she couldn't keep the pace any longer, she slowed and made her way through a park until finding a suitably isolated spot. Once her breathing steadied, she dialed the only number in the phone and waited for the connection.

"Yes?" a voice answered.

"There's been a development. I need a conference call tomorrow."

"How is 2:00 p.m. your time?"

"Good."

"Done."

Valentina took off again at a moderate pace and headed for home. She had a lot to think about.

SUNDAY, JUNE 29, 5:17 P.M. ET
Pottersmith residence—Hanover, New Hampshire
Elevation: 528 feet

Autumn gazed into the bathroom mirror and admired her handiwork. She'd trimmed a few inches of faded color from her hair and dyed it so her natural blonde transitioned starting at her ponytail to a brilliant mix of fall reds, oranges, and yellows that cascaded to the middle of her back. It had always annoyed her that friends and even some family members couldn't differentiate her from Summer, so she'd taken to using color to provide a visual distinction.

"It looks awesome," Summer said, joining her at the vanity.

"Thanks. Want me to do yours? You can change it before school starts."

"No, I don't want to risk dyeing that much. It would be way too short if I had to cut it."

"You premeds are no fun."

Summer went back into the bedroom. "Maybe, but we have to finish packing, and I don't want to be up all night. Holly will be here at four in the morning to take us to the airport."

"Did you confirm our flight yet?"

"Yes, I checked us in already. I hope we've thought of everything we need for the trail."

Autumn rolled her eyes. "I think so, and we can stop at a store in Denver if we forgot anything. There are also towns along the way, so I'm not worried about it."

"Yeah, but we should go over the list one more time."

Autumn picked up her packing list and pretended to work through the items laid out on her bed. She knew that her sister meant well, but her obsession with planning and detail could be annoying. She watched Summer for a moment and sighed. Annoying was a small price to pay to have a best friend for life, and she often thought she could never take her sister for granted. "Do you think you'll miss Mom and Dad?" she asked, causing Summer to lose place on her checklist. "I mean, I've been so excited about the trip that I haven't really thought about how long we'll be away. I think I'm going to miss them. I think I do already."

Summer's gaze met hers. "Yes, I'll miss them, certainly, but they make it sound like we're never going to see each other again. I almost felt bad for planning this when I saw Mom crying up on the mountain yesterday. Are you going to start now, too?"

"I don't think so. Not yet, at least. Mom gets emotional like that when she's sad. Or happy. I think it's cute, but maybe that's because I'm that way, too."

Summer smiled. "You definitely get that from her. It's nothing to be ashamed of, but please go back to packing. We'll have plenty of time later to discuss emotions."

CHAPTER 4

Barry Calavari stepped to the podium for his weekly press briefing on the state of the system. He hated giving these briefings. It was always the same reporters with the same questions. Why did "We're making progress" have to take an hour to convey? Being head of the Environmental Protection Agency wasn't a bad job, but Barry didn't care for the politics and environmental stuff. He'd gone into corporate finance law because that's what interested him. He was doing this only because Katherine Morgreed had called him to her office four years ago and told him he'd be taking this new job or going to jail for trading stock in her company on inside information. He'd been furious. It was inside information she'd given him while she encouraged him to buy and sell shares. He should have realized she might want to blackmail him one day.

"Good morning," Barry said in a passably enthusiastic tone. "As I trust you're all aware, we'll be starting the system nine days from now. I'm pleased to announce that we're still on track to meet that target."

Barry was pleased only in that these interminable briefings were coming to an end. Sure, he was mildly glad that the scientists were hopeful of a fix to the climate-change problem, but what he really wanted was to get out of this job and get away from Washington. Katherine had promised he'd be free to leave once the system was running, and he was counting down the days.

"Now that the safety tests have been completed," Barry continued, "the reactors are being fueled and prepared for start-up. The balloons holding the reflector arrays have completed final flight testing to the forty-kilometer service ceiling. Starting today, the system control bases will be fully operational. I will be conducting our final briefing a week from now at main control in the desert south of Phoenix."

Phoenix. Barry hated Phoenix. He'd moved there to take the legal job at Morgreed Industries headquarters and quickly found the heat to be utterly oppressive. Katherine always said it wasn't so bad, but that was easy for her to say, flying in only occasionally on her private jet from cooler climates. She never tried actually living there. The EPA job in Washington at least got him out of that sweltering desert, though he could hardly enjoy it given the stressful nature of the appointment.

"Are there any questions?" Barry asked the room full of reporters.

"Mr. Calavari," a woman in the front row said, "start-up has been delayed many times. How confident are you that this date will hold?"

"We're certain. Dr. Severnaya, our system director, has assured me that everything is ready to go. The remaining steps are formalities, and we have no reason to expect complications."

Barry wished Valentina could be the one here taking questions. She was the one familiar with the system and Pennychuck's theory, and in reality, she told him little of what was going on. Barry hadn't even started the job when Katherine ordered him to hire Dr. Severnaya. It was pointless to argue. Katherine had the president and half the IPCC bought out—and likely most of Congress, too. Barry had no authority of his own, and clearly Katherine wanted him at the EPA only to be a rubber stamp for whatever Valentina desired, which was a lot. The thought of that woman made him shudder. He didn't know what the deal was between her and Katherine, but saying no to either of them was not an option. She was like Katherine's right-hand man but in the body of a beautiful serpent. She toyed with him constantly, and he knew he wouldn't be able to resist her if it ever came to it. She had no compunction about flirting with him, even at his home, and it hadn't gone unnoticed by his wife. But what could he say? His former boss and supposed employee were calling the shots, and he had to obey or go to jail. Hopefully Katherine would be true to her word and he could leave all this behind soon.

"Mr. Calavari?"

"Sorry. What was the question?" Barry asked as his thoughts returned to the room.

"How will we know if the system is working once it starts?"

Barry thought back to what Valentina and Pennychuck had told him. "Well, we start it with the reflectors at 1.5 kilometers above sea level. Then we'll take readings of the atmosphere and determine the next step. The balloons will be raised incrementally until they reach their max altitude and the system can run automatically. Dr. Pennychuck said that if the reaction is working properly, we'll see a brief moment of golden glitter in the sky."

THURSDAY, JULY 3, 4:15 P.M. ET
Morgreed Institute for Climate Studies, Dartmouth College—Hanover, New Hampshire
Elevation: 528 feet

Late in the afternoon, Milford dialed the dreaded number again and hoped it would go to voice mail. He'd been working almost around the clock since Sunday, and he did not have the energy for this conversation.

"Yes?" Valentina answered after two rings.

"Dr. Severnaya, I've run the model again every way I can imagine, but unfortunately the results are looking even worse."

"Go on."

"We have over a ninety percent chance that everything will be fine, but the possibility of a neutral or negative reaction now looks to be about eight to nine percent."

"What condition would result in that, and can't it be avoided?"

"It's more a matter of uncertainty. This model has a more complex atmospheric profile, and regardless of how I adjust the system settings, I can't get it to calculate a successful reaction consistently."

"Have you tried working at it the other way?"

"What do you mean?"

"Have you tried to determine what settings are most likely to cause failure?"

"Oh, yes, I have identified a range, but I wasn't able to use that information to improve the positive result. If I had more time, maybe I could get the numbers to come out better."

"But you're still predicting over a ninety percent chance of success. That should be acceptable. Adjustments can be made after start-up once we see how it's working."

"No, we can't risk doing it that way. If the system is not set properly, the reaction might be off and the reactors could be damaged, or we could have other unintended consequences. The only way to do this safely is to take more time to study it. We have to delay the start-up."

Valentina was silent for a few moments. "Send me the data and also the range of failure settings. I'd like to take a look for myself before making a decision and getting Barry involved. I fear further delays may not be tolerated at this point. I'll review what you've found this evening, and we'll speak again first thing in the morning."

"Okay, I'll have it to you within thirty minutes."

"Good."

Milford heard the dial tone and returned the phone to its cradle. Dr. Severnaya had never seemed this bothered by previous delays with construction or other aspects of the project. Why was she so set on pressing ahead in the face of this concern? Perhaps it was politics catching up with good intentions. She was likely under pressure from above to meet the deadline. He'd always feared that the biggest threat to successful implementation would be the bureaucrats put in charge of it. They contributed nothing but self-promotion and empty promises, then left for the golf course while the scientists shouldered the burden.

Milford finished sending the files Valentina had requested. He could take some small consolation in the IPCC's decision to delegate most of the system work to the EPA. He generally understood the political mechanisms involved in the US and had retained sufficient influence over the course of the project to feel confident that it was going in the right direction. Dr. Severnaya was a constant thorn in his side, but things could be worse. He would feel better after taking the evening off. A nice dinner, a good bottle of beer, and a full night of sleep would be good preparation for dealing with the devil in the morning.

The sun was still high in the summer sky as he exited the building and trudged through the parking lot. He started his car and thought about where to go for dinner as he fastened his seat belt. He drove through the Dartmouth campus, waffling between pizza and the new Thai place he'd heard about. The traffic light ahead turned yellow, so he stopped at the intersection of Main Street and Wheelock. This was the decision point. He'd have to choose which way to turn when the light turned green. Pizza. Thai. They were both appealing.

A car horn sounded behind him, and he refocused on the road. The light was green. He signaled a right turn and pressed his foot to the gas. Something in his peripheral vision caught his attention, and when he turned to look, the chrome grill of a large truck was mere feet from his window and closing fast.

CHAPTER 5

Roman stood outside his command tent and surveyed the bustling camp of the Climate Freedom Militia. The Colorado division had trickled in, towing a vast assortment of supplies and weaponry as well as solar panels, firewood, machinery driven by steam and mechanical power, and other items required to live off the grid.

The CFM was a loose global network of climate-change deniers and conspiracy theorists united by the belief that the UN was using the carbon reduction system as an elaborate cover for their real intentions. The global array of electromagnetic-field generators and nuclear power plants could only mean that the UN was constructing a system to wipe out traditional electrical power sources and then force everyone to pay exorbitant rates for UN-supplied nuclear energy. Why else would all the components of the climate system be powered by nuclear reactors and shielded so well against interference? Why else would all the installations be guarded by UN troops and protected by autonomous defenses? Attacks on the system had been attempted by various factions, and the news broadcasts had shown the ensuing carnage as a warning to others not to try it. It was obvious to anyone who could see through the façade—the invasion was imminent and would occur soon after the system started.

Roman slowly strolled through the camp and inspected the preparations. He didn't share some of the more extreme conspiracy beliefs of the CFM, but their motivations aligned well with his general distrust of government, and joining them had been his ticket to the US to follow other interests. He was fairly confident that once the system started and proved to be of benign intent, the militia would lose interest and disband. But that would be another day. For now they were preparing for war in their mountain stronghold.

Well, actually for now the Colorado division was preparing to eat and then shoot off fireworks to celebrate the American independence holiday. A smoky haze that smelled of meat covered the entire camp, and the men made absolutely no effort to hide the alcohol they were consuming. There were certainly stark contrasts between this militia and the disciplined units Roman had trained with in the Russian military. To be fair, though, that was the military. The CFM divisions he'd seen back home behaved this way, too—or worse.

"Sir," one of the troops called from behind Roman.

"Yes?"

"You're needed at the mess tent."

"Is something wrong?"

"No, we need you to judge the chili competition."

FRIDAY, JULY 4, 7:39 P.M. ET
Dartmouth-Hitchcock Medical Center—Lebanon, New Hampshire
Elevation: 581 feet

Milford woke up confused. He was lying in bed in a strange room, and he didn't feel good. His vision was a little blurry, more than it usually was without his glasses, and he tried to look around, but something was preventing his head from moving.

"Ah, I see you're awake," a woman said as footsteps approached and a blurry face came into view.

"Wha . . . " Milford tried to say but let out only a whisper. His throat was dry, and the exertion almost brought on a coughing fit that he could feel would be painful.

"Good. You are alert," the woman said, "but don't try to speak yet. I just need to check a few things, and we'll try to make you more comfortable."

Milford winced as the woman shone a bright light into each of his eyes and performed a few other tasks out of his view. This had to be a hospital, but what was he doing here?

"Okay. I'm going to sit you up a little. Here. Can you squeeze my hand? Good. Do that if anything hurts and we'll stop."

Milford held her hand and felt the bed rising under his back. He was uncomfortable, but the movement didn't make it any worse. As he reached a reclined sitting position, he got a better view of the room and determined it was definitely a hospital. It looked familiar; perhaps he'd been here before.

"Here. Let's see if you can take a sip of this." The woman—probably a nurse—held a straw to his lips. "Good. Does that feel better?"

Swallowing the water was a little painful, but it was a huge relief to his parched throat. "Yes, thank you," he whispered.

"I'm Ashley, by the way, one of the nurses here at Dartmouth-Hitchcock. Do you remember what happened to you?"

"Driving home," Milford uttered after thinking for a moment. "I was on the way to dinner. That's it."

"Okay. The doctors thought you might not remember the accident. It was a hit-and-run. I saw the pictures, and I'd say you're lucky to be alive. Your side of the car was smashed in really far."

"That would be an understatement," a middle-aged doctor said as he arrived at Ashley's side. "I'd say more like crushed."

"Am I injured?" Milford asked.

"Not too badly overall, but your left arm was broken in three places. That seemed to line up with the height of the bumper of the other vehicle. We've got that all set and wrapped up in a cast. Also, you have some fractured ribs on your left side. Those will hurt, but they'll heal on their own. Your left hip is bruised and swollen but otherwise okay. The scans of your neck didn't show any injury, but we've left the brace on as a precaution, and it will likely be sore for some time. You also had a concussion. You were unconscious at the scene yesterday and have been under sedation until this afternoon. It will take a few hours for the effects to clear up. We have you on pain meds through the IV. Are they working okay, or do we need to make adjustments?"

"It's okay. When can I go home? I have work to do."

"We'll see. It could be up to a couple weeks. We have to monitor you for internal injuries, and it will be at least a few days before you can get up and start moving around. In the meantime, try to relax. You need to focus on healing. The police will want to ask you some questions, and they'll probably be here again tomorrow morning. Right now, we need to get some food in you. You must be hungry."

"Yes."

"Good. Ashley will attend to it. I have to run, but I'll be back later to see how you're doing."

"By the way," Ashley said as the doctor left the room, "your daughter has been in the waiting room most of the day. I'll bring her in soon."

"My daughter?"

"Yes, Valerie. Lovely woman. She's been so worried. She brought you these flowers. I'll have some dinner sent up, and then I'll go get her. You just sit tight."

Valerie? Milford didn't know anyone named Valerie. Also, he didn't have a daughter—or any children at all. Maybe it was a mistake. But that hardly mattered. This accident could not have happened at a worse time. He'd been unconscious for an entire day, and now he was stuck in this hospital. He had work to do. System start-up was— what?—five days away, and he had to figure out the model. And Dr. Severnaya, she was going to call him this morning. Would she even know why he wasn't at his office? He'd have to get in touch with her to explain and try to convince her to delay the start-up.

"Daddy!" someone exclaimed from the doorway. Milford wanted to see, but the neck brace allowed him only the impression of two figures in his peripheral vision.

"I'll let you two visit," Ashley said, "but only for a few minutes. He needs to be resting."

"Thanks so much." The other woman approached the bed and stood in front of him. She wore blue jeans, a Dartmouth T-shirt a couple of sizes too big, and a Red Sox hat over long blonde hair that fell around her shoulders.

"Dr. Severnaya?" Milford said. "How did you—"

"Be quiet and listen to me," Valentina said. "You need to address me as Valerie, your daughter, and you will not speak of this conversation to anyone else."

"What? Why? What are you talking about?"

"Shh," Valentina hissed. "You're supposed to be dead. Your accident was no accident. I arranged that after we spoke yesterday."

"What?"

"Please, no questions. I don't have much time. My instructions were to get rid of you once I had the information I need. I'm giving you a chance to live, but you must agree to these stipulations. You will claim to have problems with your memory after the accident. You will say you do not feel confident in your ability to work and will retire from your position. You will never discuss your recent computer model or the fact that you shared anything with me, and you will delete that model and all related data irretrievably from anywhere it is saved. You will say that you had complete confidence in the system. Do you understand?"

"Uh . . ."

"You must promise me. Otherwise you'll give me no choice but to make sure you don't leave this hospital alive. You have no idea what you're up against. Please, promise me you'll do as I've asked."

"Um, okay," Milford stammered.

Valentina leaned in to give him a hug as Ashley and the doctor entered the room. "I'm sorry," she whispered before releasing him and stepping back to greet them. "Are you sure he's going to be okay?"

"Yes, don't worry," the doctor said. "He's in good hands."

"Okay, thanks," Valentina said, then blew a kiss to Milford. "Bye, Dad. I love you."

"You look very pale," Ashley observed. "Are you feeling all right?"

"No," Milford said, slowly bringing his hand up and wiping a tear off his cheek. It wasn't his.

SATURDAY, JULY 5, 5:22 AM. MT
Camp Hale—Leadville, Colorado
Elevation: 9,200 feet

Roman woke to the sounds of hammers on metal somewhere in the distance. He checked the time. Who could be making all this racket at such an hour? Why couldn't they let him sleep? The previous day had been a disaster. The chili competition had gone well enough, but by the early afternoon, his stomach was not happy with the copious quantities of beans and spices he'd ingested. When he had to make a run for the portable restrooms, there was a long line of his comrades in similarly dire straits and he'd barely been able to withstand the wait. They had underestimated the needs of seven hundred men gorging themselves on questionably cooked meats and fatty foods, and the portable restroom truck had to come out twice for emergency service.

Then there were the campers. They hadn't given much thought to the first few people that showed up, but by midafternoon a steady stream of cars was arriving on the highway from both directions. Apparently no one from the CFM had thought to check whether there were any events this weekend or bothered to make reservations for campsites. They soon discovered that over twenty thousand people were expected for the annual Carbon 31 race and festival put on by the Colorado Climate Action Cooperative. There would be a running race on Saturday from Camp Hale to the elementary school in Leadville and back—thirty-one miles total—and a festival on Sunday with live music, rides, and food vendors. Not surprisingly, none of the CFM members were on the email lists of the environmentalist groups putting on the event, so it had escaped their attention.

Roman dressed and stepped out of his tent. Not wanting to create unnecessary conflict, the militia had moved many of their belongings and squeezed into a smaller area at one end of the valley to make room for the festival attendees. Then they'd moved everything to the other end when the trucks showed up to erect a huge music stage and sound system. Hopefully no one else would be coming to claim this end. Roman climbed to the roof of one of the tractor trailers for a better view. A group was setting up the starting line for the race. They were pounding metal spikes into the ground to anchor various pop-up structures. It was going to be a long weekend.

SATURDAY, JULY 5, 2:00 P.M. ET
Severnaya residence—Arlington, Virginia
Elevation: 272 feet

Valentina's encrypted cellphone rang at two o'clock as planned. "Hello."

"We're here," came the usual reply.

Valentina studied the scrambled number on her screen. "I've reviewed Dr. Pennychuck's work and I have what I need. The new control software will be ready before I leave for Phoenix."

"Excellent," a man said. "What result are you expecting?"

"If the model is correct, we'll overload the reactors."

"Is that wise?" a woman asked. "What about fallout?"

"It's a small risk," Katherine Morgreed said. "Under this condition they'll lose structural integrity and fly apart, but the containment domes will prevent any significant radiation exposure. It can be safely cleaned up."

"Do you have everything you need to complete the task?" a man asked.

"Yes," Valentina replied.

"And Dr. Pennychuck?" another man asked.

"He is out of the picture."

"You've done well, Valentina," a woman said. "If you succeed on Wednesday, your associate will convey you to the transfer point, and then we shall have no further communication."

"We will be watching," a man said, and then the call ended.

CHAPTER 6

On Monday morning, EPA director Barry Calavari wiped the sweat from his brow and faced the reporters gathered in the 114-degree heat of the Arizona desert. The microphones had been set up on a concrete parking area that reflected the sun. Any direction Barry looked was blinding. He longed to step back into the air-conditioned comfort of the control base, which had been the bunker for the former atomic weapons testing grounds they were standing on. Unfortunately there was not much room in the base, so the briefing had to be held outside. Barry was miserable, but at least this time Katherine Morgreed and Dr. Severnaya were here to share the discomfort. He was picturing those icy women melting into the concrete when he was given the prompt to start.

"Hello again, and thank you for joining me in the beautiful state of Arizona," Barry began. This sentiment was not shared by the crowd, judging by the silence of the reporters who had mostly flown in from elsewhere. "In exactly forty-eight hours, we will be activating the system. All preparations and tests are complete, and we're eager to begin. Standing with me today are two women who have been instrumental in bringing this project to fruition: Katherine Morgreed of Morgreed Industries, which has provided the bulk of the equipment, and Dr. Valentina Severnaya, our system director, who has overseen the implementation."

The reporters gave a brief round of polite applause.

"I was hoping Dr. Milford Pennychuck would be able to join us today. It was his research that allowed this project to begin twelve years ago. Sadly, he is still recovering from a recent automobile accident and has announced his retirement. We're all sending him our thoughts, prayers, and gratitude."

"Director Calavari," a reporter shouted, "do you have any response planned to the protest groups that will be marching during the start-up?"

"There will be designated areas for assembly as usual. We're hoping everyone can remain calm and civil."

"We have reports that the Climate Freedom Militia is gathering troops around the globe," another reporter said. "Have you had any communication with them about their intentions?"

"I have not, though I'm told they aren't planning any offensive actions."

"Director, some sources claim that the president has been pushing to get the system operational in advance of the November elections to help secure a second term. Has he spoken to you about that?"

"No, he has not." Barry wiped at his brow again and wished he could be anywhere else.

MONDAY, JULY 7, 10:17 A.M. MT
Camp Hale—Leadville, Colorado
Elevation: 9,200 feet

Roman watched the rest of Director Calavari's press briefing on his satellite television and then switched it off. They hadn't said anything new, but it was good to have confirmation that start-up was still on schedule. He hadn't planned on watching the whole thing, but the sight of Valentina by the podium kept his interest. She was rarely in the news coverage, and he hadn't seen her in person for several years. He'd tried to recruit her as a scientist for the military, but she had other plans, and it appeared they'd worked out. Maybe it was for the best. Her final months in Arkhangelsk had been hard, and he couldn't really blame her for wanting to get away. Still, it would be nice if she would write to him more. She'd promised to explain someday, but that was a long time ago, and he was getting tired of exchanging nothing but the cryptic and infrequent notes she required. He tried not to worry, but the vacant look in her eyes when the television camera zoomed in only reinforced his concerns that all was not well.

Roman let out a sorrowful sigh and exited his tent to join the cleanup effort his men had undertaken. The carbon festival had drawn a record crowd that pushed the limits of Camp Hale. It was a relief to see the last of the environmentalists head home, leaving the area to the militia again, but the mess they left was unbelievable. There had been bins arranged around the festival for refuse and recycling, but litter covered nearly every square foot of the grounds. The militia members collected trash, personal items, and thousands of food and drink containers bearing eco-friendly labels. Roman couldn't fathom how such supposedly green people could be so thoughtless, especially on this hallowed earth where soldiers of the United States Army had trained during World War II.

By midafternoon the CFM had returned Camp Hale to order and rearranged their base as they'd set it up before the intrusion.

Several roll-off dumpsters were filled with festival waste, and when the driver asked about payment, Roman arranged for the invoice to be sent to the Colorado Climate Action Cooperative's business office. He considered mailing them a bill for the hours his men worked on the cleanup effort but decided instead to provide photos of the mess to the press at an opportune time.

TUESDAY, JULY 8, 5:47 P.M. MT
Main control base—the desert south of Phoenix, Arizona
Elevation: 1,100 feet

By Tuesday evening, protesters were arriving at the main control base by the carload and setting up camp. Valentina was running diagnostics when Katherine entered the room.

"Can't we get rid of them?" Katherine peered out through the thick glass of the control bunker. "There are even more of them now. Don't the guards have fire hoses or tear gas?"

"It's just a peaceful assembly," Barry said. "They're not violating any laws as long as they stay behind the fencing."

"If I wanted your opinion, I would have asked for it," Katherine snapped. "You're the director. Go tell the guards to shoo them away. I don't want to see them."

"I'll speak to them," Barry mumbled as he left the room.

"Dr. Severnaya," Katherine barked, "are you sure everything will work as planned tomorrow?"

"Yes," Valentina said. "I've completed a trial run, and there should be no problems with the upload. I need only a minute with no one watching."

"Good. There will be several representatives from the IPCC here to witness the start-up. I'll distract them, which will be your signal to proceed. Otherwise I expect only one system operator and Barry to be in the room. It should not be hard to convince them to watch the sky. Security will be posted outside the door."

"I'll watch for your signal. Five minutes before initialization would be ideal."

"Understood. Also, are you prepared in the event that Barry or the others get in the way? Mr. Smith reports that you've done exceptionally well in your training program."

"Yes," Valentina replied, keeping her face an emotionless mask while she thought over the four years of sessions she'd endured in the basement gym. Mr. Smith—or whoever he was—had started off easy, getting her in shape, then teaching her various combat tactics consisting mostly of moves that would be illegal in any competitive arena. They'd progressed from punching bags to sparring and finally to the desperate convicts that she'd dispatched by the dozens, each one taking another little piece of her soul until she felt no remorse. She'd hated every minute spent in that dark place, but she had no choice in the matter.

"Good," Katherine purred. "I think we're ready."

"Yes." Valentina stared at Katherine. It would be so easy to kill her. They were alone in the room. No one would see. She could almost feel Katherine's neck in her hands as she squeezed with years of pent-up fury. She'd envisioned Katherine's face on every one of the convicts in that gym, and here was a chance to do it for real. But she couldn't. Not now. Not yet.

"Is something the matter?" Katherine asked, looking at her.

"No," Valentina said, "everything is fine."

WEDNESDAY, JULY 9, 6:02 A.M. ET
Dartmouth-Hitchcock Medical Center—Lebanon, New Hampshire
Elevation: 581 feet

On Wednesday morning Milford got out of his hospital bed and adjusted the pillow and sheets to approximate his form. The doctor had said it would be a few more days until they would discharge him, but he needed to get out now. He pulled a robe over his hospital gown using his right arm and slid his feet into the slippers by the bed. He'd been allowed to walk up and down the hall a bit, but the trip he'd planned this morning would be a much greater challenge. He put on his glasses, gathered his belongings, and then paused to listen at the doorway before slowly slipping into the hall. Slowly was the only speed he'd be going because of the pain in his left side, so his escape attempt would be quickly thwarted if anyone saw him.

Milford ducked into an empty patient room for a moment when he heard footsteps coming around a corner. Several doctors walked by, and then the hall was quiet again. He exited the room and continued in the direction of the elevators.

"Mr. Pennychuck?" someone called from behind him. "Where are you going?"

Milford turned around to see Ashley walking his way. He'd made it only about thirty feet from his room, so perhaps sneaking out was not going to work. Fortunately he'd considered this possibility. "Ashley," he whispered, "can we speak in private?"

The young nurse looked a bit bewildered by the request, but Milford hoped the serious expression on his face was compelling. "Okay," she replied. "Let's get you back to your room."

"No, that might not be safe. They may be listening."

Ashley led him into the empty room he'd hid in a moment before and closed the door, looking concerned. "Who might be listening? Are you feeling okay?"

"I know what you're thinking. I've been complaining of mental problems, but I need you to listen carefully," Milford began.

A few minutes later Ashley escorted him to the nurses' station and informed them that she was not feeling well and would be taking the rest of her shift off as soon as she finished giving Milford his walk. They exited the building, and she helped him into her car in the employee parking lot. "I hope you're telling me the truth," she said, buckling her seat belt and starting the engine. "I could lose my job for this."

"Yes, and thank you for trusting me. Do you know the way to my office at the Morgreed Institute?"

"I do. I passed by it all the time during construction."

After a brief drive, Ashley pulled into a space in front of the Morgreed Institute for Climate Studies and helped Milford out of the car. At his direction, she found the door card in his wallet and let them into the building.

"Once I log in," Milford said, "I can see if they've altered the settings and hopefully get this corrected before they start. If you'd be so kind, I could use some help with the computer. I'm not going to be able to type very well."

"Sure," Ashley said. "Which key is for your office?"

"That one with the bottle opener keychain."

She unlocked the door and swung it open. The lights in the room came on automatically. "Are you sure this is the right place?"

Milford followed her into the office and gasped. "No! I mean, yes, it's the right place, but all my things are gone."

Ashley gazed around the empty room. "Does this mean you can't check your climate system?"

A knock on the door startled Milford. "Oh, hi, Dr. Pennychuck," a custodian said, looking confused by the attire of the nurse and patient. "I was just mopping down the hall when I heard someone come in. Are you taking one last look at the old office?"

"Um, yes. Say, what happened to all of my things? My computer? The desk?"

The custodian shrugged. "There was a crew here packing it all up the other day. I don't know where they took it."

"Thanks," Milford said. There was no doubt in his mind—Dr. Severnaya had to be responsible for this.

"Now what will you do?" Ashley asked once the custodian left.

Milford pondered the question before responding. "I'd like to get some clothing at my home, and then I'm going to need you to drive me up to Mount Washington."

"Mount Washington? Why?"

"There's someone there who can help me."

"Oh, I see. It's just interesting you mentioned it because my sister is working there."

"Good. So you know the way?"

"Yes, but I don't like driving the Auto Road. It's so steep and narrow."

Milford nodded, taking a last look around the empty office. "It's very important that we get to the observatory, and I can't do it without you. Can you help me?"

"Yes."

likely to make it back on time. His mug of coffee was empty, indicating he'd ingested the entire dose of the substance Valentina had poured into it. She'd seen the sweat starting to glisten on his skin before he left. If the stuff worked as Katherine promised, he would be passed out on the toilet for the next hour, giving her plenty of time to complete the upload. She'd planned for different contingencies, but she had no elegant solution for the guards if they tried to intervene.

Katherine set out some glasses and a bottle of champagne on a little table by the window. "Gentlemen," she said to the IPCC representatives and Barry, "as we prepare to start, I'd like to propose a toast."

That was Valentina's signal. She pulled out the device and inserted it into the port as the engineer had instructed. The terminal displayed a status bar that started to progress but then showed three minutes remaining. It was not supposed to take that long.

"Dr. Severnaya," the chairman of the IPCC said, startling Valentina. She looked up to see him heading her way with a glass of champagne and Katherine mouthing a silent apology from her position by the window. "Here's a glass for you," he said, smiling and coming around the terminal.

Valentina glanced at the screen. The status bar was still progressing.

"What is that?" the chairman asked. "Why does this say 'System override in progress'? What is that blinking device? What are you doing?"

Valentina had no response. She started to say something, but the chairman leaned in over her and reached for the terminal. That was a mistake. Valentina was already on edge, and she reacted with trained reflexes. She put the elderly chairman on the ground, shattered the top of her champagne glass on the edge of the desk, and finished him off with the stem. As she stood, staring at the blood trickling down her hand, two gunshots rang out followed by several seconds of silence, then more shots all around her. The sound echoed off the hard surfaces of the small room, assaulting her ears with deafening force.

"You shot them!" Barry shouted.

Valentina heard footsteps hurrying her way. She turned to see Katherine approaching with a pistol drawn and Barry backing into a corner. She could hear Katherine asking her something, but it wasn't registering. She looked to the door and saw the security guards lying motionless on the floor. Then she heard glass breaking. She turned her gaze down and saw the fractured stem of the champagne glass on the floor where she'd just dropped it.

Valentina heard one of the IPCC representatives speaking, and then there were several more gunshots. They sounded far away. She looked up again to see Katherine lowering her weapon.

"Was the upload successful?" Katherine asked. "Dr. Severnaya?"

Valentina could barely hear the question. The upload? She noticed the terminal on the desk in front of her. The screen was cracked and blank, and the light had stopped blinking on the little device she'd plugged in. She started to reach for it but cried out. Her mind snapped back into focus. Katherine was still talking, but Valentina ignored her as she looked down at a spreading patch of red on her shirt.

CHAPTER 7

Milford walked to the observatory as quickly as he was able, with Laura and the others trailing. Ashley had brought him to the mountain, reluctantly driving the harrowing Auto Road to the summit. On the way he had filled her in on his research and the progress of the climate system, including further explanation of the visit from his supposed daughter and the warning she'd given him.

"Do you still have the satellite link to system control here?" Milford asked Laura as he walked into the climate research center, surprising the weather observers on duty.

"Yes," Laura said, "right over here, though we haven't used it for a number of years. Douglas," she said, addressing one of the researchers, "does this still work?"

"I think so," Douglas replied.

Laura booted up the machine. It had been installed in the observatory while the system was in the initial phases of construction. They'd used it for testing of the satellite network that would link the control bases, but once those were finished, it started collecting dust.

"Good!" Milford said as the terminal connected. It was limited to displaying only the control system status and configuration parameters, but that would be enough to show him whether the settings had been altered. "I don't know why," he explained to the group, "but I think Dr. Severnaya or someone she's working for wants the system to fail. She was too interested in my findings on calibrations that would cause problems with the reaction."

"Why would anyone want that to happen?" Laura asked.

"I don't know," he said, focusing on the screen as the control system information came up. "I don't understand. Nothing has been changed. Why would Dr. Severnaya go to such lengths to get me out of the way? I mean, I had concerns, but was it that important to stay on schedule?"

"Could someone explain what's going on here?" Douglas asked.

Milford let out a sigh. "I'm sorry. I don't really know. I thought they—someone—was going to hijack the system for some nefarious purpose, but perhaps I was overreacting. Maybe Dr. Severnaya thought I would be too vocal about delaying the start-up. Either way, I'm more comfortable up here above the field until we can find out what they're up to."

"I guess we'll find out soon," Laura said, looking at her watch. "It's twelve o'clock."

WEDNESDAY, JULY 9, 10:00 A.M. MT (12:00 P.M. ET)
Main control base—the desert south of Phoenix, Arizona
Elevation: 1,100 feet

"Valentina!" Barry shouted. He heard Katherine yelling something about locking the door, but he didn't care. Valentina was hurt.

Katherine could wait. Valentina collapsed into her seat. He called her name again. She focused on him for a moment, and he saw a brief spark of something in her eyes, but then they went dark and closed.

"Valentina!" he shouted repeatedly as he ran to her. She was leaning over in the chair at the control terminal and about to fall onto the floor when he caught her and pushed her back upright. "Katherine, she's been shot," he yelled, watching the crimson stain spreading on her right shoulder and chest.

"There. I got it," Katherine said.

"What?" Barry turned to see her sliding the locking bolts into place on the blast door. Seconds later security guards that were posted outside were pounding on the door and shouting.

"Help!" Barry yelled. He looked at Katherine, then at the door, then at Valentina, then back to Katherine. He needed help. Why was she just standing there? Why didn't she help him?

Katherine met his gaze for a moment, then pulled a first aid kit from a cabinet on the wall and tossed it in his direction. "There. Good luck. I don't need her any longer."

Need her? Luck? Huh? Barry was in too much of a panic to think about her words as he flipped open the kit and dumped the contents on the desk. It had been decades since his first aid training in the scouts, but he knew he had to do something—and quickly. He pulled the collar of Valentina's shirt aside, grabbed a water bottle, and rinsed the blood from the area. There was a bullet wound in her shoulder just below the collarbone. The skin on her back was unbroken, so it must not have gone through. He grabbed a bunch of gauze and pressed it in place, hoping the bleeding would stop before it was too late.

Katherine walked over and looked at the terminal and then at her watch. "It's 10:05. The reaction should occur any minute, if it works."

"If wh-what works?" Barry said. "What just happened here?"

A phone started ringing, and Katherine answered it. "Hello? Gunshots? No, I don't know what you're talking about. I don't know—the door won't open. What? What? You're breaking up. What was that?"

The walls of the bunker were thick, but a staticky hissing sound was getting louder outside. Barry turned his attention back to Valentina. The gauze had soaked through, so he added more and continued putting pressure on the wound. He could feel the rise and fall of her chest and the thrum of her heart beating, but she remained unconscious.

"The phone line went dead," Katherine said. "What is that sound? It's getting louder."

"I don't know. I need help!"

Katherine went to the window. "What are they looking at?"

"Who?"

"The protesters. The media. They're all looking at the sky and covering their ears. Why are they doing that?"

Barry didn't know. It was all happening too fast. Why was she asking him? He glanced at Katherine for a moment. Wasn't she going to help him? Maybe not. She was watching the crowds. He had to focus. He turned his back to Katherine and the world outside the window, and then a flash filled the room, erasing Valentina from his vision.

with their dad, and Summer had wandered onto a thin patch of ice that cracked and broke beneath her. She'd hit her head before going into the frigid water. Dad had noticed when he heard the splash, but it took an agonizingly long time for him to get her, and she wasn't breathing when he pulled her out. He did CPR, and she was revived, and then they got in his helicopter and flew to the hospital, where they said she'd be okay. It had given Autumn nightmares for years.

"Summer!" Autumn cried, desperate for a reply as her tears watered the ground. This couldn't be happening. Not again. Images of Summer's pale, lifeless face were flashing in her vision. She could barely see through the memories and the tears. She sank to her knees, sobbing and crying her sister's name over and over. She took Summer's hand in hers. It squeezed back. What was she going to do? She rubbed her tears away and looked up. There was no one around. There was no one to help. The hand was squeezing harder. Dad wasn't here. They didn't have a helicopter. If only Dad was here. He would know what to do.

"Ouch!" Autumn exclaimed as fingernails dug into her palm. The pain pulled her back to the present. Summer wasn't moving, and her grip was losing strength. "Summer!" Autumn cried again, this time with hope. She dropped Summer's hand. She had to get the tree off her. Without a second thought, Autumn grabbed the trunk and, astounding herself, lifted it and dropped it a few feet to the side.

She turned back to her sister. "Summer? Can you hear me? Are you okay?"

Summer coughed a few times and tilted her head to take some deep breaths. "Thanks," she said, her voice weak. "I couldn't breathe. It was awful."

"Thank God! I thought you were dead."

Summer nodded toward the boulder she'd been pressed against. "So did I. I probably would be if this rock hadn't been here or if I hadn't taken my pack off when we stopped . . . or if you hadn't come when you did."

Autumn swept Summer's hair out of her face. She was crying again and dizzy from the relief and emotion. "Can you move? Are you injured?"

"I don't know. That tree knocked the wind out of me. I'm scared to find out."

"Can you wiggle your toes?"

"Yes."

"Does it hurt?"

"No."

"How about your fingers?"

"They're okay."

Autumn ran a hand lightly over Summer's back where the tree had hit her. "Does that hurt? It doesn't feel like anything is broken."

Summer rolled onto her side. "No, I don't think so. Can you help me sit up and get me some water?"

"Sure. Here you go."

Summer took the bottle Autumn offered and had barely gotten a sip before Autumn leaned in and hugged her like she hadn't in a long, long time.

"I was so scared," Autumn said, her voice catching.

"Me, too," Summer whispered, beginning to tremble. Autumn held her sister tight. Her nerves were sending confusing signals all through her body, and she began weeping as the moment sank in.

She was silent for several minutes until she could feel that they'd both relaxed. Summer's racing heartbeat had calmed until it beat in sync with her own.

Autumn released Summer. Summer opened her eyes and stared at the tree that had so recently pressed her into the dirt with ponderous weight. "Autumn, how on earth did you lift that?"

Autumn turned back and looked at it and then at her hands. "I have no idea."

CHAPTER 8

Katherine Morgreed searched her memory for something comparable to what she was seeing in the desert outside the bunker. Even the prisoner executions her father had taken her to as a little girl were no match. Those had always been followed by ice cream and dinner at the governor's mansion, but she had no such comforts to rely on now. Barry was right. It had looked just like snow coming down for several minutes after the windstorm, but that wasn't what rattled her.

When her vision cleared, she was able to see part of the large crowd of protesters and journalists through the falling flakes. The majority of them were lying still on the ground, but here and there she could make out a person writhing in apparent distress. She was not one to be overly bothered by the suffering of others, but it wasn't a pleasant sight, and she was glad when a thick fog began to rise off the ground and obscure the view.

WEDNESDAY, JULY 9, 12:18 P.M. ET
Mount Washington Observatory—Mount Washington, New Hampshire
Elevation: 6,288 feet

"Look at that," Holly said, gazing out the observatory window.

Douglas put his phone away and leaned in next to her. "Wow, that's a thick blanket of fog. It must be the snow evaporating."

"I don't understand," Milford said. He was standing at the next window over. "None of this makes any sense."

"I better check on my helicopter," Craig said. He walked to the door and opened it. "That was some terrific wind and it wasn't tied down."

Holly glanced over. "I hope it's okay. That's the new one, isn't it?"

"Yeah."

"Observatory?" A crackly voice sounded from a radio on the desk. "Can you hear me?"

Douglas picked it up. "Observatory. Go ahead."

"This is Joe at Lakes of the Clouds Hut. We've lost all communication off the mountain."

"Same here," Douglas said.

"Any idea what just happened?"

"No, we think it might have been the climate system, but it's not clear."

"Well, it was intense. We're watching the fog right now. We're a little above it here, but we can see that it's coming off the snow and dissipating quickly. I'm going to go for a closer look before it's all gone."

"Okay, let us know what you see."

WEDNESDAY, JULY 9, 10:20 A.M. MT (12:20 P.M. ET)
Colorado Trail—near Breckenridge, Colorado
Elevation: 9,920 feet

"Are you sure you're okay?" Autumn asked. "You didn't break anything?"

Summer got to her feet. "Yeah, I think so, but can you check my back? It stings where the tree hit me."

"Your shirt is pretty dirty. Lift it up a bit."

"Here. Do you see anything?"

"You've got some scrapes, but they're not bleeding. Want me to put on some ointment?"

"Yes, get the antiseptic spray, too. It's in my bag."

Autumn retrieved Summer's pack and pulled out the emergency kit. It took her a minute to find the supplies and place some bandages over the area.

"Thanks," Summer said, "that feels better."

"We should call Mom and Dad. If that storm hit everywhere, they must be worried."

Summer pulled out her phone. "I don't have any service."

"Me neither."

"We're not all that far from Breckenridge. My phone was working before."

Autumn scanned the forest around them. "What do you want to do?"

Summer opened her trail map. "Well, I think we should keep going. Maybe we'll get a signal up on the ridge, and Copper Mountain is on the other side. We should be able to make it there before dark."

WEDNESDAY, JULY 9, 10:25 A.M. MT (12:25 P.M. ET)
Main control base—the desert south of Phoenix, Arizona
Elevation: 1,100 feet

"Can you see anything out there, Katherine?" Barry asked. "We should call an ambulance, but my phone has no signal."

"I think they're all dead. The fog is all gone, and so is the snow."

All dead? What was she talking about? "Who?" Barry asked.

Katherine turned. "What do you mean?"

"Who is dead?"

"All of them. Everyone outside."

"What?" She couldn't possibly mean everyone out there. That would be thousands of people. "How can they all be dead?"

"I don't know. Some of them were moving before the fog started, but I don't see any signs of life now."

Barry thought over the last half hour. "Why did Valentina attack the chairman? What happened?"

Katherine was trying the phones in the command center but threw down the last one. "Nothing works. I need to know if we were successful."

This was getting weird. Katherine was not making sense. She always seemed to have her own agenda, but more was going on here than she was sharing. "Successful at what? Katherine, what did you do?"

WEDNESDAY, JULY 9, 12:29 P.M. ET
Mount Washington Observatory—Mount Washington, New Hampshire
Elevation: 6,288 feet

"How is it?" Laura asked as soon as Craig returned from checking on the helicopter.

"It's okay," he said, "but the wind almost shifted it off the helipad. It's crazy out there. People are panicked. I heard them talking about some tourists getting blown off the observation deck, and it sounds like there were a lot of injuries."

"Wow," Laura said, envisioning the scene. She'd been on the deck during high winds. It was difficult to remain standing, and the force of the wind would carry her quite a distance if she jumped. The meteorologists enjoyed posting videos of the experience online, but for anyone not prepared for it . . . "The girls!" she said. "This might have hit where they are."

"Are the phones still down?" Craig asked, checking his again.

"Yes. Summer and Autumn are on the trail, and they're probably all alone."

"They should be fine up in the mountains."

"But we don't know until we can get in touch. What if they were hurt? What if—"

The radio crackled. "Help!"

Douglas snatched it off the desk. "Observatory here."

"I went down"—Joe coughed several times—"to see the fog." More coughing. "Need help."

"Okay, we'll be there soon."

"We'll go," Baxter said. "Cinnamon and I were planning to hike this afternoon anyway."

"All right," Douglas said. "See what's going on at the hut and call back."

"Laura, who were they?" Milford asked as the couple left the room.

"Huh?"

"Who were they? Are you okay? What's wrong?"

Laura stared at him. What's wrong? How was that even a question? Didn't he see what just happened? Summer and Autumn, her precious children, were out there—facing *that*—and she couldn't protect them. "My girls," she said, tears welling. "We can't reach them. They're on the trail."

"Oh," Milford said.

Craig's expression was worried as he put his arms around Laura. "They'll be okay. They have to be okay."

"I need to know for sure. I . . . " Words could not express what she was feeling, like something was being torn out of her. She was empty.

"They"—Craig blinked as his eyes brimmed—"they know what they're doing. They'll be okay."

Laura met his gaze and found her fears reflected. Their family . . . their daughters . . . A lifetime of memories flashed before her. Could they be . . .

"No," Craig said. Clearly he knew her thoughts. "No, Laura. They can't be." He brushed a tear from her cheek, then one from his own. "We'll find them. We will."

"Where are they?" Milford asked. "Who were . . . What?" He sounded impatient or flustered. Emotional situations—and relating to people in general—had never been his strong suit.

"I'm sorry, Milford," Laura said, sniffling as she reluctantly let go of Craig. "They're hiking in Colorado, and I completely forgot about introductions."

"That can wait," he said, frowning with concern.

"No. We may as well do it now. Does everyone know Dr. Pennychuck?"

"The climate guy," Holly said.

Laura nodded. "Yes. So, Milford, you certainly know my husband, Craig."

"Of course."

"Hey." Craig took a deep breath and closed his eyes as he leaned against the wall.

"And this is Douglas, the head meteorologist with the observatory."

"I'm a big fan of your work, Dr. Pennychuck," Douglas said, offering his hand.

"You've met Ashley, and this is her sister, Holly. Holly is one of my grad students, and she's working with me here over the summer. We've known her and Ashley forever, and they used to babysit the twins all the time."

"Ah," Milford said. "So she's the sister you mentioned."

Ashley nodded.

"And the pair that just left were Baxter and Cinnamon. They're grad students at UNH, and I guess they're soon to be married."

Milford smiled slightly. "That's wonderful—good for them. I'm happy to meet all of you, though I wish the circumstances were better."

Laura nodded. Talking was helping, though anxiety was still clawing in her stomach. "Well, what do you think we should do?" she asked.

Milford looked outside and at the system terminal again. "It seems to have cleared up out there, and this display is still frozen. I don't know what we can do other than wait and see. If this happened globally, I assume they'll shut down the system until we figure out what went wrong."

"I don't want to interrupt," Ashley said, "but I am still your nurse. We need to get you some food, and you need to stay off your feet to rest."

"You're right. Do they still have that wonderful little cafeteria up here?"

WEDNESDAY, JULY 9, 10:40 A.M. MT (12:40 P.M. ET)
Camp Hale—Leadville, Colorado
Elevation: 9,200 feet

"Sir, communications are still down," one of the militia members said. "The tents have all been put back up, and everyone is accounted for. What are your orders?"

Roman had been in discussion with the other leaders and was beginning to wonder whether there was more truth to the conspiracy theories than he'd thought. If there was a UN plot, cutting communication would be an obvious first step. Then they could move against different areas with little chance of anyone calling for backup. He'd spoken with the commanders of the Wyoming and New Mexico divisions earlier that morning, but for all he knew, they could be under attack that very moment.

"Here's what we'll do," Roman explained to his leadership group. "Double the lookouts on our perimeter. Tow the flak cannons onto the surrounding peaks, and dig them in. I want barricades on all the roads in and out, but we need to be able to get through quickly in the event we need to move. Detain anyone who approaches camp. Is that clear?"

"Yes, sir," the men replied.

WEDNESDAY, JULY 9, 10:47 A.M. MT (12:47 P.M. ET)
Main control base—the desert south of Phoenix, Arizona
Elevation: 1,100 feet

Barry finished applying a new bandage to Valentina's shoulder and turned his attention to Katherine. She was looking out the window of the control bunker. From where he sat, he could see that the sky was clear, but there was still no sign of movement outside. Katherine had been ignoring most of his questions, so he couldn't tell much more without leaving Valentina. He wanted to see what was going on out there for himself, but Katherine had refused him the few times he'd asked. What if there were a way to get help? Valentina was stable enough that it was time to start thinking of the larger situation.

Katherine's back was to him. Perhaps if he was quiet, he could sneak up behind her and . . . what? She was still holding her pistol, and she'd been on edge since the beginning of this mess. Twice already she'd fired at the ceiling when the air-conditioning kicked on. He had no doubt she'd do the same to him. It wasn't worth the risk.

Katherine turned and met his stare. Darkness clouded her already-sullen demeanor, and the hate in her eyes crushed his hope of overpowering her. He'd seen that look many times. It always came right before she tightened her screws of blackmail and control. She grabbed her large pocketbook and went around the room, collecting the guns from the security guards and checking the other bodies for anything of importance to her. Barry's stomach clenched. He'd been distracted with Valentina and hadn't even thought of obtaining a weapon, but now Katherine had taken that option from him. She was in her sixties and certainly no match for him physically, but a bullet could level the playing field in the time it would take him to get to his feet. He averted his eyes and hoped she wouldn't do anything more.

"I can see those gears spinning," Katherine said. "Believe me, Barry, I've seen how people can act out when under stress, and since I'm generally the cause of their stress, I find it's always wise to be prepared."

Barry said nothing.

"How is she doing?" Katherine asked.

"I don't know," he replied. He hadn't expected the conversation to continue—and certainly not in this direction. "I think the bullet is still inside, but the bleeding has mostly stopped. We need to get her to a hospital."

"She's not going anywhere. Not until we know what we're dealing with."

"But she could die."

Katherine motioned to the bodies around the room. "What does that matter? Why are you so concerned about her anyway? I know how she's treated you."

The question took Barry by surprise. "I'm not sure," he answered. "You're right, but that's no reason to let her die. I don't think I could live with that on my conscience."

"Conscience is a crutch for the weak," Katherine said and then turned her back to him.

Barry thought about her question. Why was he trying to save the life of this woman who had made him so miserable? Would she do the same for him? He had no idea, but in that brief second when she fell, she'd locked eyes with him and somehow conveyed a desperate plea for help without speaking a word. The image played over and over in his mind as he looked at Valentina's unconscious face. She looked so peaceful and untroubled by the turmoil of the last hour, and something deep inside kept telling him that she was no longer the malevolent serpent he knew so well.

WEDNESDAY, JULY 9, 1:03 P.M. ET
Sherman Adams Building—Mount Washington, New Hampshire
Elevation: 6,288 feet

Ashley sat at a table in the visitor center with Laura and the others, eating a slice of pizza. Something was bothering her about the room. "Hey," she said, "has anyone noticed that no one is arriving at the summit? A bunch of people left after the event, but I haven't seen a single hiker or car come up the road in at least half an hour. It's a summer day. Where is everyone?"

"Maybe they're all outside?" Holly said.

"No, she's right," Craig said. "I took a good look around before we came in here. I didn't see more than ten or fifteen people."

"That is strange, now that you mention it," Douglas said. "There were a bunch of group hikes organized for today. The Appalachian Mountain Club was holding a big fundraiser, and so was the observatory. It was really busy this morning, but like you said, it's petered out."

"I wouldn't be surprised if they shut down the Auto Road after what happened," Laura said.

Ashley shivered. "I sure hope so. Driving up that road freaks me out even when the weather is good."

"That wind was really strong," Holly said. "Anyone hiking above tree line might have been injured or decided to turn back."

"But it was so brief," Douglas said. "Most experienced hikers would probably consider it a fluke and keep going. We get strong winds up here all the time."

"Look. The Cog train is coming up," Laura said. "Maybe they'll bring some news."

"It's coming in a bit fast," Douglas said. "Something's not right."

Ashley stood to get a better view while the others lined the windows. The train chugged up the track. Without slowing down, it passed by the loading area, crashed through the barrier, and fell off the end of the trestle, where the engine and passenger car decoupled before coming to rest. She blinked. Had she really just seen that? Was this real? No, things like this weren't supposed to happen. She closed her eyes.

"Come on," Craig shouted. Footsteps pounded toward the exit.

Ashley looked again. Nothing had changed. This was real. There were people on that train, and they could be hurt. She'd prepared for this. She worked in the emergency room. She knew how to help. It was her job. What was she waiting for? She turned to Milford. "If you're okay here, I should go with them. There may be injuries."

Milford dropped the pizza he'd been holding and shifted his gaze from the train. "Go ahead. So much for your day off."

"Tell me about it," Ashley yelled over her shoulder as she headed away. She pushed through the doors of the visitor center and sprinted across the gravel to where the train sat. She tried to remember which doctors were on the schedule. They would need to be called, and she would need to get the paramedics on the way, maybe even a helicopter. The hospital wasn't far by air. Hopefully no one would be injured severely. She had nothing to work with and no one to help her.

Craig and the others were standing in front of the car, staring. Why weren't they moving? What was wrong with them? "Come on," Ashley yelled. "What are you waiting for?"

"They're all dead," Holly said.

"What?" How could she say that? She wasn't even on the train. Ashley jumped up the stairs on the back of the carriage, then stopped short at the sight in front of her. She expected cuts, injuries, and blood. She was ready for crying children, frightened people, and the sounds of suffering. This made no sense. This hadn't been in any of her training scenarios. This was . . . What was this? Some of the passengers were seated, others were sprawled on the floor, but none of them were moving. No sounds, no screams, no signs whatsoever that they'd crashed only moments before—but also no signs of life. How could that be? She knelt by the nearest person and felt for a pulse. There was none, and the same was true for the next few she tried. She hopped off the train and rejoined the group. "What happened?"

Laura was pacing. "Douglas, how long do these trains take to climb up the mountain?"

"A little over an hour."

Laura looked at her watch. "So that would put it leaving the station around the time of the system start or maybe a little before."

"Yes, I suppose."

"And the train would have been at a low enough elevation to be in the field produced by the system?"

"Definitely."

"Oh my." Laura clapped a hand to her mouth.

"What?" Ashley asked. What was Laura getting at?

Laura's expression was sheer terror. "That might mean everyone under the 1.5-kilometer reflector altitude is . . . is . . . "

"Dead," Craig said.

CHAPTER 9

Baxter took Cinnamon's hand as they hiked down the final stretch of the rocky path from the summit to the Lakes of the Clouds Hut, a shingle-sided building just above the tree line on the slope of Mount Washington. Situated next to the Lakes of the Clouds, it was the highest of the backcountry lodges operated by the Appalachian Mountain Club.

"Are you from the observatory?" asked one of the hikers milling about the premises.

"Yes," Baxter said. "Where's Joe?"

"You better get inside. That guy is not doing well."

Baxter hurried to the door. He held it open for Cinnamon and then entered behind her. A few more hikers were sitting at the tables in the dining area, and one of them motioned to the bunk rooms. The scents of coffee and baked goods fresh out of the oven seemed wholly at odds with the somber expressions on the hikers' faces, but he planned to pick up a brownie before they returned to the summit.

"Come on," Cinnamon said, tugging him to the hallway.

Baxter entered the room and found it empty except for Joe lying on a lower bunk and two of the lodge staff standing by his side, a man and woman he didn't recognize.

"What happened?" Cinnamon asked.

"We saw the big flash," the female staff member explained, "and then the wind came roaring through, and the snow started."

"It was the oddest sight," the man said. "I was watching the valley from the back windows. It started snowing down there below us, and it was like there was a certain amount and that was it."

"What do you mean?" Baxter asked. That explanation had been confusing at best. How could it snow below them?

"I mean," the man said, gesturing, "it was like the snow suddenly appeared in the air over the valley and fell. I watched the whole thing. It went down all at once, like I could watch the top of the snow going down until it was all on the ground. Imagine you were sitting on top of a cloud, watching the snow fall down from beneath you, and then the faucet was turned off and you watched the last flakes to leave get farther and farther away. It was like that."

The woman nodded. "And then the fog started building in the valley. I guess it was coming off the snow. It seemed to stay pretty close to ground level because none of it drifted up all the way to the hut, but it was close."

"A bunch of hikers wanted to see it," the man said. "They ran down the ravine trail. None of them have come back."

The woman placed a hand on Joe's shoulder. "And Joe decided to go take a closer look before it was gone, so he went after them. It lasted only a few minutes or so. He came back pretty quickly, but he was coughing terribly and having a hard time breathing. We got him some water, but he's been getting worse."

Joe nodded slowly and turned his head toward Baxter. His breathing was shallow and raspy. "Not . . . fog," he whispered, struggling to get each word out. "Burned . . . lungs . . . breathing . . . "

"Did you get to see the snow?" Cinnamon asked.

Joe shook his head. "Not . . . close . . . enough . . . "

Baxter looked at his phone. Joe's pleading gaze was unsettling. "I still don't have any signal. Are you guys out, too?"

The woman shrugged. "We've kept checking, and so have the hikers. All of the providers seem to be having the same problem, and the only place we can reach on the radio is the summit."

"We should check back with them," Cinnamon said, taking a radio from her belt.

"Yes," Baxter said, "but some of the other hikers could be down the trail and need help. We should take a look."

Cinnamon keyed the radio. "Observatory, this is Cinnamon."

"Douglas here."

"We're at the hut. Joe went to see the fog and breathed in some of it. He's having respiratory problems. There may be other hikers on the trail. We're going to check."

"Be careful. A Cog train arrived a while ago, and everyone onboard was dead. We're pretty certain it had something to do with them being in the system field. If you see any trace of that fog, don't go near it."

"We won't. We'll check back if we see anything."

"Same here."

Cinnamon returned the radio to her belt and looked at Baxter. "Ready?"

MICHAEL JAMES EMBERGER   101

"Yeah. Uh, Joe. Did you see any of the hikers that left before you?"

Joe shook his head.

Baxter glanced to the window, then at Cinnamon. "If the others were ahead of him and went deeper into the fog . . . "

"They probably didn't make it," she said, "but we don't know for sure."

WEDNESDAY, JULY 9, 1:46 P.M. ET
Sherman Adams Building—Mount Washington, New Hampshire
Elevation: 6,288 feet

"How many people live below 1.5 kilometers?" Milford asked. The group had reconvened in the visitor center. "That's close to a mile elevation. I can't fathom it."

"It has to be billions," Douglas said. "I think the majority of the world's population is close to sea level."

Milford wiped tears from his eyes. "This is all my fault. The system was my idea. I calculated the reaction. I'm responsible for this."

"No," Laura said, "that's not true. We don't know what happened. Maybe Dr. Severnaya used one of the failure conditions you were talking about and that caused this. We probably can't trust what our terminal is showing."

"I told her we had to delay. Why couldn't she listen to reason?"

"We don't know what she did," Douglas said, "or why. Dr. Pennychuck, you did the responsible thing. No one can blame you for the actions of others."

"But what if all of my models and calculations were totally wrong? What if I made mistakes that no one caught? We wouldn't be in this predicament if I'd never started the project."

"Then I bear some blame, too," Laura said. "My work enabled them to design the field network. And every scientist that reviewed the work is to blame—and every politician that voted to go ahead and every citizen that supported this project. We can blame every engineer with a hand in the design and every construction worker that tightened a bolt."

"That's ridiculous. They couldn't have known that this would happen."

"And neither could you, but you told Dr. Severnaya to wait. She's the one that put you in the hospital and went ahead. If anyone is to blame, blame her."

Ashley burst into tears. "I should be dead. I would be at the hospital right now if Dr. Pennychuck hadn't taken me with him."

Holly held her sobbing sister. "Gosh, I hadn't thought of that. And, Laura"—her own tears welled—"so would I if you hadn't asked me to help you this summer."

Laura's eyes went wide. "All of us are only here on the mountain by coincidence, well, except for you, Douglas. You're always here."

"No," Douglas said, his face turning pale. "I was supposed to be at a conference this week, but it was rescheduled."

"Wow," Craig said. "That's a lot to process."

WEDNESDAY, JULY 9, 12:04 P.M. MT (2:04 P.M. ET)
Camp Hale—Leadville, Colorado
Elevation: 9,200 feet

High up in the Rockies, Roman was pleased to see that preparations at the camp were proceeding well. Many of the men were excited about the prospect of fighting the UN, though others were beginning to worry about their families at home since they could no longer call to check in. The satellite television had stopped receiving broadcasts, and even the old shortwave radios they kept on hand played nothing but static. They were truly cut off from the rest of the world.

Roman entered the mess tent and stood in line for a cheeseburger and fries. He had to hand it to the militia—they knew how to do food. A steady diet of their menu wouldn't do for the regular army, but it was fun once in a while. He put creamer and sugar in a cup of coffee and then sat at one of the long tables reserved for the command staff.

"Sir, there's still no sign of the invasion," an officer announced as he took a seat across from Roman.

"They must know we're up here," Roman replied through a mouthful of food.

"Certainly. I think we should send out some scouts to get a better look at the surroundings and give us advance warning if anything is coming. The long-range handheld radios are still working."

"That's not a bad idea." Roman pulled a map out of his pocket and studied it. "We should send a party west to Glenwood Springs, one east to Denver, and one south to cover Colorado Springs and the approach up the valley. Tell them to be discreet."

"Understood, sir," the officer said before leaving to carry out the order.

Roman chewed in silence for a moment, then pulled out his wallet and looked at the single picture he carried in it. It was of Valentina standing on the bank of the Dvina River on a summer day in Arkhangelsk. She was laughing at something he said while they were out for a walk. He couldn't remember the conversation, just the radiant glow of her expression that had spurred him to snap the photo. Looking at it now haunted him, as it had for several years. It was the last time he'd seen her happy. He'd left on business matters the next morning, and when he returned to his apartment several weeks later, there was a brief letter waiting for him. He hadn't seen her since.

Roman put the picture away and closed his eyes. The mess tent was not a good place for emotions, and he had to maintain his tough-as-nails image for the benefit of the troops. He wondered what Valentina was doing at that moment. Analyzing climate data? Toasting the success of the project? Coordinating troop movements with the UN? He could only guess. Was she even the same person he'd known back in Russia, and would they ever meet again? He was not a very religious man, but for the first time in many years, he felt compelled to pray.

WEDNESDAY, JULY 9, 3:23 P.M. ET
Mount Washington Cog Railway Marshfield Base
Station—Mount Washington, New Hampshire
Elevation: 2,700 feet

Baxter stopped when he arrived at the bottom of the Ammonoosuc Ravine Trail. Cinnamon was crying, as she had been for most of their hike down. He pulled her to his chest and held her as he tried to think of something comforting to say.

"I don't know if I can do this," she whispered. "How many more dead people do we need to see?"

"So," Milford said, "if that was the case, the wind would be produced by air from the upper atmosphere coming down suddenly?"

"I think so."

Milford frowned. "Fascinating, but I can't imagine what would cause it. I can't think of any way the climate system would be able to change the air pressure."

"Does the snow offer any clue to that?" Laura asked.

"I've got nothing," Douglas said.

"I'll have to think about it." Milford looked at Laura. The snow was bothering him. It had to hold the key to the problem. He just couldn't think of an explanation. It made no sense.

WEDNESDAY, JULY 9, 5:00 P.M. ET
Ammonoosuc Ravine Trail—Mount Washington, New Hampshire
Elevation: 3,600 feet

"Close your eyes," Baxter said, then took Cinnamon's hand and guided her past a lone hiker curled up on the side of the trail. After leaving the Cog station, their ascent had been slow because of Baxter's insistence that Cinnamon would not have to see another dead body on the way back up. They walked several paces around a bend, and he scanned the path ahead. "Okay, it's clear for a while."

"Thank you for doing this for me," Cinnamon said, opening her eyes. "I know they're still there, but it helps. Not seeing them makes all the difference."

Baxter tucked a loose strand of hair behind Cinnamon's ear and looked into her eyes. He saw her sadness, but the love she held for him was still in there, too. It would survive this storm, and her joy would return. He was sure of it. "I promise, when this is all over, we'll go somewhere far away from here."

Cinnamon nodded. "That sounds really nice. I want to get off this mountain and then never come back. Let's go somewhere flat, like Kansas."

"You want to go to Kansas?"

"Yes, we could have a farm with horses and fields as far as you can see, and we'll go for rides at sunset and take our crops to the fair, and the kids will run and play all day long."

"The kids?"

"Of course. Lots of them."

Baxter felt tears coming to his eyes as he imagined the place Cinnamon was seeing. "That sounds perfect."

"And the crickets will chirp on summer nights, just like they are now, and we'll lay out under the stars and watch the sky."

"Crickets?" Baxter asked.

"Yes, don't you hear them?"

Baxter paused and listened. There was a faint crackling coming from somewhere. "I hear something, but I don't think it's crickets."

The radio on Cinnamon's belt squawked, and they heard a few garbled words.

She brought it up. "Hello? Please repeat."

More garble and noise came from the radio.

"I didn't catch any of that," Baxter said.

"Hello? Please repeat," Cinnamon said again.

The noises out of the radio were even worse.

"That sound is getting louder," he observed.

"Look." She pointed up.

Barry started when a hand grabbed his arm. He turned to check on Valentina, thinking she might be shifting in her sleep again, but her eyes were open. She was staring at him.

WEDNESDAY, JULY 9, 3:15 P.M. MT (5:15 P.M. ET)
Camp Hale—Leadville, Colorado
Elevation: 9,200 feet

The wind had flattened the militia's tents again, but their work to reinforce the camp limited the impact. Roman rode out the gust in his Subaru and then convened the officers for a conference.

"Have we heard from the scouts?" he asked.

"Yes," an officer said, "they all responded. They're still traveling to their positions."

"Good. I have to wonder why the UN would run the system again. What would the purpose even be since they already took out communications?"

"Maybe they needed to hit some places a second time," one of the officers suggested. "If they didn't disable everything on the first round, they might still be softening up targets before the invasion."

"That seems likely," another officer agreed. "If it was just a climate system like they claimed, they wouldn't keep it going after the first round did so much damage. That was a far cry from tiny sparkles. It's no climate system—that's for sure."

"I really wish we knew what was going on," Roman said. "This waiting in darkness is driving me crazy. Let me know as soon as the scouts report anything."

WEDNESDAY, JULY 9, 5:20 P.M. ET
Sherman Adams Building—Mount Washington, New Hampshire
Elevation: 6,288 feet

"Baxter, Cinnamon," Douglas called into the radio, "do you copy? Lakes of the Clouds, do you copy?"

"It's been almost twenty minutes," Laura said, "and they were only partway up the ravine when it hit. I don't think they made it."

"No." Milford sniffled. It was too much. He'd seen them. He'd seen their joy. Now it was gone. It hit too close to home, though *that* was not something he would share. "It's not right. They were so happy. Th-they were going to get married."

Ashley rubbed his back. "There's still a chance, isn't there? Maybe they're okay."

"I don't think so . . . "

"We don't know that," Douglas said, "but what about the hut? They were fine last time. Why aren't they responding?"

"Maybe the field got them," Holly said.

"I doubt it," Laura replied. "The altitude doesn't change unless the reflector balloons are raised or lowered. It's very precise. If they were above it last time, they would have been this time, too."

"Could they have raised the balloons?" Ashley asked.

Milford blew his nose with a napkin. What a terrible notion, certainly not one he would approve of, though no one was asking for his opinion anymore. "Yes, they could have, but why? After what the first run did, how could they?"

"What if they don't know?" Holly asked. "Could it have worked normally at the control base?"

"No," Milford said. "I'm confident of that. Whatever we saw here would have happened globally." Unless . . . Whatever had happened, it was not within the design parameters. Was his confidence warranted?

"Where is the control base?" Ashley asked.

"It's south of Phoenix at an old bomb testing range in the desert."

"Maybe they got hit by the field," Holly said.

Milford thought. Even if something had been changed, the system was built to create an even field distribution. There was no way to alter that. The problem they observed *had* to be global. "That base is at a fairly low elevation," he said. "All of them are. So, yes, it would have been under the field. But main control was put in a sealed bunker in case of unintended side effects of the system or almost any other conceivable disaster. It's operating if the system is still running."

"So why don't the people there do something?" Douglas asked. "Could they be dead?"

"I doubt it," Milford said. "From what I heard, the bunker is nearly indestructible. They said it could take a nuclear shock wave that would level most buildings. It's electrically shielded, radiation shielded, and it even has a positive air pressure system in case of chemical attack. I think they'd be fine unless someone opened the door."

"And if someone did?" Douglas asked.

Milford shuddered. "Then they would probably be dead."

The door slammed behind Craig as he entered the visitor center. "The helicopter is okay. It's a good thing I tethered it down after the first time."

"Good thinking," Laura said.

Douglas tried the radio again. "Why don't they answer?"

Holly got up from the table. "I'll run down to the hut and check."

"No," Ashley said. "It's too dangerous."

"I'll be careful, and I'll come right back. We need to know what's going on there."

"We could fly down in the chopper," Craig offered.

"No, it's not that far. I won't be long."

"Call us on the radio when you arrive," Douglas said. "In the meantime, I'll be in the weather center. I should check if we logged any readings during the second event that can tell us anything new."

WEDNESDAY, JULY 9, 3:38 P.M. MT (5:38 P.M. ET)
Main control base—the desert south of Phoenix, Arizona
Elevation: 1,100 feet

In the control bunker, Barry and Valentina had locked eyes for several tense minutes, but he had no idea what Valentina was thinking. Her expression shifted between anger, fear, confusion, pain, and a few other unclear emotions. Barry was unsettled by the intensity of her focus on him. His instinct was to avert his gaze as he'd always done when she approached him with provocative intent, but he couldn't do it. That aspect was missing from her countenance. It was something else in those piercing eyes that held him transfixed. They were boring into him with uncertainty, sadness, or perhaps even despair. It was a look that Barry had caught glimpses of before, and it had always caused him to wonder.

He finally glanced down, realizing that Valentina's hand remained on his arm. When he opened his mouth to say something, she tightened her grip. He stayed silent, but she winced and let out a whimper of pain since she was holding him with her right arm on her injured side. Barry checked to see whether Katherine was watching, but she was still glued to the window. When he turned back to Valentina, she signaled with her left index finger for him to be silent and then made a couple of gestures indicating she wanted his phone. He placed it in her hand.

Barry was watching Katherine at the window again when he felt Valentina bumping the phone against his elbow. He took it from her and read the short message she'd typed.

"She shot me. Don't trust her. We need to talk."

Barry looked up with alarm. Valentina's intense stare had softened to an imploring expression of worry. "Her?" he mouthed, pointing in Katherine's direction.

Valentina nodded.

Barry was more confused than ever. He hadn't seen who fired those first shots. He'd been focused on watching Valentina attack the chairman and assumed it was one of the security guards doing the shooting. His mind raced as he thought back over the event. After dispatching the chairman, Valentina had stood facing his direction. He was near Katherine in front of the window. The shots rang out, and the red spot blossomed on Valentina's shirt. It was on the front of her shirt, but the guards were off to her side. Then the other gunfire started.

Barry looked at the control terminal screen on the desk in front of him. Based on the shape of the hole and pattern of cracks surrounding it, the bullet had hit it straight from behind. That was Katherine's shot. It had to be. Why hadn't he thought of any of this before? There had been more gunfire but from more than one source. The guards must have been shooting at Katherine. He looked at the front wall of the bunker, where she'd been standing. There were pock marks on the concrete under the window, probably from bullets. So she exchanged fire with the guards and won. He'd seen what happened next when she shot the rest of the officials. But why? Why would she want to shoot Valentina? Wasn't Valentina Katherine's most trusted associate? That's what he'd thought.

"Why?" Barry mouthed to Valentina, handing the phone back to her.

Valentina slowly typed a reply with her left hand and turned the phone so Barry could see it. "Long story. Not now. Don't tell her I'm awake. Need water."

Barry opened a water bottle and handed it to her. She gulped down half of it, watching Katherine out of the corner of her eye, and then gave it back.

Barry took the phone and quickly keyed in his own message. "What's going on?"

Valentina read it and put down a reply. "Get her to leave and we'll talk. I have questions, too."

Barry was going to reply, but Valentina shut her eyes after giving him the phone. For some reason she didn't want Katherine to know she was conscious, and it was probably a bullet-shaped reason lodged in her shoulder. Barry observed Katherine in a different light. She hadn't moved from her spot at the window for quite some time. What was she looking for out there? What had she been scheming, and what were her intentions now? He needed to think of a way to convince her to leave the bunker, at least for a few minutes. So far she'd been intent on not letting him out of her sight, so it had to be something she couldn't trust him to tag along for.

Barry turned to Valentina again. Though her eyes were closed, her expression betrayed the pain she was enduring. If Katherine looked at her with any level of scrutiny, she would see that the blank serenity of sleep had disappeared. He had to think of something soon.

WEDNESDAY, JULY 9, 6:03 P.M. ET
AMC Lakes of the Clouds Hut—Mount Washington, New Hampshire
Elevation: 5,030 feet

Holly completed her inspection of the hut and sat on an outdoor bench to radio the observatory. Her heart ached for Baxter and Cinnamon. They were nowhere to be seen, confirming her fear that they'd been too far down the mountain. She'd known them for a couple of months since starting her summer work with Laura and had grown to really like them. Baxter had been so nervous about his proposal, and he'd peppered Holly with questions every chance he had when Cinnamon was not around. Would Cinnamon like this or that better? Should he do this thing or that thing? He'd even trusted Holly's opinion on an engagement ring, returning three or four she rejected until finding one that was perfect.

Cinnamon had also been a good friend and was sharing a room with Holly at the observatory for the summer. They had conversations about everything. She had so many dreams for the future and would talk long into the night as they lay in their bunks. She was such a sweet and caring person, and now none of those dreams would come true.

"Observatory, do you copy?" Holly said into the radio.

"Yes, this is Douglas," came the reply.

"I'm at the hut. There were several hikers here, but they're all dead. So are Joe and the other staff. I don't see Baxter and Cinnamon."

"Did you find anything that could help to explain this?"

"Not much. The windows are blown out, and the inside is a mess, but otherwise things look normal, except for the people."

"Okay. Come back up right away."

"Understood. You don't have to convince me. This is creepy."

Holly returned the radio to her belt and set off up the trail. She'd been trying not to think of the ramifications of everyone she knew being caught in the event, but it was impossible to block out those thoughts entirely. She was grateful that Ashley was on the summit with her—and Laura and Craig, too. They were the closest family and friends she had. The Pottersmiths had always been like a second family to her. She'd helped watch the twins when they were little and had shared countless meals and experiences with their family.

She'd always admired Laura and had chosen her college major and graduate studies in the same field. Getting to work with her was great, but that didn't mean Craig was any less important in her life. He'd given her part-time and summer jobs with his business since she was in high school. She'd started with office work, but during her college years she began learning about the helicopters and flying. She was ecstatic when Craig offered to help her get her pilot's license, and by the time she was working on her master's degree, she was flying charters on the side. She couldn't imagine a better life, and now she couldn't imagine better people to be with.

CHAPTER 11

What did Katherine seem to want the most? Several minutes of observation brought the obvious answer to Barry's mind. She'd been checking for a phone connection ever since service was lost, and she seemed desperate to contact someone.

"Katherine," Barry said, startling her after they'd gone so long without speaking.

"What?"

"I was just thinking. All those news vans outside probably have satellite links, or the police may have radios or something. We should go out and check."

"Hmm," Katherine said, peering out with renewed interest, "that's true."

"We should also gather more food and water if they have any," Barry added. "We don't have a whole lot here, and who knows how much longer we'll be waiting?"

Katherine thought for a moment. "I'll go out and check. You're staying here, and don't even think of running or trying to lock me out of the bunker. There's nowhere to go for miles, and I have the access code to the door and the emergency key."

"Okay," Barry replied in a somewhat-disappointed voice. He was playing on Katherine's distrust of him, assuming that she too would think of all the police out there with guns that he might go for if given the chance.

"Open the door and then stand back," Katherine ordered, pointing her pistol at him.

He complied, glad to see she was going along with the plan.

"I won't be long," Katherine said, and then she was gone.

Barry ran to the window and waited until he could see her walking out to the news area. Then he rushed to Valentina's side. "Okay. We have a few minutes."

Valentina didn't reply or open her eyes. Barry's stomach clenched. Had she died? He leaned closer. She was breathing, and her countenance was peaceful again. She'd fallen asleep. He reached for her but paused, thinking of their stormy relationship over the last several years. She'd bullied, manipulated, threatened, and blackmailed him and coerced him to do her and Katherine's bidding, all while keeping up the appearance that they were having an affair, which kept him tiptoeing around the office and his family.

All that time he'd struggled with resisting her advances. She was gorgeous and, to be honest, far out of his league. He never knew whether she actually had some twisted desire for him, despite the way she treated him otherwise, or whether it was just a calculated act for some purpose known only to her. He'd been focused on tending to her wound earlier and hadn't thought about it, but now he was hesitant to touch her. Her being unconscious helped keep the reality of the situation out of his mind, but now would be different.

Barry labored over how to do it for a few moments. He didn't want to aggravate her shoulder, so he'd have to be gentle, but that made him feel awkward. None of the ways he woke his wife seemed appropriate. He didn't want to convey the wrong idea. But time was wasting. Barry took Valentina's left hand and squeezed it. She didn't respond. He brushed a palm over her shoulder. No response. "Valentina, wake up." He gathered some of her hair and tugged a bit, which got her to scrunch her eyes closed a little farther. "Dr. Severnaya," he said louder than he'd wanted to, "wake up!"

Valentina opened her eyes. "Bar . . . " she said, then coughed.

Barry offered her the water bottle again, and she drank.

"Barry, where's Katherine?"

"She's outside checking for a working phone."

"Why?" Valentina asked, confusion obvious on her face.

Barry was hit with the realization that Valentina had slept through the system running. "I guess you don't know what happened, do you?"

"The chairman lunged at me, and I reacted, and then Katherine shot me, and then . . . "

"What were you doing?"

"An upload, but what happened then? Did the system start?"

"Um, yes, but it was crazy. The sky flashed bright white, and there was a massive windstorm, and then it was snowing, and then that turned to fog. Everyone out there is dead, and we have no way to reach anyone."

Valentina's eyes had been widening as she listened to Barry's description. "No, it wasn't supposed to happen like that."

"What do you mean?"

"Is there anyone else here?"

"No, Katherine shot everyone in the room, and the rest were outside. It's just the three of us."

Valentina took on a pained expression. "Barry, we've been working against this climate system from the start. Katherine . . . and the Society . . . You have no idea."

"I . . . " Working against it? The Society? What was she talking about? "I don't understand."

"No, you wouldn't know. I'm sorry. I doubt we have much time, and I really have to go to the restroom."

"Wait," Barry said but not before Valentina attempted to sit up. She groaned and fell back on the couch.

"Your shoulder," he said. "I was just going to say take it slow or it's going to hurt. I think the bullet is still in there. I managed to stop the bleeding and bandaged it, but you really need to get to a hospital."

Valentina glanced down as she clenched her teeth. "Argh, I wasn't thinking. Help me up."

Barry propped her up on the couch and assisted her to her feet. "Take it slow," he said. "You lost a lot of blood, and I don't want you passing out on me."

"You saved my life," Valentina said as Barry helped her out to the hallway. "Why?"

Why indeed? He still didn't know the answer to that question. "I had to. I can't fully explain it. I hope it was the right choice."

A tear rolled down Valentina's cheek. "Barry, I'm sorry. For everything. I know what you must think of me, but Katherine forced me to do it. She's evil. She made me do things, say things, act with cruelty. I couldn't say no. She was watching me constantly. I'm not who you think I am."

These revelations were too much for him to process. Valentina was sorry? Katherine forced her? How could that be? She wasn't who he thought she was? "Who are you?"

"That's not important," she said as they reached the restroom. "I think I can manage, but check on me if I'm more than a few minutes."

Barry held the door and then waited in the hallway. His feeling had been right. This was not the Dr. Severnaya he knew. Whatever hold Katherine had on her must have been broken or no longer mattered. He was intrigued to say the least. He knew his position—do Katherine's bidding or go to jail for his stock trading—but what could she be holding over Valentina?

Valentina came back into the hall. "I'm starving. Do we have any food?"

"Yes, we have some things in the control room."

"Okay. Let's get back there. Maybe I can figure out what happened with the system."

Barry's spirits lifted for a moment; then he remembered. "Didn't you see? Katherine shot the control terminal. We can't use it."

Valentina stopped walking. "You're joking."

"No. I assume the other bullet was meant for you but hit the screen."

"And you said everyone outside died after the system ran?" She turned toward the exit door.

"Yes, and I think the flash must have woken you when it went off the second time."

Valentina's head snapped to face him, her eyes wide. "Ahh!" Her hand shot to her shoulder and she grimaced. "It ran twice?"

"Yes. Are you okay?"

"How long between?" she asked through clenched teeth.

Barry looked at his watch. "Um, five hours."

"It's on auto," Valentina whispered.

"Huh?" Auto what? What did she mean? He reached toward her awkwardly. She was clearly in pain, but what could he do? He dropped his hand.

She took a deep breath and relaxed her posture. "If it ran again, that means it will keep going every five hours on automatic control."

"For how long?"

"I don't know. We need to move."

"What were you uploading?" Barry asked as they entered the bunker.

"System failure conditions."

"Did they work?" Wait—what did she just say? Failure?

"Maybe," Valentina said as she sat on the couch, "but it should have fried the system. It shouldn't still be working."

Barry opened a packaged sandwich and handed it to her. Whatever was going on with her and Katherine, they hadn't included him, but he needed answers. "Is that why Katherine is so anxious?"

"I suppose. If communication is down, then she hasn't been able to reach her associates, but she must also be wondering what went wrong."

"What should we do?"

"I don't know. You can't trust her. I should have known she'd never keep her promise."

"What promise?"

Valentina went even paler than she already was, and her eyes started watering. "Even if she meant to . . . if all the people outside are . . . he's not . . . unless . . . Barry, you have to get her to talk. She has to believe I'm still unconscious, or she'll most likely kill me. I have to think, and I need to hear what she says to know for sure. Get her talking about why she did this. If she brings up the Arctic Circle Society, you're on the right track, but you can't mention that directly, or she'll get suspicious. I need to hear what her plans were for me."

Barry checked out the window and spotted Katherine walking back from the news vans. "I think we're out of time. She's coming back. I'll see what I can do. Is your shoulder okay?"

Valentina nodded and finished the sandwich, and Barry helped her lie on the couch as she'd been before. "Thank you," she said before closing her eyes.

"How did she force you to do this?" Barry asked.

"I . . . I can't talk about that, not yet. You'll understand. I'm barely holding on. I won't be able to if I say it out loud."

Barry ran to the window. Katherine was almost to the bunker. He took a deep breath to calm his nerves and then sat on the couch by Valentina as if nothing had changed. "I'll get us out of here," he said, adjusting her hair to how he thought it had been. "I'll figure something out."

WEDNESDAY, JULY 9, 7:12 P.M. ET
Sherman Adams Building—Mount Washington, New Hampshire
Elevation: 6,288 feet

Milford was sitting in the visitor center lounge, thinking. He'd been wary of Morgreed Industries and Katherine for a long time, and it seemed his distrust was warranted. Katherine and Dr. Severnaya had always seemed to be working on their own agenda, but he could never pinpoint what it was that bothered him. Katherine had made little to no effort to conceal how profitable the system contract was for her company, but that wasn't out of the ordinary. Neither were the fraud, waste, and mismanagement of the construction. All of those were normal aspects of large government projects.

But what had bothered him most was the secrecy. Morgreed Industries, the EPA, the IPCC . . . all of them shared as little information as possible, even with him. It was his plan, yet he'd had to constantly push to get the design details he needed to refine his software models. Even so, he'd never been confident that they were giving him correct information. It should have raised more of an alarm in his mind, but he'd been too busy to step back and think about it, and until the events of the last couple of weeks, he had no reason to suspect anyone of foul play.

And what had really gone wrong with the reaction? Dr. Severnaya had wanted his calculated conditions for system failure. It seemed likely that for some reason she had started the system using one of those configurations. Why would anyone want to do that? What purpose could it serve? Who would benefit? All good questions, but figuring out what happened was the far more pressing concern.

None of the computer simulations predicted anything even remotely close to the type of event that occurred. The reaction was supposed to make such a small change that it would be barely noticeable after only one run. The amount of energy required to achieve that result was enormous, and he could only guess at what it would take to do what they'd seen.

Had his calculations been incorrect, or had their estimates of reactor output been wrong? That avenue was worth consideration. He'd never run models using power outputs higher than a certain range, but if the power was increased by orders of magnitude, what would that do? It would probably result in greater changes and maybe even extend beyond affecting only the carbon. His process had been finely tuned to that substance, but with more power . . . The possibilities started to become frightening.

Laura and Craig joined him at the table. They'd disappeared into the kitchen for a while and prepared dinner for everyone from the food left when the staff headed home. Holly entered the building with Ashley, who'd been waiting outside and watching for her. Douglas was the last to join them when he came over from the weather center.

"Friends," Laura said to the group around the table, "I want to say something. I don't know what's going on exactly, and I'm trying not to think about what's happened at lower elevations, but I feel like we're all here for a reason, and I thank God that all of you are with me. If this is the end, well, I love you all."

Craig put an arm around her. "There's no place I'd rather be."

Holly and Ashley shared a brief look. "Us, too," Holly said.

"I'll drink to that," Milford agreed.

Douglas sat in silence for long enough that it was clear he was not going to join in the sentiment. "Um," he said, "I hate to put a damper on things, but, Laura, you might be right about this being the end."

"What do you mean?" Laura asked.

"I looked at the readings from the second event and compared them to the first. The duration of the windstorm was slightly longer. The max wind speed was slightly faster. The local pressure and other variables fall in line with why the hut was hit on the second run. We know the system was set at an altitude of 1.5 kilometers the first time. By my calculations, it was raised to 1.6, which is a difference of a little over three hundred feet."

Milford groaned. "This can't be!" Douglas had confirmed his worst fear.

"It has to be," Douglas said. "You guys said earlier that if everything looked good after the initial run, they would set it on auto, and it would rise incrementally until reaching operating altitude."

"But it didn't look good after the initial run."

"No, but the data matches a 0.1-kilometer increase."

"Then somehow the control system was set to keep going," Laura said.

"And there's probably no one there to stop it," Milford added.

"So what will happen?" Holly asked.

Milford turned to face her. "If no one stops it, the system runs every five hours until the carbon target is met."

"How long will that take?" Craig asked.

"If it was running as I'd intended, it would take several years, but we don't know what it's doing now."

"Won't it run out of fuel?" Ashley asked.

Milford frowned. "Dedicated nuclear plants were constructed to power everything related to the system, and the burst reactors are nuclear as well. Unless something breaks, it could be ten years or more until refueling is necessary. With the technology now, they'll run quite happily even if no one is there to watch."

"We can't wait up here for ten years," Holly said.

"No, we can't," Douglas said, "but it won't matter. If the system altitude keeps increasing, the summit will be hit by the field within three or four runs. We have approximately thirteen to eighteen hours."

"When will it run next?" Craig asked.

"Ten o'clock tonight, assuming the schedule was set before it started the first time."

"What are we going to do?" Holly asked.

"If we could get to main control," Milford said, "we could shut it down."

"But that's all the way across the country," Ashley said. "We have less than three hours until it runs again, and we'll get hit by it once we're off the mountain."

"That's true," Milford replied. There had to be some other way. He needed more time.

"Can we break it?" Holly asked. "What if we take down a reflector balloon or go to a power plant and figure out how to shut it down?"

Milford laughed. "No, sorry. I wish it were possible, but we don't have the resources to do either of those things. If we could, it would cause an error that would pause the system until corrected, but all of the infrastructure is military grade. With the automatic defenses, we'd be dead well before reaching the doors of the power plants. Surely you've seen the news footage of that. And the balloons are massive and well protected, too. I observed some of the testing. They have multiple bullet-resistant skins with self-sealing membranes and hundreds of separate internal compartments. The engineers tethered one at two hundred feet and spent a day shooting at it with small arms, and it was still okay, and that was without pumping any replacement gas up the tether. In flight, the tethers supply lifting gas and power. We'd need an army at our command to bring one down, but short of that, it's not possible. We need to go to main control. I just don't see how we can."

"Craig," Laura said, "I can see you're thinking about it."

Craig nodded. "We can fly there. We'll have to jump from one airport to another to refuel and stay above the field when the system runs, but we can do it."

"Are you up for flying, Milford?" Laura asked.

Milford looked at her, then at Craig. Of course! Craig was a pilot. The answer was sitting right outside. "I think so. Yes!"

Craig turned to Holly. "I'll need a copilot."

"Of course."

"And a nurse," Laura said to Ashley.

"At your service."

"And a weatherman," Craig said to Douglas.

Douglas shook his head. "No, sorry. I can't."

"Why?" Laura asked.

"It's a medical condition. I can't fly. I've had it for years. I used to be able to, but then on one flight I got a bad headache. I assumed it was something else, but when I flew again, I had a seizure and spent a week in the hospital. The doctors aren't sure what it is, but they said if it happened again, I might not survive it."

"Oh my," Laura said.

"What about antiseizure medications?" Ashley asked.

Douglas shrugged. "It would be a gamble. I can't risk it."

"There must be something we can do," Craig said.

"No. Don't worry about me. I'll keep taking readings, and you do what you need to do. I'm sorry I can't go with you, but it can't be helped. Maybe something else will work out, but if not, I wish you all the best. You need to get going."

"I'm sorry, Douglas," Craig said, "but you're right. We can't delay. Hopefully this will work out for all of us. I'll prepare the chopper. The rest of you gather some food, water, medical supplies, extra clothing, and whatever else seems useful. We have a long trip ahead of us."

CHAPTER 12

Summer and Autumn navigated the lawn chairs, tables, and other items scattered by the wind as they approached the lodge at Copper Mountain, where the clean and orderly lobby was an odd sight after their ordeal on the trail.

"Twin hikers?" the man at the desk asked.

"Yes," Summer said, "we're doing the Colorado Trail."

"Are your phones working?" Autumn asked.

"No, everything went down this morning right when they were starting the big climate system. We weren't that busy today to begin with, but most of the guests have left."

"Can we stay the night?" Summer asked. "We wanted to get inside in case those winds keep coming."

"Certainly, and there's no charge. We're operating under emergency conditions right now. We have power and water, but that's about it. Television and internet are out. Were you on the trail when the wind hit?"

"Yeah," Autumn said, "both times."

"Wow, that must have been scary. Our weather instruments were showing gusts over a hundred miles per hour. We've had some damage around the property, but fortunately it was minimal. You must have come from Breckenridge. How did it look over there?"

"We don't know about the town," Summer replied. "We left a couple hours before the wind started, but our phones didn't work on that side of the ridge either."

"Well, I'm sure they'll get things fixed soon. Here are your room keys. I put you on the first floor. It should be one of the safest spots if this gets any worse. Also, we have some food set up in the breakfast area. Help yourselves."

"Thanks," the twins said together, then took the keys and headed down the hall.

"Hey," Summer said, turning around, "is there a hot tub?"

"Sure. It's that way. Just follow the signs—you can't miss it."

"Thanks."

"A hot tub?" Autumn asked as they continued down the hall.

"Why not? If we're going to stay in a hotel, I want to take full advantage of it."

"All right. Let's get cleaned up and eat, and then we can check it out."

WEDNESDAY, JULY 9, 6:35 P.M. MT (8:35 P.M. ET)
Main control base—the desert south of Phoenix, Arizona
Elevation: 1,100 feet

Katherine Morgreed had returned in a foul mood since none of the satellite links or other communication systems in the news vans were working. She'd slammed the door when she got into the bunker, kicked over a trash can, and then emptied a full magazine into the trash can. Barry had seen it coming, and since Katherine's back was to him, he cupped his palms over Valentina's ears to warn her and protect her from the shock of the gunfire.

Barry had done more thinking while Katherine sulked and swore at the window. How widespread was the problem? Had it hit the whole state? The whole country? The whole world? What about his family back near Washington? Was his wife worrying about him? Had she seen anything on the news? Was she even alive? He'd also thought about how to engage Katherine in conversation based on what Valentina told him. He'd come up with some ideas but needed to wait for the right opportunity.

"She should be tougher than that," Katherine said. "Why hasn't she woken up yet?"

"Uh, I don't know," Barry mumbled.

"Well, she's the scientist. I want answers. She probably has them."

"Katherine, we can't go on like this forever. What if no one is coming? It's been hours. Someone would have already come to check on us if they could."

"Do you think I don't know that?"

"No, but I want to know what's going on. Did the Climate Freedom Militia have something to do with this? The reporters were asking about them."

Katherine laughed. "Not at all."

"How do you know?"

"Because they weren't part of the plan."

"What plan?"

Katherine stared at Barry for a long minute before seeming to make up her mind. "Well, I may as well tell you. It will be more entertaining than sitting here doing nothing, and I can shoot you later if I need to, but I don't think either of us is going to be getting out of here."

"Maybe not," Barry said, fighting to keep a straight face despite his fear. Movie scenes flickered in his head. Villains always said something like that when they had the hero trapped. They could never resist boasting. His mouth began to curl, so he coughed to mask the smile. He still had to be careful. Katherine was anything but predictable.

Katherine turned a chair around and took a seat several yards from him. She placed her pistol on a table beside her and pulled another from her bag. "What do you know about the East India Company?"

"They traded tea and spices?" Where on earth was she going with this?

"Yes, as well as many other things. The company traded goods from India and the Orient and gained enormous wealth and political power over the course of several centuries. My ancestors invested early and made their fortunes, and for a time business went well, but they foresaw the beginnings of decline that ultimately ended the company. Britain and other governments were not going to let a commercial organization maintain such power and control indefinitely, so they slowly took over until India was under British colonial rule."

"Okay," Barry said. What did this have to do with anything?

Katherine ejected the empty magazine from the pistol she'd used to dispatch the trash can. She returned the gun to the table and rummaged in her bag, then pulled out a box of ammo. "My point being," she said, opening the box and plucking out a bullet, "my ancestors understood that the world worked best when the civilized nations maintained strict control through force and subjugation, but they could see the way things were headed. Popular opinion turned against the slave trade. Empires dwindled as colonies gained independence. Third world nations began to industrialize and chip away at our rightful place on top." She pressed the bullet into the empty magazine. *Click.*

"Look at us now. Europe and North America are a shadow of what they once were while Asia and India are raking in profits at our expense. The Morgreeds and their associates realized long ago that something would have to be done, but it couldn't be through another overt play at control like the East India Company. So they founded the Arctic Circle Society."

The group Valentina mentioned! "I've never heard of that."

Katherine took another bullet from the box. "Of course you haven't."

She pushed it into the magazine. *Click.*

"We've kept our existence secret for over two hundred years, but in that time we have grown. Membership is restricted and by invitation only. We have politicians, industrialists, the rich, and the powerful in our ranks . . . mostly from Europe, North America, and Russia, with a few exceptions. Trade was power in the old world, but now power comes from the ability to influence."

Click.

"Influence what?" Barry asked as Katherine selected another round.

"The course of civilization. We control from behind the scenes and within the power structures. We influence the outbreak of wars. We influence trade treaties. We influence the trends of social media. We don't always get what we want, but we've been biding our time while profiting from our losses. We've invested our money in numerous businesses in the developing world. It's not ideal, but they make profits that fund our efforts."

Click.

"I don't understand. What does that have to do with the climate system?"

Katherine gave a wicked smirk. "That's all background, Barry. In modern times, the Society has had one setback after another with the civil rights movement, the end of apartheid, the rise of the oil-producing states in world affairs, and many other undesirable developments. But we saw the potential of climate change from the earliest days it was theorized."

Click.

"Potential?" Was she crazy? What kind of potential could there possibly be in climate change?

Katherine seemed to look through him. Her fingers paused before taking the next round from the box. "Yes, potential for control, for power, for putting the world back as it should be. Think of it! Warmer temperatures in the north would open up the arctic sea lanes. We could tap the resources of Siberia, Greenland, and the Canadian arctic. Scandinavia would have longer growing seasons. It would usher in a new age of prosperity. At the same time, the equatorial regions will become increasingly hot and uninhabitable. Water will dry up and businesses will fail. They'll be put back in their place as we restore the balance of power and empire."

Click.

"But your company built the carbon reduction system. I don't understand."

Click.

Katherine grinned, and her eyes gleamed as her gaze returned to him. "It was a beautifully orchestrated coup. Billions of dollars have been funneled into the Society on top of the profits I've made. The majority of the delegates to the IPCC are either Society members or controlled by us, so my company has operated free from any effective government oversight. The Society has been working for decades to increase pollution and dirty energy in the third world, and now we've been controlling the construction of the system that is supposed to fix the problem."

Click.

"It was never meant to work. Sure, Dr. Pennychuck's plan was valid, but he was a screen of legitimacy over our real intentions. We caused delays and overbuilt at great expense. We could have met Pennychuck's power requirements with a small fraction of the infrastructure we built, but that wouldn't have been nearly so effective at draining the world of money to put to our uses."

"But won't the people turn against you?"

Click.

"Not at all. Remember, the Arctic Circle Society doesn't officially exist, but we had plenty of blame ready to place for the failure of the system. Terrorist attacks, faulty components from suppliers in China and India—the list goes on. All of it engineered to shift public opinion in the direction we want. It wouldn't be long until we'd get the mass deportations and immigration restrictions necessary to see the third world devolve into a wasteland of chaos and war, and then the Society would finally come out of the shadows."

Click.

"Wow," Barry said. "I had no idea. Was Valentina a member?"

Katherine leaned back and looked to the side. "No, though at one point I thought she had the potential. Like you, we've used her for a purpose. She was an orphan in Russia with no future, but she was smart. We were notified, and we put her on our watch list when she was young. We made sure she was placed in the right schools, and she was given a college scholarship so long as she went for the course of study we chose. Most of the Society members are assigned candidates, and she was one of mine. Some of them develop appropriate views and talents and are invited to join us, but others do not and are either turned loose or eliminated if they know too much." She returned her gaze to him. "Valentina's case was special."

Valentina was growing tense on the couch behind him. They were getting close. He had to keep Katherine on this track. "How so?" Barry asked.

Katherine sighed. "It became clear to me she would never see the world our way, but I'd envisioned this role with the EPA that she would fit perfectly, and by the time she was working on her doctorate, we had no better candidate. I wanted her for the job. I could tell she didn't like me, so I determined the only way I could get her to work for us was to force her into it. I fed her some information to influence her decisions and gave her a lot of space to make life choices—all under surveillance, of course, though she didn't know. She got pregnant and tried to hide it from me, and she was making plans to run away."

Click.

Valentina started to shake, and Barry hoped it wasn't visible. She was pregnant? Now? No, that couldn't be. Katherine was talking about before. Still . . . her? A mom?

Katherine had that faraway look again. "So I waited, and at the appropriate time, I took the baby and gave her a choice: she could do exactly what I demanded, or the child would die in front of her. She came here thinking we'd keep our promise to return him to her. In that regard she's misjudged us completely. He's been under the care of a Society family, and that's where he'll remain. They send pictures a few times a year, which I've given to her to keep up her hope and obedience, but now that she's completed the task, she's nothing but a liability."

Click.

"That's awful," Barry said, fidgeting to mask Valentina's silent sobbing that was shaking the couch. He was fairly certain that the control terminal was blocking Katherine's view of Valentina's face, which was most likely betraying her efforts at composure. He shifted a hand subtly to hold hers. "How could you do that to her? Do you have no heart?"

Click.

Katherine shrugged. She tried to press another round into the magazine but returned it to the box. "At one time I did, but compassion gets in the way. Our work requires sacrifice." She picked up the empty pistol and slid the magazine home.

WEDNESDAY, JULY 9, 8:52 P.M. ET
Mount Washington Observatory—Mount Washington, New Hampshire
Elevation: 6,288 feet

Laura stowed a duffel bag of clothing in the helicopter, then turned to face the summit building. Her heart ached. She was leaving this place. It had been her home away from home, full of laughter and love, and she missed it already. "I feel kind of bad taking things from the gift shop," she said. "It's like we're stealing."

Craig sighed. "I know what you mean. I topped off the fuel, but there's no one to pay."

"I'm ready." Ashley adjusted the hood of the Mount Washington sweatshirt she'd procured.

"As am I," Milford said, walking slowly beside Ashley and carrying a large backpack. "I found some interesting snacks for the road."

"You mean for the air," Laura pointed out. "We're flying."

"Quite true."

"What's our range?" Holly asked.

"About 300 to 350 miles," Craig replied, looking over the helicopter. "Cruise speed is 135 knots."

Holly looked to the sky. "We're lucky to be under a full moon. If the field really hit everywhere, there may not be lights on the ground."

Craig nodded. "That's a good point."

"Good luck," Douglas said as he stepped onto the helipad.

"Are you sure you can't come?" Holly asked. "The helicopter is a lot different than commercial airliners."

"I'm sure. I don't know what triggers it, so I'll have to take my chances here."

"You've been most helpful," Milford said, shaking Douglas's hand. "Thank you, and good luck."

"It's been an honor, Dr. Pennychuck."

"Ashley"—Milford reached for her arm—"will you help me up the stairs?"

"Sure, and watch your head on the door."

"Goodbye, Douglas," Holly said, giving him a hug. "Thanks for letting us stay up here."

"It's been a pleasure," Douglas said with a shaky voice. "Now, go before I get all emotional, and, Craig, take good care of them."

"I will," Craig said. "I'm sorry, Douglas. It feels so wrong leaving you here. Can't you come with us?"

Douglas grasped Craig by the shoulders. "I can't. I've made my decision. It's my choice. You have your job to do, and I have mine. Now, please, be on your way."

"All right," Craig said. "Everyone aboard."

Laura waited for him to complete one last walk around the helicopter. He stopped at the door to the passenger cabin, and she looked up to meet his gaze.

Craig took her hands in his. "It's not the romantic picnic I planned."

"I know," she said, smiling at the thought of their earlier conversation. "Did you find your wife?"

Craig took in a sharp breath. "I did." He hugged her, and she knew it was all he'd be able to say without breaking into tears. Her own were already building.

She squeezed his solid chest and breathed in the comfort of his scent. "Let's go."

Craig stepped back and nodded. Laura climbed in, and he closed the door behind her. Moments later the machine came to life.

The intercom crackled. "I'm going to stop at our house in Hanover first to get some things," Craig said. "It's a short flight. Is everyone buckled in?"

"Yes," Laura said.

"Okay. Here we go."

Laura watched out the window as the rotor picked up speed until reaching a steady beat. The helicopter lifted off the ground and rose into the night sky. Douglas waved from where he stood at the entrance to the observatory. She waved back and started to cry as the twinkle of lights on the summit she loved faded into the distance.

CHAPTER 13

"The little brat is probably dead anyway," Katherine stated from her spot at the window, having resumed her lookout after talking with Barry.

"What?" Barry said, interrupted from his thoughts.

"Dr. Severnaya's little boy. His parents live in Finland in a mansion by the sea. It looks like everyone out there is dead, so he's probably dead."

The tremors behind Barry had been increasing, but there was nothing he could do to hide Valentina's gasp as she broke down and cried.

"She's awake," Katherine snapped, grabbing her pistol and chambering a round before approaching.

"No, don't kill her," he pleaded.

Katherine stopped several feet away. "Oh no, not yet. I have some questions for her when she's finished with her little outburst."

Katherine walked over to one of the dead security guards and removed a pair of handcuffs from his belt. "What are you doing?" Barry asked.

"Make her sit up," Katherine ordered, waving her pistol at Barry.

147

"But—"

Katherine fired a round into the back of the couch. Barry flinched and squeezed his eyes shut. Anything to lessen the pain in his ears.

"No *buts*. I'm a good marksman, Barry. Don't try me."

Barry pulled Valentina up until she was sitting. Her eyes were open but not focused, and she made no effort to help him.

Katherine tossed the handcuffs onto the couch. "Cuff her, hands behind her back. Make sure they're tight, Barry."

"Why?"

Another bullet ripped into the cushions. "Do it now! You have no idea what I've made her capable of."

Barry picked up the handcuffs and fastened one half in place around Valentina's left wrist. "I'm sorry," he said as it clicked closed.

"Hurry up," Katherine barked.

Barry took Valentina's right hand and was about to put the other half of the cuffs on her wrist when another shot whistled by within a couple feet of his head. He cringed. The room was buzzing. He didn't know eardrums could hurt this much.

"Behind her back!"

Valentina was whimpering and offered no resistance as Barry pulled her arms back, but she cried out when he brought her wrists together and clicked the second cuff closed. They were connected by a short chain, and the stress on her injured shoulder had to be unbearable.

"Katherine, she's been shot," he said, turning to face her and hoping for some compassion. "Is this really necessary?"

Katherine made a strange face, displaying something like incredulity. "She's lucky to be alive."

Barry turned back to Valentina as Katherine retreated to her post at the window. "No, no, no!" The bandage was getting red. He rifled through the contents of the first aid kit he'd used before, but the gauze was nearly depleted.

"What now?" Katherine asked.

"It's bleeding again and we're out of gauze. I need more."

"Can't you use a shirt or something?"

"No, it has to be sterile. I need another first aid kit."

Katherine rolled her eyes and groaned. "'I need this. I need that.' I should shoot both of you."

"Please," he pleaded, "she'll die. I thought you wanted answers."

"Fine!" Katherine stomped to the door. "I'll get your stupid kit. I'm sure there are plenty out in the parking lot."

Barry ripped off the bandage and pressed the remaining gauze on the wound.

"Ow!" Valentina cried between shallow, rapid breaths.

"Sorry. Hang in there."

"It hurts!"

"I know. I'm sorry," Barry said, glancing at the door and the dead security guards. A thought hit him. "Can you hold this in place with your chin? Just for a few seconds?"

Valentina nodded once, and Barry guided her head into position over the gauze.

"Hold that. I'll be right back." He dashed over to the guards. He searched the belt and pockets of the one that still had a pair of hand-cuffs until he found the key, then returned. He tried it on Valentina's cuffs to make sure it worked but left them in place.

"Mmmph?" she squeaked, trying to keep her chin from slipping as Barry pressed a hand into the back pocket of her pants.

"Valentina"—Barry put his fingers back on the gauze and took her chin in his hand—"I put a key to the cuffs in your left pocket. I'm sorry I can't unlock them now. Katherine will be back. If the time comes, remember you have it. Do you understand?"

Valentina's eyes were red as she focused on Barry. "Yes."

Footsteps pounded in the hall, and Katherine stormed in and quickly dumped several first aid kits on the couch. "There. I was feeling generous."

WEDNESDAY, JULY 9, 9:24 P.M. ET
Pottersmith residence—Hanover, New Hampshire
Elevation: 528 feet

The flight from Mount Washington to Hanover had been quick and was a route Craig could fly with his eyes closed. Scattered lights dotted the countryside and some of the towns they flew over, but they'd seen no signs of movement that would indicate life below.

Craig touched down on the lawn of the home he and Laura had purchased once his business got off the ground. It was situated on the outskirts of town and had a large enough yard for games and helicopter landings, though this was the first time he'd ever taken advantage of that feature. He jumped out and opened the passenger door as the rotor spun down.

"It's hard to believe this is home," Laura said, looking at their house in the moonlight. The landscaping was a mess, with fallen trees and debris from the neighborhood all over. Shingles were missing from the roof, and the windows had shattered.

"Hmm," Craig agreed. "I'm going to get my maps. The GPS isn't working, so we're going to have to navigate on basic headings and eyesight. We should get some flashlights, and I'll grab my shotgun. Holly, can you give me a hand carrying stuff?"

"Sure."

"If it's all right with you," Milford said from his seat in the cabin, "I'll stay put. We have only thirty minutes until the system is likely to run again, so we should be in the air before ten."

"Ashley," Laura said, "if you don't mind, could you help me get some things?"

"Of course."

Craig led the group to the house and opened the back door.

"It looks like a hurricane went through here," Ashley remarked as she entered the kitchen.

"Oh no," Laura said, looking at a fallen shelving unit. "This was my best pottery. It's all broken."

"I'm sorry," Holly said. "Did you bring your favorite mug from the observatory?"

"I did. I guess that's all I have left."

Ashley opened a cabinet. "Nope, this one is still all right."

Laura let out a mournful laugh as Ashley handed her a misshapen lump of a mug. "The twins made this for my birthday when they were four."

Craig took it from her. It was large and heavy, holding roughly twenty-four ounces, but he could fit only one finger in the tiny handle. The girls had pressed and molded some of Laura's favorite polished rocks into the outside of the clay and painted "Love You Mommy" in a heart on the side. He traced the heart with his finger and then handed it back. "I fired it in the kiln for them. We made a great team."

"I hope they're okay," Laura said, setting the mug on the counter. "This might not be useful, but I'm definitely taking it."

"We should hurry," Holly said.

"You're right." Craig headed for the hallway. "Follow me."

Several minutes later they loaded the helicopter with the items scavenged from the house. Laura brought some photo albums and other keepsakes, and Ashley had raided the pantry for additional food and drinks. Craig opened some maps and discussed a route with Holly before taking off.

Craig switched on the intercom as they ascended. "What altitude will keep us above the field?"

"Six or seven thousand feet should do," Milford answered, "but we have only a few minutes."

"Thanks. Our next stop is Albany."

Holly turned off the intercom. "Craig, what about the wind? If we get a two-hundred-mile-per-hour downdraft, it could knock us out of the sky. What's this rated for?"

"Not that. Believe me—I've been worrying about it. I think our best bet is to get up high enough that we have some margin to regain control before hitting the ground."

"This is going to be a bumpy ride."

"I hope that's all." He turned the intercom back on. "Laura, everyone, make sure you have things secure back there, and be ready to hold on tight. If that wind hits us, I expect we're going to take a beating."

"Got it," Laura replied.

"Look," Holly said as they passed seven thousand feet. The static sparkles that had been visible during the day were remarkable in the dark, like a thick blanket of fireworks bursting continuously in the sky. From their vantage point, they could see the curve of the field as it followed the horizon, and the dark masses of several reflector balloons perched atop the shimmering sea of light.

"It's beautiful," Craig said, watching in awe as the light intensified.

"Eyes closed," Milford ordered.

Craig gripped the controls firmly. "Hold on, Holly."

The sky below them flashed as expected, and then it felt like the floor dropped away. Warning lights blinked and buzzers sounded as the helicopter plummeted, rocking and spinning as the mighty gust enveloped it. Craig was forced to let go or risk having his arms broken by the control stick bucking all about, but then the storm subsided, and they slowly halted their downward trajectory as the blades of the rotor dug into the air and he regained control.

"Aa-ah-uh," Milford moaned.

"Are you okay?" Ashley asked.

Craig's stomach finally settled out of his throat. "What's going on back there?"

"We're fine," Laura said.

"Oh boy, did that hurt," Milford said. "I think I may have broken those injured ribs."

"I doubt it," Ashley said, "but I'll check."

"Hey, guys," Laura said. "Look! It's snowing!"

"What's our altitude?" Craig asked, focused on climbing as quickly as possible.

"3,500," Holly said. "We dropped like a rock."

He turned on the wipers. "Phew, good. I can't see anything through this snow."

"But we made it!" Holly said, and seconds later the snow abruptly ended.

"We made it." Craig closed his eyes for a moment and breathed. That had been close, but they could do it again if the helicopter held up. He checked the instruments, set a course, and continued his ascent into the moonlit sky.

WEDNESDAY, JULY 9, 8:00 P.M. MT (10:00 P.M. ET)
Main control base—the desert south of Phoenix, Arizona
Elevation: 1,100 feet

"It's eight o'clock," Barry said. "Are you up for it?"

Valentina sat up. Her head ached but not enough to overcome her curiosity. "Yes. I want to see."

Katherine leveled her pistol in their direction as Barry helped Valentina to her feet and over to the window. Once he'd stopped the bleeding again and she calmed down, Barry had described what they observed during the previous events.

"So you're sure the upload was completed?" Katherine asked.

"Yes," Valentina said, "it would have run only once if the patch was not installed fully, and I can't envision what you've described happening without my new settings."

"It's starting," Katherine said.

The static charge built and intensified. Valentina closed her eyes on Barry's warning, and then she gazed in wonder at the windstorm, snow, and fog until the scene was clear.

"What does it mean?" Katherine demanded. "What did it do?"

Valentina's mind raced. What had she just observed? She knew the reaction inside and out, nearly as well as Milford. There was no way it could cause such a dramatic event. The system wasn't capable of it, no matter the calibrations. "Katherine, you saw the people out there die after the first flash, right?"

"No, I couldn't see anything well at all until it had been snowing for a while. I could see some of them were definitely moving, but they looked to be in terrible distress. They were all dead after the fog cleared."

"And you said you overbuilt the power systems. By how much?"

"I don't know. I told the engineers to grossly underrate the reactor power and design the system for far more output than was necessary. No one else knew about that."

"Do you have a rough idea? Double the power? Triple?"

Katherine pondered for a few seconds. "I told them 'Make it a thousand times what Pennychuck needs,' but I don't know what they ultimately came up with. They were paid off very well to keep it a secret, even from the rest of the company."

Valentina stumbled, and Barry had to keep her from falling. "Katherine," she said after recovering her bearing, "you should have told me about that. This is your fault."

"Why? What are you talking about?"

"The plan. It would have worked if you kept to Pennychuck's power level, but you got greedy, and you ruined everything. Everyone is dead because of you!"

"I don't see how."

"No, you wouldn't, because you never asked and you never bothered to understand the science. You keep staring out that window, waiting to hear from your precious Society, but they're gone, Katherine. They're dead. Everyone you know is dead. My . . . my son . . . "

Barry helped her onto a chair as she started sobbing again.

Katherine stared, her expression blank, and for the first time since Valentina met her, she had nothing to say.

CHAPTER 14

"This was a great idea," Autumn said as she relaxed in the hotel hot tub surrounded by bubbles and steam, leaning her head back after watching the winds rage outside.

"Mmm-hmm," Summer replied from across the tub.

Autumn closed her eyes and let the jets massage her muscles. This beat cowering on the side of the trail. "How are you feeling? Does your back still hurt?"

"No, I'll probably be sore and have some bruises from the tree squishing me, but so far I feel all right. I'm certainly happy to be alive. Thanks again for what you did. I was worried you wouldn't make it in time. It was . . . awful . . . "

Autumn breathed in, filling her lungs with steam, then breathed out. Her chest rose and fell. There was nothing preventing it. She was free to breathe as she'd been all her life. It was a simple but terrifying concept. That freedom could be taken in an instant. "I was scared. I used to get nightmares about losing you. Those fears came rushing back when I saw you stuck under the tree."

"You had nightmares?"

Autumn opened her eyes. Summer was looking at her, clearly waiting for her answer. "Yeah, for a while after that time we went ice fishing with Dad."

"Oh." Summer shivered despite the warmth of the water.

"And I guess today made me start thinking about what's going to happen to us, like after we graduate. Am I going to lose you?"

Summer frowned. "Why would you think that?"

"Because you'll be going to med school and I'll be—I don't know. But we won't be in the same place anymore."

"I know."

"And then we might get jobs far away, or what if you get married or I get married? I mean, guys are great, and kids and all, but I don't want to end up living miles apart and hardly ever seeing you again."

Summer plucked a duck thermometer from where it bobbed next to her. "You're thinking all this because a tree fell on me?"

"Well, I guess. It just put things in perspective, like how life is fleeting and we hold on by the smallest thread sometimes and we may not even know it. I couldn't stop thinking—what if you were actually gone?"

Summer was quiet for a moment. "I can't imagine it. I think I'd feel empty."

"If you were gone or if I was gone?"

"You, silly." Summer laughed and threw the thermometer at her. "You're my best friend—or something more than that. I don't know. It would be like losing half of myself. I don't like to think about it."

WEDNESDAY, JULY 9, 8:15 P.M. MT (10:15 P.M. ET)

Camp Hale—Leadville, Colorado

Elevation: 9,200 feet

Roman was helping to set a picnic table upright when one of his men approached.

"Sir, the scouts have reported in."

"Good. What did they say?"

"Not much from Glenwood Springs. They only saw another horizon flash and wind from their location. The group watching Denver described some sort of electrical field that covered the city before the flash, with a snowstorm following the wind. They said the whole area was covered in a thick fog, so they were planning to head down out of the mountains for a closer look."

Roman dropped his end of the table. "A snowstorm in July?"

"That's what they said, but they were too far away to give a more accurate description."

"What about Colorado Springs?"

"They didn't see anything over the city but described something similar to Denver in the lower elevations, and they said some areas lost power."

"All right." He brushed his hands against his fatigues. "We'll see what they find in Denver. Tell the other groups to hold position."

"Yes, sir."

"Perhaps," one of the other officers said, "the attack isn't coming as quickly as we thought. From the sounds of it, they need to hit an area repeatedly to knock out the power."

"Strange, though," another said, "that Denver would be affected. That's the Mile-High City. The news said they'd start the system lower than that. I wonder if something changed?"

"It does seem to be following a five-hour interval," Roman said, "so I expect the scouts will see the next event at one in the morning. Tell them to pay attention to any elevation changes. Also, let's set an alarm to get everyone up in time to brace for another windstorm if that happens, and we'll all convene to hear what the scouts say on the radio. In the meantime, I'm turning in. I'll be in my Subaru."

WEDNESDAY, JULY 9, 10:40 P.M. ET
Albany International Airport—Colonie, New York
Elevation: 285 feet

The rest of the forty-five-minute flight to Albany had gone smoothly. Following the snow, they'd watched as thick fog blanketed the earth for several minutes before clearing. They passed north of the city, which was dotted with lights in some areas but dark in others.

"I wonder if it's not as bad as we thought?" Holly said as they approached the airport. The facility was brightly lit and appeared normal from this distance. Perhaps Dr. Pennychuck was wrong after all. Maybe the field had affected only one area.

"I don't know," Craig said, "but based on what we found on the Cog train, I'm not too hopeful. We haven't seen a single plane in the air, and I don't see any activity here."

"True, and there's nothing on the radio from the tower. Even a handheld should work from this range, but maybe they've just lost communication."

"Look there," Craig said, pointing ahead. "That's not a good sign."

Holly leaned forward and squinted, then drew in a sharp breath. "Oh my." She clutched the straps of her harness. Several planes had crashed on the runway, and the tail section of another was protruding from where it had slammed into the terminal. Only a minute ago they had looked like planes in queue for departure, but now the scene was unfolding into something from a disaster movie.

"They probably went down when the wind hit the first time," Craig said.

"And they just left them there? Where are the emergency trucks?"

"No, Holly. Think about the train. Most of the passengers hadn't even left their seats. Whatever effect the system is having, it's quick."

"Right . . ." The mangled wreckage held her gaze. She couldn't look away. Each one of those planes held hundreds of passengers with seat belts fastened . . . tray tables secured . . . personal items stowed. Had they died instantly, or did they suffer? Were they scared? Did the pilots have time to react? "There was no response . . . because there was no one alive to help."

"I'm afraid so," Craig said as he circled over the runway. "There. I'll land by that fuel truck. I hope the equipment is working, or this trip is not going to end well."

WEDNESDAY, JULY 9, 9:22 P.M. MT (11:22 P.M. ET)
Camp Hale—Leadville, Colorado
Elevation: 9,200 feet

Roman woke to the sound of frantic knocking on his car window. What was going on? Where was he? He squinted and blinked. An officer was standing by the car.

Roman opened the door. "Sir," the officer said, "the scouts called in from Denver. Everyone is dead!"

"What are you talking about?"

"All the people, sir. They're dead."

"All what people?"

"The people in the city. Everyone in Denver. They're all dead."

Roman rubbed his eyes. This had to be a dream. "Are you serious?"

"Yes, that's what they said. It looks like a tornado hit the entire city."

A tornado? In Denver? Did they get those? No, he only said it looked like one. He was talking about the system. The UN plan. That couldn't be right. "Who's going to buy the power?"

"Sir?"

"The UN plan—to sell power. How is that going to work if there are no customers?"

"I don't know."

"Did they see any signs of troop movements?"

"No, they said there were no signs of life at all, but they're still searching."

"Okay." This didn't sound right. Maybe the officer had misunderstood something. It could probably wait until morning. "Let me know if there are any further developments before our meeting, and tell the scouts to get back to their position before the next event hits."

WEDNESDAY, JULY 9, 9:38 P.M. MT (11:38 P.M. ET)
Main control base—the desert south of Phoenix, Arizona
Elevation: 1,100 feet

Barry helped Valentina through the bunker door as they entered following a trip to the restrooms under Katherine's supervision.

"I need some water," she said.

"Here." Barry held a bottle for her to drink. "How are you feeling?"

"Terrible. Exhausted. Everything hurts."

"So," Katherine interrupted, "explain to me why this is my fault."

Valentina grimaced as she sank onto the couch. "If you have so many questions, why did you shoot me?"

"Perhaps that was a little rash, but I panicked. Anyway, I want to know why you blame me."

"Katherine, she's exhausted," Barry said. "Can't it wait until the morning?"

"You stay out of this. I've been patient enough with her sulking."

"I hate you," Valentina said, glaring at Katherine.

Barry perched on the couch next to her. He looked back and forth between the two women. Neither spoke for a few seconds, but a struggle seemed to be taking place between them.

"I don't doubt that," Katherine finally said, "but I still want to hear your explanation. Start talking, or I'll make you less comfortable."

Valentina took a deep breath, and her glare faltered. "Dr. Pennychuck calculated the power necessary to make his reaction work. Too little and it would fail to make enough of an impact. Too much and there would be risk of damaging the system due to feedback, which has always been a shortcoming of the burst reactors. I studied his failure cases. The most promising route for ruining the system was for the field frequencies to be out of sync with the carbon enough that the energy was not taken into a successful reaction. Then I played around with the model far out of range of what he would have considered and came up with settings that would guarantee reactor overload."

"How?" Barry asked.

"Did your engineer program the override as I instructed?" Valentina asked Katherine.

"Yes, as well as some provisions against tampering."

"Okay. Then my theory should be correct. I set the field frequencies to target nitrogen and oxygen instead of carbon. Those gases make up about ninety-nine percent of the atmosphere, so the system would never generate enough power to affect them. Below a certain threshold, Pennychuck's reaction doesn't occur at all, so the feedback on the system would be catastrophic."

"Then why didn't it break?" Katherine asked.

"Because *you* changed the power output. *You* threw off the whole equation. You gave the system enough energy to complete a reaction with the gases that make up the main part of the atmosphere, and we're not talking about a slight change like Dr. Pennychuck planned for the carbon. Based on what I saw out the window, we put enough energy into the field to turn those gases into solid phase. It makes perfect sense. Gas to solid is a huge decrease in volume. That creates a vacuum, which is filled by the atmosphere above the field. Thus the sudden windstorm. The solidified gases then fall, but they would be highly unstable and quickly sublimate, dispersing back into the atmosphere until the system repeats the process."

Valentina stopped, and the room fell silent. Barry looked at her, though her focus remained on Katherine. She reminded him of his high school chemistry teacher. He'd struggled with the concepts of pressure, temperature, and volume, and his teacher had given him that same look when he failed to understand. Valentina should have taught that class. He understood. This was bad.

"And that killed everyone?" Katherine asked.

Valentina nodded. "You can't breathe in a vacuum, and if it hit suddenly, it would probably damage or rupture your lungs."

"But the wind was over in seconds," Katherine said. "That would bring more air, and I saw people still moving through the snow."

"Yes, you could potentially survive it, but God only knows what kinds of compounds were created that made up that fog. We can produce terribly lethal substances from nitrogen and oxygen using electricity, so I assume breathing the fog would be fatal."

Barry's chest ached and his breathing sped up. Not enough oxygen. He was going to faint. His heartbeat pounded in his head. He shivered, and his skin itched all over. He knew it wasn't real, but it didn't matter. He'd always suffered from intense psychosomatic responses. What Valentina described lodged in his mind, and his body was reacting with real symptoms.

The room had fallen silent again. Valentina was looking at Katherine. Katherine was glaring at Valentina. Neither spoke. A minute or two passed, and then Katherine started pushing a table toward the door.

"What are you doing?" Barry asked, his voice shaky.

Katherine didn't reply as she dragged more tables and chairs and stacked them in a barricade, blocking off a little corner of the room with the door behind it. She slipped in around the edge and pulled the furniture tight against the wall, then turned the lights out, put her pocketbook down as a pillow, and lay on the floor.

"Katherine?" Barry said.

"I'm going to sleep," she said in a strained voice. "Don't bother me."

"We should get some sleep, too," Barry whispered to Valentina. He could see her worried expression in the moonlight coming through the window. She slumped over on her left side, trying to find a comfortable position with her arms stuck behind her back. She was shivering, so he covered her with a blanket he'd taken from the break room.

"Thanks," she whispered, and moments later she fell asleep.

Barry rolled his suit jacket under his head and stretched out on the floor in front of the couch. He had calmed down, and he thought about everything that had happened over the course of the day. Had it been only one day? It felt like a week ago when they were preparing to start the system, but within only one day his world had been turned upside down. He refused to think about his family. Denial was easy when all he could see was endless desert out the window. The rest of the world was fine, no matter what Valentina said. He could believe it until he was forced to face the reality. For now his reality consisted only of Katherine and Valentina and this bunker.

He despised Katherine. How could she do such things? Did she feel any remorse or guilt? Was she capable of those emotions? And Valentina—he felt so bad for her, which seemed strange given their history, but so much had changed, and now he realized that she'd been bearing burdens far worse than his own. What would become of them? Would they live to see the morning? Even if they did, what then? It seemed hopeless.

WEDNESDAY, JULY 9, 11:51 P.M. ET
Wilkes-Barre/Scranton International Airport—Avoca, Pennsylvania
Elevation: 962 feet

Craig landed the helicopter outside the terminal of the Wilkes-Barre/Scranton airport and started the shutdown sequence. They'd been flying for nearly an hour since leaving Albany, and he needed to stretch his legs.

"Are we here already?" Holly asked, having fallen asleep on the way.

"Yes," Craig said. "I'll top off the fuel, and we should all take a bathroom break while we're here. Do you want to take over for the next leg?"

"Sure, if I can wake up. Some fresh air should help."

Craig got out and started the fuel pump, then opened the passenger door. Laura greeted him with a yawn as she descended the stairs and nestled against his chest.

"Can we go to bed?" she asked.

Craig held her tight. "I wish, but not yet. I thought we could use a bathroom break or at least walk around a bit."

"Oomph," Milford said as he got up from his seat. "I believe your helicopter is more comfortable than my hospital bed was, Craig."

Craig nodded. "It better be for what they charge for these things. Is Ashley coming?"

"I'll wake her," Laura said. "She was on a double shift this morning before leaving the hospital with Milford. She must be exhausted."

"All right," Craig said.

Laura climbed back into the helicopter and took a seat next to Ashley. "Ashley." She shook her arm.

"Mom?" Ashley asked, her eyes still closed.

"No, honey. It's Laura. Time to wake up."

"I had the worst dream. We were stuck on the mountain, and everyone was dead."

"I'm sorry, but . . ."

Ashley blinked a few times and focused on Laura, then looked around the softly lit interior of the helicopter before her gaze landed on Craig at the door. "No . . . "

"It wasn't a dream," Laura said. "Come on. We've stopped to use the restroom."

Ashley stepped out and folded her arms against the night chill, then walked with Laura to the terminal, where Holly and Milford were waiting for them before entering.

Craig had just replaced the fuel nozzle when he heard the screams. He grabbed his shotgun from behind the pilot's seat, then sprinted to the building, burst through the door, and almost ran into his companions, who were huddled inside the entrance. Hundreds of bodies lay motionless on the floor amid luggage and shattered glass, illuminated by the flickering glow of the overhead lights.

"No," Laura whispered, reaching for him. He took her into his arms, staring at the scene before him while Laura shook and Holly and Ashley sobbed a few feet away. Craig couldn't think. He couldn't take his eyes off the horrible sight. So far he'd sort of comprehended the scale of death on an intellectual level, as they all had, but the reality in motionless flesh and blood froze him to the spot.

"Let's make this quick and get out of here," Milford said quietly, leading the way into the building with his head bowed.

WEDNESDAY, JULY 9, 10:33 P.M. MT (12:33 A.M. ET)
Copper Mountain Resort—Copper Mountain, Colorado
Elevation: 9,720 feet

"Autumn," Summer whispered, "are you asleep?"

"No." Autumn turned to face her sister in the king-size bed they were sharing.

"I've been thinking," Summer said.

"Oh?"

"Do you think Mom and Dad would be mad if I decided not to go to med school?"

Autumn tried to make out Summer's expression in the darkness of the room. "No, I don't think so. Why?"

"I'm not excited about it anymore. I don't want to spend all those years killing myself to get a job that I don't really want."

"Did that tree hit you on the head?"

"No, I'm serious."

"But you've been planning to go for years."

"I know, but I've been thinking about it a lot while we've been on the trail. Like Dad said, we won't be able to do things like this once life gets busy. But I love this. I love the freedom. I was watching you the other day while you were painting that sunset, and I realized you were exactly where you wanted to be, doing what you love. That will be your life. You'll have a family, and you'll paint, and you'll have adorable little kids that will hug you at any time they want. And then I pictured one of them asking you if Aunt Summer was going to visit for Christmas, and you said no, that I wasn't able to get away, again. I don't want that. I can't do that."

"What do you want?" Autumn propped her head up. This would not be resolved in a few seconds.

"I don't know. I haven't thought that through yet."

"Maybe you could work with Dad."

Summer laughed. "You mean fly a helicopter?"

"Why not?"

"I guess it never even crossed my mind. Dad is so, like, macho adventure guy. That's not me."

"Holly does it."

"True, but she's got the personality. I don't know. I don't see myself doing that."

Autumn shifted her pillow. "Did I ever tell you about my art major conversation with Mom?"

"Not that I remember."

"It was back in high school when we were applying to Dartmouth. I wanted to go for art, but I was worried that it wasn't practical like what you were doing. I asked her what she thought. We had a long conversation, but the thing I remember most is her asking me what job I would do even if no one paid me for it. She said if you love your work, you'll find contentment that no amount of money can buy, and if you can get paid for doing what you love, then you're on the right path."

"Hmm."

"She also said I could get lots of boring jobs that pay the bills as long as I have a college degree, in case art doesn't work out, but I didn't think that part was nearly as motivational."

Summer sighed. "I should talk to her."

"You should, and you should pray about it. But whatever you decide, I hope my adorable little kids get to see you all the time."

"I'm going to be hearing about that for a long time, aren't I?"

"Oh, yes, Aunt Summer."

CHAPTER 15

Valentina lay in bed in the maternity ward, singing softly to the newborn baby boy she cuddled to her breast. He was perfect, and he looked just like his father. She ran a finger through his soft black hair and watched his little eyes open momentarily. "We'll be going home soon," she said. "Your father will be so excited to meet you, and we'll travel far, far away from here where she'll never find us. I promise."

The nurse entered the room and strode to Valentina's bedside, where she added something to the IV.

"What's that?" Valentina asked, wondering at the change in the normally pleasant and talkative woman.

"To help you sleep," the nurse said, then left as quickly as she'd come.

Valentina started to feel a little dizzy, and the hand she was holding on her baby's head grew heavy and dropped to her side, just as the other would if not for the pillow supporting it.

"What?" she whispered. Then, hearing the door close, she looked up and froze.

"Miss Severnaya," Katherine Morgreed said as she approached.

171

"What are you doing here?"

"Did you think I wouldn't know?"

"How did you . . . "

"Did you think you could hide this from me?"

"I thought—"

"Did you honestly think I would let you run away?"

"I . . . " Valentina said, tears coming to her eyes, "I don't want to work for you. I'm done."

"It's too late. I know your plans. I've known all along. You can't hide anything from me."

"Please, just let me go."

"No, Valentina. Not after all I've invested in you. I have a big job for you, and you'll need to be focused on your work."

"I'm sorry. I can't . . . "

"Let's see this child of yours."

Morgreed pushed her lifeless hand off the baby and pulled him away. He tried to clamp on to continue nursing, and Valentina felt the pain of him being yanked from her. She couldn't move. Whatever the nurse put in the IV had paralyzed her, but she could feel everything in excruciating detail.

"Please, no," she pleaded, still able to speak softly as the drugs coursed through her body.

"If you ever want to see him again," Morgreed said as she turned away, "you will do everything I ask, without question."

"No!" Valentina screamed, the word a gentle whisper.

"I'll return tomorrow for further instruction. You will not speak a word of this to anyone," Morgreed said, walking away as a bright light surrounded her.

"No!" Valentina screamed inaudibly again and again as she was racked with sobs that no one heard.

The light grew brighter, obscuring Morgreed.

"Goodbye, Miss Severnaya."

Valentina's eyes flew open as the dazzling flash of the atmospheric reaction lit up the walls of the bunker and the sandstorm began. She was soaked with sweat and breathing heavily, her heart racing from the nightmare she'd had nearly every night since it happened. And like every other time it had woken her, she couldn't stop the memories from replaying in her mind. She'd remained on the bed, unable to speak or move. The comforting warmth of her son pressed against her skin was replaced by the air-conditioned chill of the room that she could do nothing about. It was a cruel reminder of what Katherine had just ripped away. When the nurse finally returned, she averted her eyes and said nothing as she adjusted Valentina's hospital gown and pulled up the covers. She reached up for the IV again, and then Valentina woke the next day to find Katherine waiting for her.

Valentina watched the snow falling on the desert under the light of the moon. It would be pretty under different circumstances. She remembered being a little girl in the orphanage, standing at the window at night and peering out over the snow-covered city. She would gaze at it for hours, mesmerized by the way it sparkled, and she would dream of herself as a ballerina twirling as the flakes danced around her. She never got to be a ballerina, but her dreams of being free had been so close. Katherine was busy in America and was out of touch for months between visits while Valentina was working on her doctorate. Valentina didn't understand what Katherine wanted from her, and she planned to part ways once her program was finished. She'd been so naive to think it would be that simple and to think her secret actions were not known. She was in love, and her future looked bright.

They'd been so excited on that cold winter night as they met the priest in the forest outside Arkhangelsk. He didn't inquire about their reasons, having agreed to perform the secret ceremony in the hour after midnight for a generous payment. Valentina felt like a princess, standing in a clearing with the moon reflecting off the snow and the sparkly white dress she'd borrowed, and he looked so handsome as he held her hands and they exchanged vows. There were no guests, no flowers, no rings—just a kiss and a certificate signed and filed with the state like so many others. It was a certificate, among other things, that Valentina was horrified to see in Katherine's hands a year later in that hospital room as she tore it into pieces.

A lock of hair fell across her eyes, and Valentina tried to brush it aside but was reminded of the handcuffs biting into her wrists. Her arms had gone numb, but that didn't lessen the stabbing pain in her shoulder or the renewed aching of her broken heart. Katherine had brought her nothing but misery. What had she ever done to deserve this? Why did Katherine have to choose her? She wished she could go back and warn that little girl watching the snow at the window. Say no. Run . . .

THURSDAY, JULY 10, 1:01 A.M. MT (3:01 A.M. ET)
Camp Hale–Leadville, Colorado
Elevation: 9,200 feet

Roman joined the other officers in the back of the box truck they'd converted into a command base since the tent kept getting blown over. Most of the men had likewise resigned themselves to coping with the storms and were sleeping in their vehicles. The truck was outfitted with a conference table and several radios so they could communicate with the scout groups on different channels.

One of the radios crackled. "Denver here. We're seeing something in the air."

"What do you mean?" Roman asked.

"What the . . . " someone said from Glenwood Springs.

"What is it?" an officer asked.

"Like sparkling or fireworks. It's all around us."

"What's your location?" Roman asked. "Didn't you leave the city?"

"It's all glittery!"

"Can you describe it?" the officer asked.

"We're at . . . " Garbled words followed.

"Repeat that."

"We're seeing it again," the Colorado Springs scout announced, "and it's definitely up higher than last time."

"It's . . . spark . . . " The Denver radio sputtered.

"Static," Glenwood Springs said, followed by gibberish.

"It's getting more intense," Colorado Springs said.

"Please repeat," Roman said.

"It flashed!" Colorado Springs shouted. "Did you see that?"

Roman braced himself. The box truck command center rocked as the wind gust bore down on it.

"Denver, do you copy?" he yelled into the mic.

"Glenwood Springs, do you copy?"

Both radios emitted only static.

"—blinding," Colorado Springs was saying. "Wind just knocked us over."

Roman handed the Denver radio off to another officer and took over on Colorado Springs. "Are you okay?"

"Yes, we're up on the mountain and watching it. It's snowing. Not over the city but some of the lower areas around it."

"Please come in," another officer was saying, still trying to reach the other groups.

"Do you see any signs of attack?" Roman asked.

"No, sir. It's really quiet."

"Have you heard from the other scout groups?"

"No."

"Can you try them on the radio?"

"Just a second."

Roman waited, listening to the other officers still attempting to contact Denver and Glenwood Springs.

"Negative. We're only getting static on their channels."

"You said this field is higher than it was last time?"

"Yes, we're certain."

"Can you retreat to higher ground and maintain your view?"

"Um, yes, we can. It looks like the snow ended. Now there's a fog."

"Okay," Roman said. "Get up higher, and we'll see if this happens again in another five hours. But report back if you see anything else."

"Understood."

"What are we dealing with here?" an officer asked.

A terrible thought hit him. "I don't know, but if it keeps advancing, we might not need to worry about the UN invasion."

THURSDAY, JULY 10, 5:42 A.M. CT
St. Louis Lambert International Airport—St. Louis County, Missouri
Elevation: 605 feet

Craig descended on the St. Louis airport as the sun was peeking over the horizon. He was tired even though Holly had been helping with the flying. She'd taken them to Pittsburgh; then he'd done the leg to Columbus, waiting out the system event before landing. They'd tried going to a higher altitude before the storm hit and found the winds to be much less severe. Holly had then flown to Indianapolis, and now Craig was completing his turn.

He was grateful to have Holly along for the trip. She was a skilled pilot, and without her, there was no way he'd be able to continue nonstop through the night and beyond. The fact that he could sleep while she was at the controls was a testament to the trust he had in her, as he was generally too anxious to rest while flying commercially as a passenger. He often hoped Holly would decide to fly for him full time, though he knew she was torn between her love of the air and the research she did with Laura. He wondered whether there was any line of work combining the two.

Craig thought of Laura, Ashley, and Milford. No doubt they had many things to worry about, but they'd all been able to get some sleep during the flight. He envied their position, though he was glad to help the mission in such an important way. What would they do if he hadn't flown up to the mountain on that fateful morning? They would be stranded, and if their predictions were correct, that would be the end. It was amazing how things sometimes had a way of working out, and that was even true of the helicopter. What were the chances that the new one would be ready a week ahead of schedule?

They were usually finished on time at best. What would he have been flying if it wasn't available? The two-seater? He couldn't say, but they were fortunate to have room for everyone.

"St. Louis, the Gateway to the West," Holly said with a yawn as they touched down. "How are you holding up?"

"Okay," Craig said. "We're almost halfway to Phoenix."

"Ugh, we've been at this for—what?—ten hours? It's no wonder helicopters haven't caught on for long-distance flights."

"I can't argue with that, but in this case I'm glad. We haven't seen a single runway clear enough to attempt a landing with an airplane."

Holly grimaced. "Gosh, you're right. I wonder, if some of those planes were high up when the system hit, do you think they came down to land after and couldn't find a safe spot?"

"That would be tough. Even if they made it down, where would the people go?"

"That's a scary thought."

"Good morning," Laura said over the intercom. "Can we get out?"

"Go ahead," Craig said. "We'll take off in fifteen minutes, and I could go for some breakfast if we have anything."

"We have plenty of cold chili and pizza from the visitor center."

"Sounds good."

THURSDAY, JULY 10, 6:06 A.M. MT
Main control base—the desert south of Phoenix, Arizona
Elevation: 1,100 feet

Barry was awakened by a bright flash that his eyelids did little to hide. Startled, he checked his watch. It was time for the system to be running.

He must have slept through it when it went in the middle of the night, but he couldn't imagine how. He rubbed his eyes and sat up as the wind blew outside, then watched the snow fall under the early-morning sun. The bunker was quiet except for loud snoring coming from Katherine's barricade by the door. He smirked, thinking of how his kids used to arrange cereal boxes in little forts at the breakfast table and duck behind them to eat. The thought tugged at his heart. He was trying not to think of them, but it was hard. They'd be fine if he could block them from his mind. He had to keep them separate from the grim reality he could see through the window. He had to keep his thoughts in the bunker.

Barry got to his knees and shuffled over to check on Valentina. She wore a troubled expression, though she did appear to be sleeping. Her face was obscured by her hair. He gathered it and moved it to the side, but as his hand brushed her forehead, he felt perspiration and heat. He checked again and compared it to his own skin. She was definitely running a fever. This was not good. Had her wound developed an infection? He'd been so careful trying to keep the gauze and bandages sterile, but there was only so much that could be done in their situation.

Barry folded the blanket down a bit and pulled her collar aside to check on the bandage. He was relieved to see that nothing had changed since the night before. The bandage was still clean, and the skin around it looked normal. He didn't want to wake her, so he refrained from further inspection. Instead, he put the blanket back and went over to check the first aid kits for anything useful. There were some pain relief pills and antibiotic sprays and creams but nothing stronger. If she was sick, they'd have to hope her body could fight unaided.

Barry sat on the chair at the broken control terminal and stared at the window. He wondered what they were going to do if no one ever came. They had food and water for a few days, but then what? If they left the bunker, where could they travel in five hours that would be safe from the system? Katherine had checked some of the vehicles around the base and said they wouldn't start, so driving probably wasn't an option. That left only walking, but it was many miles through the desert in all directions to any form of civilization. That was important in the days when they tested atomic weapons at the site. He had no idea which way to go, how far it was, or even what they would find when they got there. And even if they did have somewhere to go and Katherine allowed it, he doubted Valentina was in any condition to make that kind of journey. Staying put seemed like the only option, but it wasn't a good one.

THURSDAY, JULY 10, 6:18 A.M. MT
Camp Hale—Leadville, Colorado
Elevation: 9,200 feet

Roman and the command staff were gathered around the radio in the box truck, listening as the scouts watching Colorado Springs finished describing the event as they saw it cover the city. Roman rested his elbows on the table and pressed his palms to his eyes. The news was not encouraging. What were they dealing with?

"So," Roman said into the radio, "it's clearly hitting higher elevations each time they run it. I want you to return to camp. At this point I think we can watch from the mountains immediately surrounding us."

"That sounds good, sir," one of the scouts replied. "Our situation here is getting dicey if we don't move to higher ground."

"Okay. Come back and we'll figure out what to do."

"Yes, sir."

Roman turned to the officers. "What's the elevation at Colorado Springs?"

"A little over six thousand feet," one of them said after checking a map.

"So we're above them by about three thousand?"

"Yes."

"Hmm, and Denver is at about a mile?"

"Yes."

He thought through the math. "So this might reach us in two days, give or take."

"That's about right."

It wasn't enough time. What was he going to do? "Okay. We need to think about our options. We can stay here and wait, or we can move out, but neither sounds very good. We'll meet later today, and I want to hear some ideas."

The officers nodded and agreed.

"Good. I think I smell bacon, so breakfast must be ready. Let's enjoy it while we can."

THURSDAY, JULY 10, 7:04 A.M. MT
Copper Mountain Resort—Copper Mountain, Colorado
Elevation: 9,720 feet

Summer and Autumn sat together at a table, eating breakfast, having slept soundly through the night in the comfort and safety of the lodge.

"I wonder," Autumn said while sipping a cup of coffee, "do you think we should wait here until they get the phones working again so we can call Mom and Dad?"

"It would be nice," Summer said, "but we don't know how long that will take. I think we should keep going. Plus, the longer we stay here, the harder it will be to go back on the trail."

"You think we'll get spoiled with the hot tub, showers, and a real bed?"

"I know it. I already don't want to give them up."

"I suppose you're right, but I'm worried that Mom and Dad will try to reach us and they won't be able to."

Summer pulled out her trail map. "Look. If today goes well, we'll make it to Camp Hale before sunset. Then we'll be hiking to the west of Leadville and the other towns along this highway for a while before we're in the wilderness again. We can keep checking for service, and we'll need to stop in one of the towns for food anyway."

The man from the desk walked up to the table and glanced at the girls' packs on the floor. "Are you two heading back on the trail?"

"It looks like it," Autumn said.

"Wow, you're brave. Those winds are fierce. I wouldn't leave the building if I was you. You know you're welcome to stay until this is over."

"Thanks," Autumn said.

"Did you get more damage through the night?" Summer asked.

"No, nothing major. So far it's only been cosmetic stuff. I checked in with our operations guy after the last one. He said the gusts peaked well over a hundred again, but they're so short that it's not the same as a sustained wind like a hurricane or something. But seriously, you could get injured or worse out in the open. Are you sure leaving is a wise decision?"

"No," Summer said, "but we'll find good spots to ride out the storms. We did it before, and it's not so bad if you're expecting it. Besides, our dad has put us through stuff way more intense than this."

Autumn chuckled. "Yeah."

"Well, I can't stop you, but I want to make sure you're considering the dangers."

"Thanks," Summer said, "and thanks for letting us stay. It was really great."

"No problem. I hope we'll see you again someday. We have great skiing if you're into that."

"You never know," Autumn said.

Summer stood and picked up her pack. "Are you ready?"

Autumn put down her empty coffee cup. "Yes, let's go."

CHAPTER 16

"Barry," Valentina whispered. Barry had been sitting and worrying for a while as he waited for her and Katherine to wake up.

"I'm pretty sure Katherine is still sleeping," he said quietly, picking up a water bottle and crouching by her side. "How are you feeling?"

Valentina coughed and winced. "Not good."

"Can you sit up?"

"No, you'll have to help me."

"Here we go," he said, pulling her upright, then offering her some water. "We need to make sure you stay hydrated. I think you might have a fever."

"I'm cold," Valentina said, shivering without the warmth of the blanket.

"Let's see." He pressed a hand to her forehead. "You definitely feel hot. Here. Take this. It's only a Tylenol, but it might help, and I need to check the bandage."

She swallowed the pill. "Okay."

He pulled off the bandage and felt the skin around it. "I think it's okay. It doesn't feel hot, and it's not red, but you might still have an infection. I sure wish we had a doctor."

184

"We don't."

Barry sprayed an antibiotic on the area and applied a new bandage. "Is that okay?"

"I guess so."

"Valentina," he whispered in a serious tone, tilting her listless head up until her sad eyes met his, "we haven't had much of a chance to talk since, you know . . . "

She nodded.

"When we arrived here yesterday, it would be fair to say I wished you were dead. I hated you, as I'm sure you can understand."

Another nod.

"But hearing your story, I get it. Even thinking back on the time I've known you, those memories look different when put in perspective. I want you to know, whatever happens here, that I forgive you. You made me miserable. You caused me so much heartburn and stress, I would have quit if I could. You nearly cost me my marriage. But I can't blame you for the things Katherine made you do. You had it even worse than me. I see that now."

Tears welled in Valentina's eyes as she looked away and then back again. She was trying to say something, and though the words weren't coming, the meaning was clear.

"It's okay," Barry whispered, pulling her into his arms. Her tears fell on his shoulder, and he held still until he sensed she was ready to speak.

"Thank you," she finally said. "You don't know how much that means to me. I've hurt so many people. I've hurt you. I'm so sorry."

"It wasn't your choice. I forgive you. I mean it. I wish things could have been different, but we can't go back to change it. That's all in the past. It doesn't matter now."

"It matters to me. I've ruined people's lives. I've killed people. Who knows how many are dead because of me? I can't live with that. I don't deserve to."

"No, don't think that way. You did what you had to do. No one can fault you for it. If one of my kids was taken, I would do anything to get them back. Katherine is the one to blame, not you."

Valentina sighed. "You can say that, but it doesn't change how I feel. I've been fighting to keep it together for so long, but now I've lost everything. There's nothing left for me."

"You don't know that. You've been through a lot. I can't fathom it. I can't imagine the pain you must feel, and I wish I could make it go away. Maybe that's not possible, but it can get better. I never thought you had a heart, but I see it now. It's in there—battered, I'm sure—but it can heal. Don't you want that?"

"Yes, I do, but I'm tired, Barry. I'm sick. I can't keep fighting. My strength is gone. I feel like I've been treading water for a long time, but I'm drowning. I have nothing to cling to. You've been kind, more than I can understand, but I'm not going to survive this. You'll have to let me go."

"I won't do that." He wrapped the blanket around her and took a seat next to her. "If we get out of here, I'll find help. Don't give up hope. It's all we have. I know it looks bad, and maybe there's nothing left out there, but I need something to believe in. I need hope. Please, promise me you'll try. I need you to try."

"Why?"

"I don't know exactly. When you were shot, I just knew I had to help you. I'm glad I did, and something tells me you need to keep going. I can't explain it. I just know. Please, hold on."

"Maybe," Valentina said.

Barry sat in silence for a while. "Valentina?"

"Yes."

"I was just wondering, if you had a child, what happened to his father?"

"He's dead, too," Valentina said, shuddering with emotion.

"I'm sorry."

"I thought I would see him soon, once I got my son back, but now . . . "

"The system?"

"Yes."

"Did you love him?"

"With all of my heart, but I haven't seen him since . . . she took me. I had to walk away. It killed me inside. You can't imagine what that feels like, pretending to be someone I'm not all day and then going to bed alone with the memories haunting me. And then she made me treat you the way I did."

"I could never understand that. It didn't make sense, but, um, thanks for never pushing it, uh, that far, you know?"

"I know, but that's only because she never ordered it."

"Oh." He'd never considered it from her perspective. If Katherine had demanded and she had to go through with it . . . Would he have let her? Honestly, yes, but now that he knew what was behind the scenes . . . If only she'd had some way to get free of Katherine.

"Barry," Valentina said, finally relaxing in the warmth of the blanket while she leaned against him, "thank you. All those times you were a perfect gentleman. I'm thankful you're here. You've been so kind."

The sound of furniture grating on the floor broke the serenity of the moment as Katherine pushed her barricade to the side, picked up her pocketbook, opened the door, and ordered them to come with her for a restroom trip.

"Milford, what are you eating?" Laura asked, watching the professor sipping something out of a small pouch. They'd stopped in Springfield, Oklahoma City, and Amarillo and were now en route to Albuquerque. Milford had downed several of the packets throughout the morning and opened another after they leveled out following the last run of the system.

"This, Laura"—Milford grinned—"might be what I've been searching for all these . . . years."

"For the carbon system?"

Milford shook his head and burped. "No, no. More years than that. I found these in one of the . . . airports we stopped at. It's a truly remarkable product."

"What is that?"

"Oh. Yes, you asked that. This is beer concentrate for hikers. They brew it with no water, so you only need to carry these little pouches and add your own water and . . . carbonation from special packets."

"Where's the water and carbonation?" Ashley asked. "I've only seen you drinking those packets."

Milford burped again and waved away her question. "You need a special bottle. I didn't realize that when I picked these up, but it's quite good . . . anyway."

"Milford, are you drunk?" Laura eyed him. He was acting out of character.

"Ha ha, no, I've only had a few of these."

"Let me see one." Ashley took a pouch from the bag on his lap and read the instructions. "Milford, one pouch makes a liter of beer! You've had at least four of these this morning."

"Well, they're very good. To Douglas!" Milford raised the pouch.

"Douglas?" Laura was at a loss. What was he talking about?

Milford finished the rest of the packet, crumpled it, and shoved it in his bag. "Douglas. The weatherman. You know, the one on the summit. You were there."

"Yes, of course I know him."

"Dead!"

"What do you mean?"

"The last event. By my reckoning, that one was over the summit."

"Oh," Laura said, "that's right." She'd tried not to think about the schedule. The observatory, Douglas . . . She didn't want to picture it.

"Wouldn't he be okay in the observatory?" Ashley asked. "Wasn't that built for this type of stuff?"

"Nope!" Milford let out a rumbling burp and stifled a sob. His odd demeanor was giving way to tears.

"I doubt it," Laura replied. "The summit buildings can withstand ordinary weather but not this."

"I'm sorry," Ashley said.

"Good man." Milford sniffed and rummaged in the bag. "H-he was a good man."

"Oh, no, you don't." Ashley yanked the bag away and put it out of reach. "You've had *too* much already. As your nurse, I'm ordering you to stop."

"Milford," Laura said, "you may not realize it, but you're drunk. Trust me—a little of that stuff is going a long way. We need you thinking sharply."

"I'm thinking as sharp as your rocks. Give me that."

Ashley put a restraining hand on him, but he fell back against the seat and started sobbing. "Now I see why it smelled like alcohol in here," she said.

Laura took his hand in hers. "Milford, what's bothering you? I've never seen you drink like this."

Milford's eyes were red with tears when he raised his head. "I'm sorry, Laura. I'm so . . . sorry."

"Why?" Was this about the system again—or something else?

"I didn't see it. I couldn't . . . stop it. Douglas and those kids . . . They died. It should be me, not them."

"Milford, no. It—"

"Did you see them?" His expression was tortured. "They loved each other. They"—he burped—"didn't deserve to die. Why did they have to die? Why did Douglas have . . . to die? S-Summer and Autumn. Why did they have to die?"

Laura squeezed his hand and fought back her tears. "Please don't say that. We don't know that."

"Why does everyone have to die? It's not . . . f-fair. I wanted to help them. I gave up . . . ev-ever . . . Everything." He dropped his head as sobs racked his body.

"Milford"—Laura put a hand on his shoulder—"It may seem like that, but—"

"You don't understand!"

Ashley held out a tissue. "Here."

"Understand what, Milford?" He wasn't making sense. What was he getting at?

He blew his nose and wiped a sleeve across his face. "I gave up everything. I gave up . . . her."

"Who?" He'd never mentioned a *her* that she could think of.

Milford squeezed his eyes closed and put a fist to his forehead.

"Milford, it's okay."

"I . . . I never told you. I was engaged once. It w-was in grad school, j-just like those kids. She wanted to settle down and have a family, b-but I was too focused on my . . . research. We fought . . . and she left me. I n-never told her I was sorry. I loved her, b-but now she's gone . . . "

"Milford, I—"

"She was wonderful. Sh-she always saw the good in people. She was so kind. She played . . . the piano. We played together. She p-pushed me to pursue my music. She was . . . such a good influence, but I drove her . . . away. I didn't make time. I didn't . . . think about her. I p-put her in second place . . . to my work. She t-tried to talk about . . . it, but I got angry. I . . . I shouted at her, and the l-look in her eyes . . . it doesn't go away. I'm sorry. It's m-my fault. It's all my . . . fault. I thought"—he burped—"I'd drink it away, b-but it didn't help."

Laura rubbed his shoulder and dabbed at her eyes. She'd had no idea, but it explained so much. "I didn't know. I'm sorry. I understand, but, Milford, drinking isn't the answer. It will only make it worse."

"I know. I'm sorry."

Laura sighed. "We can talk about this when you're feeling better."

He groaned. His head slumped back against the cushion, and he started snoring.

Laura turned to Ashley. "Will he be okay?"

Ashley sniffed and looked through the bag. She looked at the ceiling, and her fingers ticked off unspoken digits. "He's had a lot, but I don't think he's in any danger. Fortunately, this stuff is low proof."

"That's good." Laura sat back and put a hand over her forehead. "He's never mentioned anything about that. I guess with everything that's happened . . . it's got to be hard for him. I've never seen him drunk before. I hope he sleeps it off."

"She must have been great," Ashley said.

"What do you mean?"

"The woman he loved. If he's still this torn about her after all that time, she must have been great."

Laura's eyes brimmed over. "I guess so."

THURSDAY, JULY 10, 12:02 P.M. MT
Main control base—the desert south of Phoenix, Arizona
Elevation: 1,100 feet

"Barry," Katherine barked, "I have a job for you."

Barry turned to look at her while licking powdered sugar off his fingers. He and Valentina were finishing a lunch consisting of vending machine snack foods.

"I want these bodies out of here," Katherine said, "and the ones in the hallway. You can drag them outside with the others."

"All right." It was actually not a bad idea, and they should have taken care of them earlier. He took hold of the IPCC chairman's feet and pulled him toward the door. Katherine opened it and followed as he moved the body down the hall and outside into the parking area, where he deposited it next to a security guard. Barry stood straight and shielded his eyes from the sun. The scene was disturbing enough viewed from the bunker window, but standing there in the open, viewing it firsthand, was very different. He felt queasy, and rivulets of sweat streamed down inside his clothing because of the brutally hot temperature outside. His stomach turned, and he wretched the lunch of cookies and doughnuts onto the pavement.

"Come on," Katherine ordered. "Let's go get the others."

Barry spit to clear his mouth and staggered back to the bunker. This was harder than he'd thought it would be. Couldn't they have done this in the cool of the night? Why was she forcing him to endure this insufferable experience? He entered the control room and looked over at Valentina as he took hold of another body. The sight of her put an instant reality check on his self-pity party. All things considered, he had it easy. He wasn't sick. He wasn't injured. He could move freely. What did he have to complain about? He opened a water bottle and took a long swig, then continued his task with determination.

THURSDAY, JULY 10, 3:36 P.M. MT
Flagstaff Pulliam Airport—Flagstaff, Arizona
Elevation: 7,014 feet

Holly brought the helicopter down on approach to the airport south of Flagstaff. She'd offered to fly the long stretch from Albuquerque, and Craig had taken the opportunity to stretch out for a nap in the passenger section. The helicopter was flying well, and their high-altitude strategy was paying off in minimizing the turbulence caused by the system, so they didn't anticipate any problems that she couldn't handle solo.

"This is Flagstaff tower," said a voice from the radio. "Please identify yourself."

"What?" Holly said, taken off guard. She'd become accustomed to radio silence as they flew across the country. A voice seemed so out of place.

"This is Flagstaff tower. Please identify yourself."

"Um, I'm Holly. This is a Pottersmith Air Charters private helicopter. We don't have a flight plan scheduled."

"Where did you fly from?"

"Albuquerque."

"What's going on there? We've lost all communication besides local radio."

"Uh . . . " How could she possibly explain this? She'd seen it all firsthand, but putting that experience into words . . . "I think we'd better discuss that after I land."

"Okay. Come on in. We haven't seen any flights arrive since yesterday morning. I hope you can shed some light on what's happening. You may as well land in front of the main terminal. I'm the only person still here. I'll come over to meet you."

"Understood," Holly said, adjusting her heading toward the terminal building. She brought up the intercom. "Hey, we're about to land, and there's actually someone at the tower."

"Really?" Craig asked.

"Yes, I was on the radio with him."

Holly set the machine down and saw a young man jogging their way. By the time she shut down and they got out, he'd arrived.

"Holly?" he asked, a little short of breath.

"Yes, it was me on the radio."

"I'm Stewart. What's going on out there? We haven't heard a thing since they started the climate system yesterday."

"I'm going to refuel," Craig said.

"Well," Holly said, "there seems to be a problem with the system." Best to start into it gently.

"It's killing everyone," Milford stated. So much for gently.

"What?" Stewart asked, alarm in his voice.

"Something went wrong," Laura said. "There's no easy way to say it. Everyone caught in the field is dying."

"Everyone?"

Holly nodded. Her hopes of limited devastation had dissolved. "Yes. We left New Hampshire yesterday, so we've seen it all across the country."

"Where are you going?"

"The control base near Phoenix," Laura said. "We're hoping to stop it."

"Wow, that would explain . . . So is that the cause of the flashes we keep seeing around the horizon—and the wind gusts?"

"Yes," Laura said. "The system is running every five hours, and the altitude keeps increasing."

"Increasing? Like, it will hit here?"

"Very soon!" Milford blurted.

"But," Stewart said, pointing to the east, "that thing hasn't moved. I didn't think they were running it here."

Holly looked in the direction he was pointing to where one of the massive reflector balloons sat at ground level near a reactor facility. Even at a distance of a couple of miles, its size was intimidating.

"I saw that on the way in," she said. "They're everywhere."

"What's the elevation here at the airport?" Laura asked.

"7,014 feet," Stewart answered.

Milford looked at his watch. "Not this time. Probably next."

"What do you mean?" Stewart asked.

"The next run will start at four o'clock," Laura said, "but it's not going to cover this far up yet. We do have a pretty good idea of the elevation schedule."

"But in another five hours it will be here?"

"We think so," Laura said, gazing at the balloon. "The installations at higher elevations don't engage until the system is at a high enough altitude to tie them into the field. That one is still on standby, so it's not going to be included this time."

"We're set," Craig announced, joining them after fueling the helicopter. "We need to be going now to get above this."

"No," Laura said, "we're actually high enough that we could sit this one out on the ground, as long as the helicopter will be okay in the wind."

"Oh," Craig said. "Yeah, that won't be a problem. I'll lock it up and adjust the blade angle so it doesn't get pushed around so much."

"Do you need some help?" Holly asked.

"No, I've got it."

Laura turned to Stewart. "It looks like the terminal has held up so far. We should all take shelter inside before the system runs and those winds arrive."

"Certainly."

"Do you have a snack shop?" Milford asked.

"Milford . . . " Ashley and Laura said together.

"No, no more beer. I need something to clear my head."

"Come on." Ashley took his arm and pushed him toward the building. "We'll find you something."

They entered the terminal and found some seats. "All set," Craig said, rejoining them. Several minutes later they watched the flash on the horizon and the ensuing winds.

"Look," Ashley said, pointing toward the balloon in the distance. Holly moved to the window for a better view. The balloon's navigation lights had lit up and started blinking, and it was rising off the ground as the tethers spooled out. It was only fabric and metal, but seeing it come alive made her uneasy. She hated it for what it would do.

"That confirms it," Laura said. "This elevation will be under the field in five hours."

"My wife. My kids," Stewart said, looking around in panic. "What am I going to do? I have to go get them."

"Stewart." Laura placed her hands on his shoulders and looked him in the eyes. "Our next stop is the control base. We should be there in plenty of time to shut this down. They should be fine."

"But what if you don't make it?"

"Do you have a car?" Craig asked, scanning the horizon.

"Yes."

"Where is the highest place you could drive to within five hours with your family?"

"Um, maybe Elden Mountain. It's over nine thousand feet. I've gone up there before."

"Okay," Craig said. "Go home, pack up some supplies, and take your family there just in case. You'll know if we've been successful at nine o'clock tonight."

"All right. I can do that. Thanks."

"The clock is ticking," Holly said. "Let's hit the restrooms and get out of here."

THURSDAY, JULY 10, 5:42 P.M. MT
Camp Hale–Leadville, Colorado
Elevation: 9,200 feet

Roman took a seat on the grass in the mess area, the tent having been packed away, and dug into his dinner of steak and potatoes. It had been a busy day in the camp as the men reinforced the barricades and built several sturdy pavilions to protect their more delicate equipment from the winds. His radio squawked as he was chewing on a piece of meat.

"Commander Muscovite?"

"Yes."

"We have a situation here at the north barricade. Can you come over?"

"I'll be there in a minute." He folded his plate to go and dug his car key out of his pocket as he walked to his Subaru. After a brief drive, he pulled to a stop behind the roadblock they'd erected on Highway 24 north of the camp.

"They're on the other side, sir," one of the men said.

"Who?"

"They say they're refugees headed for Leadville."

"Okay," Roman said, climbing up the barricade to take a look. A line of cars stretched down the road as far as he could see, and people were milling about, obviously frustrated by the delay and wondering at the heavily armed soldiers on top of the wall. One of his men was speaking with a young couple standing by the closest car.

"What's going on?" Roman yelled down.

"Refugees, sir," the militiaman said. "They want to drive through to Leadville."

"Why?" He knew the answer as soon as he'd asked the question.

"We have to get away from the climate system," the young woman from the car said. "It's killing people. We saw it."

The militiaman climbed the barricade and stood next to Roman. "There could be UN spies among them, sir. What are your orders?"

Roman surveyed the people within view. Young couples, elderly people, cars with only women and children. Could there be spies? Perhaps, but if so, they were probably seeking refuge, too. No UN conspiracy could have intended this. "Let them through, escort them along the road, and radio the southern barricade to allow them to pass."

The militiamen moved the barricade out of the roadway, and soon the caravan of vehicles was proceeding up the highway. Roman recognized some of them as family members of the troops, and by the time the last car had passed, most of his men were reunited with their loved ones. Roman discovered that the wives had planned a retreat in Vail while the men were "playing army." They decided to come join them when they realized the severity of the situation and that the men's concerns were apparently well founded.

CHAPTER 17

"Do you hear something?" Katherine asked from her perch at the window.

"No," Barry replied, concentrating on changing Valentina's bandage. He was feeling more hopeful as it seemed her fever was subsiding.

"You don't hear that?" Katherine asked again.

Barry finished and looked toward the window, listening. "I don't know—maybe the air-conditioning?"

"Hmm," Katherine said, scowling.

Barry gave Valentina a drink of water, and then she cocked her head as if she heard something, too.

"It's getting louder," Katherine said, peering out the window.

Barry heard it. The sound was faint, but it was a low, throbbing beat of some sort.

"How about now?" Katherine asked.

"Yes," Barry said. "I do. What do you think it is?"

"It's a helicopter," Valentina said, surprising them. She hadn't spoken a word all day other than in whispered conversation with him.

"You're right," Katherine said, still looking out the window.

200

"Who could be coming?" Barry asked. Hopefully not the people Katherine was waiting for. They would likely be interested in saving only one person in the bunker. Not Valentina. Not him.

"I see it!" Katherine said. "It's headed towards us."

Barry went to the window and found the little dot in the sky that was slowly growing. "I hope they're coming to help."

"It's descending," Katherine said. "They must intend to land here."

"I agree," Barry said, turning to Valentina. Her gaze was indifferent, but a glimmer of hope flickered in her eyes when she noticed him.

The sound of the helicopter grew louder, and they watched as it came down and settled in the parking area amid a cloud of dust and sand.

"Can you see what that logo on the side says?" Katherine asked.

Barry squinted, trying to make it out through the haze. "Pottersmith . . . Air . . . Charters."

"That sounds familiar," Katherine said. "Why does that sound familiar?"

"I don't know." It did sound familiar, but was that a good thing? He'd worked with so many people, both from the government and connected to Katherine.

They watched as the doors opened, then Katherine pointed her pistol at Barry. "Get back. This could be our chance to get out of here. You let me do the talking. If you try anything, Dr. Severnaya gets a bullet in her head, and then so do you."

"Katherine, they're probably here to help. We can all get out of this." He stared at the gun. If there was a time to act, this was it, but what could he do? Katherine was focused.

She checked the safety. "I don't think so, not if you two start talking and try to blame this on me. No, our story is that Dr. Severnaya was behind it. She's responsible for this mess, and we're lucky I was able to subdue her before she killed us, too."

"Will you never stop, Katherine?" Valentina asked.

"Not while there's a chance of survival. Now, quiet, both of you. They're headed for the bunker."

Barry retreated and took a seat as Katherine concealed her weapon and opened the door. The voices grew louder, and then footsteps echoed in the hallway. A tall man entered the room, followed by two women and then another woman escorting an older man they all recognized.

"Milford?" Katherine said.

"Katherine?" Pennychuck replied. "Dr. Severnaya? Director Calavari? What happened?"

"We had a terrorist network operating under our noses," Katherine said. "They destroyed the control terminal. Dr. Severnaya was their leader. She killed everyone here, but I managed to stop her."

"What?" Pennychuck bellowed.

"Yes, terrorists."

"Is that why you tried to kill me?" Pennychuck asked, turning to Valentina.

"I wouldn't put it past her," Katherine said.

"Did you say they destroyed the control terminal?" one of the women asked, walking toward it.

"Yes, Dr. Severnaya shot it. It's unusable."

Pennychuck leaned on another of the women for support. "So we came all this way for . . . nothing?"

"She's right," the woman near the terminal said. "It's not working."

"What did you do to my system?" Pennychuck shouted at Valentina, his face reddening.

"I'm sorry . . . " she said weakly. Barry shifted closer to her.

"Don't believe anything she says," Katherine snapped. "She's been telling nothing but lies."

"So there's no way to stop the system from this facility?" the woman at the terminal asked.

"No," Katherine replied.

"Is that why you came here?" Barry asked.

"Yes," she said. "We flew all the way from Mount Washington in New Hampshire."

"Did this"—Barry pointed out the window—"happen everywhere?"

"Yes," Pennychuck said, "and the balloons are rising higher each time. Flagstaff is next."

"Flagstaff?" Katherine asked with interest. "You mean it's unaffected so far?"

"Yes," the woman replied. "Our last stop was the airport there."

"Are the hangars intact?"

"I think so," the tall man said. "All the buildings looked okay. Why?"

Katherine gave a sigh. "Oh, just wondering."

Barry tensed. Katherine wouldn't have asked out of mere curiosity. She never just wondered. If she wanted to know something, she demanded, ordered, or forced an answer. What was she thinking?

"Have you communicated with the other control bases?" Pennychuck asked.

Katherine shook her head. "No, we can't reach anyone at all."

"So we can't stop the system?" the young woman standing by the tall man asked.

"I don't know, Holly," Pennychuck said.

"Excuse me," Katherine said, "but Barry and Dr. Severnaya were just about to use the restrooms before you landed. Barry, would you please escort her down the hall for me? I'll help her from there. The rest of you, please have a seat. I'm sure we'll be able to think of something."

Barry was about to object, but he saw the imperious look on Katherine's face and knew he'd have to play along. As their visitors began talking among themselves, he helped Valentina to her feet, and they walked out the door with Katherine close behind.

"Follow me," Katherine whispered, heading for the exit.

"What are you doing?" Valentina asked.

"Be quiet. I'm getting us out of here."

"Where are we going?" Barry asked as they stepped out into the parking lot.

"To the helicopter," Katherine replied, rooting around in her pocketbook and pulling out a pill bottle. "Hurry up."

"We can't fly a helicopter."

"I can," Katherine said. "I have three of them."

"What about the others?" Barry asked, pointing back to the bunker.

"What about them? They can stay here. Now, open the passenger door—quickly."

While Barry pulled the door open and the steps folded down, Katherine shook a small pill out of the bottle and forced Valentina to swallow it along with some water.

"What was that?" Barry asked.

"Insurance," Katherine said. "Put Dr. Severnaya in the back, and make sure her seat belt is securely fastened. You'll ride up front with me."

Barry helped Valentina up the stairs and into one of the soft leather seats. "Should we make a run for it?" he asked, buckling the seat belt.

"No," Valentina whispered, "I can't." She looked forlornly at him, her eyes appearing glazed and starting to close.

"Remember your key, left pocket." He paused, but there was nothing more he could do. He backed down the stairs and closed the door. Katherine had started the rotors already, and they were picking up speed. Barry opened the cockpit door and climbed in. He glanced over toward the bunker and saw the tall man coming out and running their way.

"Out!" Katherine ordered, her pistol pointed at him.

What? She'd said he was going with her. "But you—"

"Out!"

Barry stepped back to the ground. "Valentina . . . " His voice was lost in the beat of the blades. She was trapped, out of reach. He couldn't get to her.

"Close the door!"

The tall man was getting closer. Barry swung the door closed and crouched in the wash of the blades. He shut his eyes against the sting of whirling sand and heard several gunshots. The helicopter lifted off the ground and ascended. As soon as he could, Barry opened his eyes and saw the tall man lying motionless on the sand. He turned back to the sky. The helicopter was speeding away on a northernly heading. He ran a few paces after it, then stopped.

Katherine was gone. Valentina was gone. He dropped to his knees and wept.

Katherine could see the Phoenix skyline in the distance, and from there she would know the route to Flagstaff by sight. How fortuitous that Pennychuck and his companions had made such an effort to deliver transportation to her doorstep as well as the news that Flagstaff was not destroyed. If the hangars were intact, then one of her many private jets would be safe where she kept it.

She would fly to her own bunker and live out the rest of her years in comfort deep underground. She was set with supplies and provisions to last for decades no matter what ravages the climate system inflicted on the surface. She would finally be free of the droning annoyance of so many idiots surrounding her, and she would live in peaceful seclusion.

It was unfortunate that the Arctic Circle Society would not see its dreams come to fruition. Was Dr. Severnaya correct that her greed had caused this catastrophe? If so, she'd undone centuries of hard work accomplished by her predecessors. She couldn't accept that. No. What did Severnaya know? She'd been nothing—an orphan, probably destined for a life on the streets. Who was she to assign blame? Everything Katherine did was in the interests of the Society, and she could not be faulted for that.

The sedative would keep Dr. Severnaya asleep for a couple of hours and prevent her from causing any trouble. She had no use for

"That explains the snow," Milford said. "It's solidified."

"So this *was* a terrorist attack?" Craig asked. Barry's explanation wasn't adding up.

"It was more like an accident," Barry said. "Valentina uploaded some sort of software right before the system started, and then Katherine shot her and everyone else in the room. It was Katherine that destroyed the terminal, and since then, we've been sitting here waiting."

"I don't understand. Why would she shoot Dr. Severnaya?" Milford asked. "She and Katherine were so close. I've always thought they were up to something together."

"They were, sort of, but everything I thought I knew about Valentina was wrong. The things Katherine did to her were unspeakable. She had no choice but to comply. Once she'd served her purpose, Katherine was going to be rid of her. I don't know why she didn't finish her off, but now I'm afraid she will."

"That might make sense of what she said at the hospital," Milford said. "She was supposed to kill me, but she didn't want to."

"That woman that just left was Valerie?" Ashley asked. "The one who pretended to be your daughter?"

"Yes, that was Dr. Severnaya."

"Wow."

"So where did Katherine go?" Laura asked.

"And why did she take my helicopter?" Craig added.

"I have no idea," Barry replied. "She kept waiting and watching out the window, but she didn't say anything about going anywhere."

Craig turned to the window. "So she's just going to leave us here? Why?"

"Unless she has another way to stop the system, it's not important," Milford said. "What are we going to do?"

"What can we do?" Holly asked. "Without the helicopter we're stuck here."

"How could you stop the system without the computers?" Craig asked.

"It's impossible," Milford said.

"But there must be a way. What would make it stop?" There had to be a weakness. Every system had one, just like the opposing team on the football field. His coaches always said that. No matter how bad it looks, you find the gap and go for it.

Milford frowned. "You'd have to damage something, like bring down a balloon to crash the field or stop a reactor so the safety protocols would cause a shutdown."

"We can't do those things," Laura said.

Maybe . . . Craig thought. If his memory was correct . . . "Dr. Pennychuck, you said the balloons are next to impossible to shoot down, but is there another way they could be damaged? There are several not far from here."

"I don't know," Milford said with indifference. "Maybe if you destroyed the reflector array that hangs off the bottom, that would do it, but they're out of our reach."

"What if they weren't?" Was this the right place?

"What are you talking about? Katherine took the helicopter."

"What if I could get us another one?" It had to be. He'd specifically mentioned the control base.

Milford laughed. "Well, that would be nice. Perhaps you could pick up a pizza for me as well."

"Craig?" Laura asked. "What are you thinking?" She could always tell.

"I have a friend who does restorations of old military aircraft. His shop is only a few miles west of here. He's mentioned several times how he can see the main base from his property. I think I could get there. He's bound to have something ready to fly."

"Katherine said none of the vehicles outside were working," Barry said. "She tried a bunch of them. It seems that the system knocked them out somehow."

"Yes," Craig said, "I was curious about that on our way here. I kept checking things at the airports while I was refueling. Some worked, others didn't, but it seems like only machines with a lot of computerization are getting knocked out. Simple stuff works just fine. My helicopter would probably be dead if it got caught under the field, but something much older . . . it should be okay."

"This is madness," Milford said. "Even if you could find some old relic, what would you do with it?"

"If we latched on to a balloon, could we pull it free of the tethers?"

Milford's eyes narrowed a bit. "How much can a helicopter lift?"

Craig shrugged. "Depends. Maybe a few thousand pounds on average."

"No, that won't do. You'd be like a fly trying to lift an orange."

"Maybe we can figure something else out if we can get a closer look."

"How far is this shop?" Laura asked.

"I think it's only a few miles." He hoped that was right.

"How will you even get there?" Milford asked.

"I'd have to run."

"Craig," Laura said, looking at her watch, "we only have about two hours until the next event. What if you get lost or it's farther away than you think or there's nothing there?"

Laura's questions were valid. It was a long shot. He wasn't going to lie, but he also couldn't pass this up. "I know. It's risky, but we didn't fly all the way out here to hide in a bunker. This could be our only chance."

"You're right," Holly said. "We have to try, but you can't do this alone. I'm going with you."

Barry got up from his chair. "Me, too."

"Are you up for running a few miles?" Craig asked, eyeing the politician. Was Holly? Yes, certainly. She could outdistance him any day. He wasn't worried about her, but this Barry guy struck him as a benchwarmer.

"I ran cross-country in my college days, and I've kept it up."

"Okay."

"I hope you'll excuse me," Milford said, "if I sit this out."

"I wouldn't let you go anyway," Ashley said, then smiled as she picked up on his sarcasm.

"Promise me you'll be careful," Laura said.

"You know I always am," Craig said, holding her tight. He wanted to say more, but there was no time.

"I know, and I know there's no talking you out of this, so you better get going."

"We'll be back," Holly said, giving Ashley and Laura a hug.

Barry handed out a few water bottles. "Let's go. Oh, and make sure to close the bunker door before the system runs."

CHAPTER 18

Following a long day of hiking, Summer and Autumn were descending the trail toward a dirt road on the floor of a valley north of Leadville when the outskirts of the Camp Hale site came into view.

"It says in the guidebook," Summer said, "that they had about fifteen thousand soldiers here during the Second World War, training for skiing and mountain warfare."

"That's cool," Autumn said. "Hopefully it's a good spot to camp."

"It should be. There won't be many trees around."

"Do you think we can use the tent?"

"We may as well try. Dad said it's rated for the worst—"

"Stop right there!" a man dressed in camouflage ordered, stepping out from behind a rock outcropping by the side of the trail and leveling a rifle at them. "Who are you, and where are you going?"

The twins froze. A second sentry appeared and circled around behind them.

"Please, don't hurt us." Autumn moved closer to her sister and linked arms. She could sense the tension building in Summer's body, and her thoughts went to the pepper spray canisters they each kept in the shoulder straps of their packs.

"No one's going to get hurt," the sentry said, "as long as you cooperate. Please answer my questions."

"I'm Autumn. This is Summer. We're hiking the Colorado Trail." Who were these guys? What did they want?

"Where did you come from?"

"We left Copper Mountain this morning." Could they run? Would they be shot if they tried? Where would they go? There was no one around for miles.

"What's your purpose here?"

"The trail crosses this valley," Summer said. "We were going to camp here tonight."

"Do you have identification?"

"Yes," Summer said. Autumn nodded.

"Show me—slowly."

They each pulled out their driver's license and held them up. The sentry took them and looked closely. "Wait here." Then he walked down the trail to have a conversation on the radio.

"I don't like this," Summer whispered.

"Neither do I, but they have guns."

"What do you think they want?"

Autumn had no idea. A lot of things had flashed through her mind, but the situation wasn't making any sense. "Are you sure this isn't still an army base?"

"Yes. That was closed a long time ago."

"Then what are they doing here? They look like soldiers."

"He's coming back."

"All right." The sentry returned their licenses. "Our commander said to bring you down to camp to see him. Please follow me."

"What camp?" Autumn asked. What had they got themselves into?

"Commander Muscovite will explain."

THURSDAY, JULY 10, 7:18 P.M. MT
Flagstaff Pulliam Airport—Flagstaff, Arizona
Elevation: 7,014 feet

Katherine landed the stolen helicopter at the Flagstaff airport. Pennychuck and his companions had been correct—the system had not reached it yet. She got out and peered through the rear window to confirm that Dr. Severnaya was still sleeping, then went to her hangar and punched in the code to open the door. As it rolled aside, she entered and ascended the stairs to the door of her plane.

Everything looked to be in order, so she went back out to remove the wheel blocks and prepare the jet for departure. Few of her colleagues or peers could ever understand why she insisted on flying her own aircraft, but who was laughing now? The Morgreeds had a long and proud history of self-reliance despite their wealth and privilege, and she had kept up the tradition. She remembered the lectures she'd received as a young girl about never depending on others so much that she'd be helpless without them, and now more than ever, she could appreciate the wisdom behind that philosophy.

Katherine completed her inspection and ensured that the plane was fully fueled before starting the engines. Some of the satellite instruments weren't working, just like in the helicopter, but the essentials checked out okay. She buckled in and taxied out to the runway, where she lined up the nose and paused to check all the controls before takeoff. Satisfied, she pushed the thrust levers forward and sped down the pavement until lifting into the air.

She eased into a slow banking turn as she gained altitude and the airport grew smaller beneath her, but something ahead caught her peripheral vision, and she turned to see a massive reflector balloon in her path. She rolled the plane into a tighter turn and pushed the nose down to avoid the balloon, holding her breath and cringing as the jet narrowly avoided a collision, but then one of the tethers loomed ahead.

There was nothing she could do. The high-tensile cable ripped into the wing, slicing through the thin metal and taking off a huge section. A cacophony of alarms sounded in the cockpit as the engines stalled and the jet descended out of control. Katherine fought to keep it pointed straight and engaged the flaps to slow her fall, but before the landing gear had locked into place, the plane hit the ground, sliding several hundred feet until coming to a jarring halt against a boulder.

THURSDAY, JULY 10, 7:38 P.M. MT
Private aircraft restoration facility—the desert south of Phoenix, Arizona
Elevation: 1,150 feet

"Wow, Craig," Holly said, breathing heavily, "you're really slowing down in your old age."

Craig took a gulp of water and turned toward her. "Slowing down? I don't think so, and who are you calling old?"

"I'm just saying, that wasn't as quick as I remember from last time we ran together."

"I was pacing myself. I didn't know how far we'd need to go."

"Right . . ."

"Is this the place?" Barry asked, slowing to a walk as he caught up with them.

"Yes." Craig looked over the sprawling complex of buildings, old aircraft, and parts. "We better get moving—there's not much time. Holly, let's go check out those helicopters. Barry, we're probably going to need tools. Can you look for anything that would be useful for taking things apart and breaking stuff?"

"Sure."

"All right. Come on," he said, jogging toward an area with several helicopters in various stages of completion. They went from machine to machine, finding nothing that appeared flight ready. "I really thought he'd have something." Worry began to build in his chest.

"There might be another one behind that hangar," Holly said.

Craig looked to where she was pointing. The tip of a rotor blade was poking out several feet. "Maybe." He hoped she was right. If not, they would have to run again, and the thought was not appealing.

They reached the building and rounded the corner. "Wow," Holly exclaimed. "That's an old one."

"It's a military Huey. I'd guess it saw service in Vietnam."

"Do you think it will work?"

"I don't know. Let's see." He opened the cockpit door and climbed in.

Holly clambered in from the other side. "It looks like new. What's in that folder?"

Craig picked up a manila folder sitting on the instrument panel and opened it. "It's an invoice," he said, scanning the pages. He read the notes and grinned. Thank goodness, they wouldn't have to run.

"According to this, it's been fully restored and is ready for the customer to take it."

"So it should fly?"

"I would think so." He studied the control panels and flipped a couple of switches, then shut them off again. "It has power, but we better check it over before we try."

"Okay." Holly got out and walked around the machine. She opened one of the large sliding doors of the rear section and climbed in. "It has plenty of room, and there's a cable winch."

"That could be useful," Craig said, standing on the lip of the door opening and inspecting the rotor mechanisms on the roof. "I'm no mechanic, but there are a lot of new parts up here. I'm inclined to think the invoice is right. It's ready. Can you jump in the cockpit and test out the controls? I want to make sure everything is moving correctly."

Holly took a seat in the front and manipulated the stick and pedals as Craig confirmed they all did what they should. Everything looked good. The connections were secure. It was ready to fly. His friend had come through. He wouldn't likely see him again, but he'd be sure to thank him if he did.

"Okay," he said, joining Holly in the cockpit. "Let's try it."

"Are you sure you know what you're doing? This is a lot different than any of your machines."

Craig gave her a mischievous grin. "It's been a long time, but I trained on one of these. You know, back in the dark ages when I could run faster."

Holly rolled her eyes and watched as he went through the start-up procedure, and soon they were circling above the compound.

Once he was satisfied it was fully operational, they landed near the pile of tools that Barry had been collecting.

"That's a relief," Barry said as they joined him. "For a minute there, I thought you were going to leave me."

"Of course not," Craig said. "We needed to check that it was working."

"And is it?"

"Yes. The fuel tanks are full and it's good to go."

"Great." Barry motioned to the pile of tools. "I hope this is what you had in mind. I found wrenches, hammers, cutting torches, hacksaws. Unfortunately they were all out of rocket launchers."

"It will have to do," Craig said with a smile. "Good work, Barry. Let's load up."

THURSDAY, JULY 10, 8:00 P.M. MT
Main control base—the desert south of Phoenix, Arizona
Elevation: 1,100 feet

"One hour to go," Laura said, checking her watch. "I hope they make it."

"They will," Ashley said, "and if they don't find Craig's friend's place, they'll come back in time."

Laura sighed. "I hope so, but I'm still worried. What if they don't?"

"They will. Craig won't let anything happen to them."

"But he can get so determined. I'm worried he won't leave enough time to get back." She tried to push the thought down, but there was no denying it. Craig was always running late because of his eternal optimism. It didn't typically bother her, but this was a deadline he couldn't miss. The emptiness she'd felt in the weather center had returned—but worse.

"He'll leave enough time," Ashley said. "He has to. Holly always says how he takes safety so seriously. She trusts him, and I'm sure she's watching the time, too."

"We shall see," Milford said, "but even if they find their helicopter, I don't see what good it will do."

"Craig will think of something," Laura said. "He always does." She had to believe it. She had to trust him. Milford's pessimism was not helping, but that was nothing new.

"Perhaps," Milford said. "I'm sorry. I'm being awfully negative, but I can't accept that my life is going to end like this. We should have been celebrating by now, not waiting to die in this bunker. I can't stop thinking that this never would have happened if it wasn't for me, but at the same time, I'm outraged that Katherine went behind my back and ruined what could have been a wondrous achievement. Politics and profit always make a mess of things. I should have known this would never have a chance of succeeding."

Laura looked at him. "You have every right to be mad. I'm mad, too, and I'm sick with worry for Craig and for my girls, but anger and worry won't help them. I've known you a long time, Milford, and we both know that dwelling on the negatives prevents you from thinking creatively and making progress."

"That's true."

"You need to put what happened behind you and start focusing on what we're going to do now, in the present. We're still alive. We need you, and as long as I have hope of bringing my family back together, I'm not going to give up."

Milford stared at the floor for a few minutes in silence, then looked at Laura and Ashley. A faint smile grew on his lips. "Laura, you're right. I'm being selfish. If Craig doesn't succeed, there must be another way, but I'm starting to think he's going to pull it off."

"Why is that?"

"Because I hear a helicopter."

THURSDAY, JULY 10, 8:09 P.M. MT
Camp Hale–Leadville, Colorado
Elevation: 9,200 feet

Autumn had looked about with apprehension as she and Summer were led off the trail and into the military-style encampment of the militia. The commander was busy, so they'd been asked to wait until he was free. In the meantime, Autumn observed that the camp consisted of women and children in addition to the camouflaged soldiers, and on more than one occasion, a small child wandered over to stare at them and comment on their identical appearance.

"Hello," a man said, approaching them. "Sorry for the delay. I'm Commander Roman Muscovite of the Climate Freedom Militia, Colorado division."

"Summer and Autumn," the twins replied.

"Pretty names," Roman said. "Anyway, I told the sentry to bring you in because I wanted to ask you about what you've seen out there."

"Do you mean the winds?" Autumn asked.

"Yes. Please tell me what you've experienced."

"Every five hours," Summer said, "there's a bright flash on the horizon, and then it gets really windy for a few seconds."

"Is that all you've seen?"

"Yes."

"Have you had any communication since the start of the climate system?"

"No," Autumn said. "We left Breckenridge, and our phones haven't worked since then."

"Copper Mountain was out of service, too," Summer said.

Roman looked a little disappointed. "I was hoping you'd seen more than that."

"Like what?" Autumn asked. This was weird. What could they possibly tell him? Did he know something? Was this a test? He had hundreds—or thousands—of people. She and Summer were just two hikers.

"Our scouts have had a closer look at what's happening. The lower elevations have been getting hit by those flashes and the winds that follow, and it appears that everyone caught within the electrical field is dead."

"Dead?" Autumn refocused on him. Had she heard that right?

"Yes."

"Everyone?"

"As far as we can tell."

Autumn stared at him, speechless. Was he joking? She looked at Summer, but her sister's expression mirrored her own confusion.

"Why?" Summer asked.

"I don't know. Our militia is organized around the belief that there's a UN conspiracy behind the climate system, but we don't know what to make of this, and it's getting closer."

"Closer?" Autumn asked. What was that supposed to mean? The system didn't move. Mom said it went up and down—that's it. And she'd heard about this militia. The news reported on them occasionally, but most people dismissed them as a backward-thinking hate group.

"Yes, the field is being raised each time it goes off. We estimate it's up to around seven thousand feet now, and it will cover us here in less than two days. Denver has been hit already, and so has Colorado Springs. We're running out of time."

Summer looked doubtful. "Are you sure? Mom didn't say anything about killing people, and Dr. Pennychuck would have told us."

"Dr. Pennychuck, the climate scientist?" Roman asked.

"Yeah, he's like our third grandpa. Mom worked with him."

"Wait a minute. Do you mean the Dr. Pennychuck behind the Pennychuck carbon plan?"

"Yes."

"How do you know him?"

"Mom got her doctorate working with him," Autumn said, "and his office is at Dartmouth. We see him a lot." She eyed Roman in a different light. Did he know Dr. Pennychuck?

Roman's thoughts were obviously racing. "Does your mother know you're here in Colorado, on the trail?"

"Of course," Summer said.

"Was it her idea?"

"No," Autumn said. "She was reluctant to let us go." That was an understatement, but it also wasn't any of his business.

"So she would have been happy if you stayed home, around Dartmouth?"

"Yes," Summer said, "although she's busy with her work on Mount Washington, so it's not like we'd see much of her."

"Has she told you about her work on the climate system?"

Autumn shook her head. "She tries, but it's above our heads."

"Hmm, so as far as you know, it was intended for what they claimed?"

"Yeah," Summer said. "Mom was definitely excited to see it work."

Roman's brow furrowed. "Did she have plans to travel before they started the system, or did Dr. Pennychuck?"

"No, Dad was going to meet her on Mount Washington to watch. We talked to her on the phone that morning."

"This doesn't make any sense."

"Dr. Pennychuck said there was no way the system could hurt us," Autumn said. "Are you sure it's killing people?"

"We're sure."

"You said everyone under seven thousand feet," Summer stated.

"About."

"No," Summer said. "That would mean Mom and Dad and, like, everyone. No way."

Autumn didn't want to believe it either, but Roman's expression was dead serious, and what would he have to gain from convincing them of some wild conspiracy? He believed it, and that meant Mom and Dad and everyone she knew . . .

"Listen," Roman said. "I can't force you to do anything, but would you mind staying at camp tonight? We can find a vehicle for you to take shelter in. We're going to have to come up with some sort of plan tomorrow, and it's possible you might know something that could help. I'm guessing you've made it this far by sheer luck, hiking up into the mountains ahead of this thing, but it wouldn't be a good idea to continue on the trail."

The twins looked at each other for a moment, coming to an unspoken decision. "Okay," Summer said.

"Good. I'm sorry if my men may have frightened you at the checkpoint. They're being overly cautious due to our present circumstances, but they're a great bunch of guys. You'll see if you get to know them. Actually, the two that met you are elementary school teachers."

"Oh," Autumn said, "I never would have guessed that. They were pretty scary."

"Well, we're all very tense. I'll have someone come and get you situated for the night, and please join me for breakfast in the morning."

"Okay," Summer said.

"And," Roman added, "before you go. One more question. Do you know anything about Dr. Severnaya?"

"Do you mean the lady that works with Dr. Pennychuck?" Autumn asked.

"Yes."

"Hmm," Summer said, "we've only seen her a few times, but Dr. Pennychuck would certainly have some things to share. He doesn't like her."

"She's pretty, though," Autumn added, trying to say something nice but feeling silly for sounding so shallow. Dr. Pennychuck had shared plenty about her. *Dislike* didn't begin to describe how he felt, but she didn't know Dr. Severnaya personally, and Dr. Pennychuck had his rough spots, too.

"Um, yeah," Roman replied. "Thanks. Good night, then."

CHAPTER 19

"I didn't realize they were so big," Holly said as Craig piloted the old Huey toward the balloon nearest to the control base. It was a long cylinder tapered at the ends like a blimp, with the reflector array hanging off the middle of the underside and ground tethers trailing down out of sight from their attachment points near each end.

Craig whistled. "That has to be—what?—two hundred yards long?"

"At least," Holly said. "I can see why Dr. Pennychuck said this was impossible."

"I'm going to take us under to have a look at the reflector array. Let me know if you see anything."

Holly examined the array as it came into view. "It's huge!"

"Hey!" Barry said, checking the view out the rear door. "Look at the tube frame that's holding the array to the bottom of the balloon. There's a ladder going up inside of it. Maybe there's a way to get in there."

"There could be an access hatch up on top," Holly said. "I watched an old movie once with a blimp that had a hatch in the top."

"You never know." Craig backed the Huey away and slowly ascended until they could see the top of the balloon.

"There!" Holly said. "Do you see it?"

"Yeah, you were right. Holly, tell me if this sounds crazy, but I think we could set down on top of the balloon."

"That does sound crazy. We could slide right off."

"Not if we tie down. Look. There are anchor points along the top. If you keep it steady, I'll hook up on the winch and go down to connect the tethers."

"You're assuming those are strong enough. They could rip right off the skin."

"Maybe, but I'm sure they put them there for a reason. Look how heavy the loops are. They must be able to take a load."

"All right, but I won't be able to see you, so watch your head."

"Of course, and I'll need to take off my headset. I can signal to Barry when it's safe to land. You just need to keep it steady a foot or two off the top before then."

"That won't be easy in this wind."

"No, but I know you can do it, and I wouldn't say that about many pilots."

Holly took the controls and felt the force of the wind pushing the aircraft. "Okay. I'll try, but I don't like this." She corrected, returning the helicopter to position, but the wind shifted, and she overshot her mark. She adjusted again. It would be a constant battle. This was crazy.

Craig moved to the rear of the helicopter and fastened the end of the winch cable around his chest. He took up an armful of tether straps and had a brief conversation with Barry, then slid open the door.

Holly inched the Huey forward until they were over the access hatch, then brought it down to a hover above the balloon's surface.

She didn't dare look back to see what was happening but focused her concentration on keeping the machine as stable as possible. It was one thing to do this above a landing pad at ground level, but it was a completely different story at seven thousand feet in an unfamiliar helicopter with a variable wind blowing.

The controls pushed and pulled against her, communicating the effects of the wind. She steadied her breathing and relaxed, letting the beat of the blades and her honed reflexes guide her movements. The stick pushed; she pushed back. It pulled; she corrected. The tail swung; her feet responded. It was a precise, nuanced dance, and she *was* good at it—best in her class. Her instructors had drilled her until she could feel the helicopter as if it were her own body. She'd been offered a position flying high-altitude mountain search and rescue, a dangerous job for the most skilled pilots, but she'd turned it down. She hadn't told Craig. He didn't need to know.

"Bring it down," Barry finally said. Holly lowered the Huey until the skids touched the balloon, then adjusted the collective until the full weight of the helicopter was supported from below. She glanced over her shoulder and was relieved to see Craig at the open door.

"Keep it just like this," he said, having put his headset back on. "I don't want to risk shutting down in case we need to get off of here in a hurry. I've got the hatch open, and there's a ladder all the way to the bottom. Barry and I are going to take some tools and head down."

"When will you be back?"

"I don't know—hopefully before nine o'clock—but if this works, it shouldn't matter."

"What if it doesn't work? We're burning fuel sitting here like this. I can't wait forever."

"Then just sit tight and ride out the storm. You won't get knocked off. If we don't make it back, leave when you need to. Don't wait. You can cut the tethers from the rear doors. I tied them within reach just in case."

"All right. Be careful, Craig."

"I will."

THURSDAY, JULY 10, 8:36 P.M. MT
Flagstaff Pulliam Airport—Flagstaff, Arizona
Elevation: 7,014 feet

"Where am I?" Valentina asked herself, opening her eyes and feeling as if she was being pulled from a deep and dreamless sleep. Her head was throbbing with a pain so intense that she wanted to check whether her skull was split open. She'd had headaches before but nothing approaching this. Her throat felt dry and parched, like she'd had nothing to drink for days. She was sitting in a helicopter, and she could see through the windows that it was at an airport. Light from an open hangar spilled into the night nearby. She remembered walking to the helicopter with Katherine and Barry. Then Katherine had given her that pill, and then . . . now.

Valentina looked around the cabin and spotted the time. 8:37. How long had she been out? Was it hours or days? She shook her head, trying to clear her thoughts but worsening the splitting pain. Dr. Pennychuck and the other people had arrived. They'd talked . . . Flagstaff was okay . . . Katherine seemed excited to hear that . . . Katherine took them to the helicopter . . . Barry said something . . . The system was going off next at nine . . . It's 8:37 . . . That's before nine . . .

Valentina's eyes popped open with the realization. She tried to sit up, but she couldn't. She was buckled in tightly, and her arms were pinned behind her. "Think. Don't panic," she muttered. She had to get the handcuffs off, but how? The key. Barry had given her the key. Left pocket—he'd made her repeat it. Could she reach it? She tried moving her fingers. They were heavy and numb, at least on her left hand. She couldn't tell about the right. She squirmed in her seat, trying to get her hand lined up with the pocket. Her head was pounding, and searing pain coursed through her shoulder.

She paused to catch her breath. This was hard. The shoulder straps all but prevented her from moving her hands up, and she was forced to push against her injured shoulder with each effort. She wiggled the fingers of her left hand, trying to get some feeling, and tried again. She was about to give up when she felt the lip of fabric brush her fingertips, and she slipped her hand in. The key was in her grasp, thanks to Barry thinking ahead.

Pinching the key between her index and middle finger, Valentina pulled her hand out of the pocket until she could curl the key into her fist and get a better grasp. The movement and exertion were helping restore some dexterity, though it was still only at the level of frustratingly numb. She held the key between her thumb and index finger and twisted her wrist to find the lock. Metal scraped on metal until the end of the key slipped into a hole. She took a deep breath and turned. *Click.* The cuff on her right hand sprang open.

Valentina tipped her head back and exhaled, then wriggled her left arm out and around in front of her. She tried the same with her right, but she couldn't move it. There was a painful numbness in her upper arm, but it wouldn't respond. Assuming it to be asleep from lack of circulation, she stuck the key between her teeth and unlocked the remaining cuff, then let it fall to the floor. She quickly found the buckles to the five-point harness and freed herself.

The compartment where she sat was full of bags and boxes, probably supplies that Pennychuck and his crew had brought for their journey. The clock said 8:41. She had to hurry. She bit the cap off a water bottle sitting in a nearby cup holder and downed the contents. It didn't help with the headache, but her throat felt better.

She tried her right arm again. It was the same. Something was wrong. She pushed the collar of her shirt aside and checked the bandage. It looked all right. She'd been worried that it would start bleeding again in her efforts to get free, but at least she didn't have that problem to contend with right now. She sat up a bit, leaned to the right, and was able to bring her arm to her side. She grabbed her wrist with her left hand and pulled it onto her lap, wondering at how foreign it felt. Something would have to be done to keep it stationary until feeling returned, or it would swing and wreak havoc on her shoulder. There was a sweatshirt sitting on the next chair. She pulled one arm around her back and placed it between her teeth, then reached for the other and brought it around her front before tying a knot as tightly as she could and pinning the lifeless arm to her side. It would have to do.

The clock read 8:43. She had to find somewhere safe—and soon. Valentina pushed herself off the seat and opened the door of the helicopter. What was she facing? An instant vacuum. Hurricane-force wind. Deadly fog. Why had their bunker protected them? It was sturdy enough to withstand the pressure difference and the wind, and the climate was self-contained with a recirculating filter system. She had fifteen, maybe twenty minutes at best to figure something out. Valentina scanned the buildings and vehicles in the vicinity and started to piece together a plan.

THURSDAY, JULY 10, 8:45 P.M. MT
Morgreed Industries reflector balloon—Arizona airspace
Altitude: 7,218 feet

Barry and Craig were working at a feverish pace as they attempted to remove the reflector array from the bottom of the balloon. It had been a long climb carrying tools down the ladder until they reached the access port on the underside. As Barry had pointed out, the ladder went down the inside wall of a cylindrical tube frame attached to the balloon like a circular jungle gym where the passenger compartment would typically be positioned. An aluminum mesh floor extended across the bottom of the structure, and the reflector array was connected underneath with bolts and nuts. A thick cable ran down through the center of the structure from an attachment point on the balloon to the array beneath the floor. They'd quickly given up on removing the bolts with wrenches, as they were large and torqued too tightly, and were using the cutting torches to burn through the cable and tube frame instead.

Craig stood on the mesh floor, guiding his torch through one of the thin-walled tubes of the structure and hoping his assumptions were correct that the cylindrical frame provided stability and the thick cable was for supporting the weight of the array. He looked back over his shoulder to check on Barry, who was kneeling by the cable and making slow progress cutting through. Craig was fairly confident that once they weakened the attachments sufficiently, they would see things starting to bend or give way and have time to get back to the ladder, but "fairly confident" wasn't completely certain, and he felt his fear rising with each tube that snapped under the flame of his torch. As he started cutting another, he looked down at his feet and the metal grid. The moonlit desert floor was visible far below through the array. It was a long way down.

THURSDAY, JULY 10, 8:48 P.M. MT
Flagstaff Pulliam Airport—Flagstaff, Arizona
Elevation: 7,014 feet

Valentina pushed through an access door to the operations section of the terminal and walked down the hallway, searching for a basement. She carried a face mask and air tank over her left shoulder. She'd found them in one of the fire trucks outside, as well as a large roll of duct tape from the helicopter. She stumbled and leaned against the wall for a moment, still suffering from the pounding headache and dizziness, and wondered what was in that pill that Katherine had given her. It couldn't possibly be legal, but of course, Katherine had never been concerned with that.

There was a door ahead that appeared promising. Valentina pushed it open and saw stairs heading down. She followed them to a basement corridor that ran the length of the terminal. Somewhere there had to be a room she could work with. She adjusted the tank on her shoulder and continued down the passage, finding a mechanical room and a few locked doors until coming to a janitorial supply closet.

She opened the door and turned on the light. It was a small space with no windows or vents. It would do. She put down the tank and slid the roll of duct tape off her wrist, then tucked it under her chin and worked the end loose with her fingers. She closed the door and then taped around the seam, applying layer after layer around and around until she'd used up the roll. Then she pulled the air tank to the back wall and sat down, put on the mask, and began counting down the unknown minutes remaining.

THURSDAY, JULY 10, 8:53 P.M. MT
Morgreed Industries reflector balloon—Arizona airspace
Altitude: 7,218 feet

Barry was making progress, but the support cable was thick, and he was not even a quarter of the way through with the torch. He was keeping an eye on Craig, who kept moving across the structure and cutting tubes in a star pattern as if he were tightening lug nuts on a wheel. He'd figured taking them out evenly around the circle would be safer than moving along in one section and risking the array suddenly swinging down beneath them like it was on a hinge.

Barry focused on the cable again. The little torch was hardly adequate for the job, and it was taking forever to heat up and burn the metal. He felt a tap on his shoulder and paused.

"I've cut through most of the supports," Craig shouted over the wind. "I have a few left, and then the structure will be free, so be ready to hold on."

"Got it," Barry yelled, returning to cutting the cable as Craig moved off. Barry spread his knees on the mesh floor and held on to the cable above his head with one hand, keeping the flame in place with the other. He glanced over to see Craig finish a tube and felt a vibration start in the grating. Craig went out of sight behind his back to cut another. The vibration increased. Barry bent to check his progress. He was halfway through or a third, maybe—it was hard to tell. Craig must have cut another tube because the structure groaned and vibrated even more.

"Last one," Craig said in Barry's ear as he passed by. Barry held the torch steady and watched as Craig cut through the final tube of the cylindrical cage. As the metal gave way, there was a shudder and the platform started to bobble and turn on the cable as the wind spun the array like a large ceiling fan. Craig had to steady himself on the unstable platform, but then he came over and knelt by Barry.

"That's it," he yelled. "Once we're through this cable, the whole thing drops."

Barry looked back at the ladder running up the side of the cage. "There's no way we'll make it off of here. It's too far."

Craig checked his watch. "We're running out of time. I'll cut with you."

"No. Get out of here. Once this goes, we go down with it."

"I know that," Craig yelled, "but there's no other way."

"All right," Barry yelled, swaying as a gust jolted the array. "Let's finish this."

Craig put his torch to the cable on the opposite side and started cutting, but then his flame sputtered and went out. He checked the gas cylinder.

"I'm out," he shouted.

Barry thought for a moment. "There's another torch in the helicopter. Go!"

"Are you sure? I only saw these two."

"Yes. It's up there. Hurry."

"I'll be back."

THURSDAY, JULY 10, 8:58 P.M. MT
Vicinity of Flagstaff Pulliam Airport—Flagstaff, Arizona
Elevation: 7,008 feet

Katherine groaned as she woke in the cockpit of her jet. She touched her forehead where she could feel a nasty bruise forming and cursed her misfortune for not seeing the balloon. How could she have been so careless? She silenced the alarms and buzzers still going off on the instrument panels and then got out of her seat and walked to the rear. Looking out the windows at the moonlit landscape, she could see the tattered remains of the wing that hit the cable, and she was amazed that the plane had been controllable at all.

Katherine was about to open the door when she noticed faint sparkly lights in the sky outside. "No . . . " She backed away from the window and looked around the cabin. This couldn't be happening. She was supposed to be cruising at thirty thousand feet far above this on the way to her bunker. Maybe she could still do it. She hurried to the cockpit and tried to start the engines, but all she got were alarms and warning lights until she cut the power again. The sparkles in the sky were getting brighter.

THURSDAY, JULY 10, 9:00 P.M. MT
Main control base—the desert south of Phoenix, Arizona
Elevation 1,100 feet

"Craig . . . " Laura sighed. Nine o'clock was here, and the lights sparkled through the bunker window.

"It's starting." Ashley walked up and put an arm around her.

Laura turned to her with tears in her eyes. "It's so hard not knowing if they're okay or if they'll even come back."

"I know . . ."

Milford was watching the sky. "I hope they make it, but if not . . . if this is it . . . This is fascinating up close. I never would have thought it was possible."

Laura and Ashley held each other and closed their eyes as the sparking intensified. Laura prayed that Craig and Holly would return safely. She didn't want to watch. She couldn't. The thought of Craig out there, up there—somewhere—was too much. Where was he, and what was he doing? Was he okay? Was he watching this, too? And the twins . . .

"I'm scared," Ashley said, trembling and hugging Laura tighter. "I don't know what I would do without Holly."

"I know," Laura said. "God," she prayed, "please help them. Keep them safe. Bring them back to us. Please watch over my girls."

THURSDAY, JULY 10, 9:04 P.M. MT
Morgreed Industries reflector balloon—Arizona airspace
Altitude: 7,218 feet

Craig clambered down the ladder through the bottom of the balloon and stepped onto the revolving platform. "There was no torch!" he shouted, approaching Barry.

"I know," Barry yelled, glancing up from his work. He was over halfway through the cable.

Craig could feel the presence of the field just yards below his feet, and he caught himself staring at it. It was a truly beautiful sight to behold. The ocean of crackling energy pulsed and sparked, lighting the underside of the balloon and the array structure in sharp contrast to the twinkling stars in the night sky above. The feeling was magical, reminiscent of sitting around a campfire or lighted swimming pool on a perfect summer night.

"Get out of here!" Barry yelled as a strand of the cable snapped with a loud twang.

"No!" Craig hooked an arm and leg around the ladder and reached a hand out. "You've almost got it. When it starts to go, run and grab on to me."

Barry nodded and kept cutting. Another strand popped, and the rest started to stretch. Barry dropped the torch and rose to his feet as the platform lurched and groaned, then ran across to where Craig was waiting and took his hand. He pulled it free a second later.

"What are you doing?" Craig shouted as Barry went back.

"It wasn't enough."

The sparkling was intensifying, and Craig knew it would flash soon. "Come on!" he yelled, stepping onto the platform to go after Barry.

Barry was almost there. Craig could see it. The metal was hot and pinching inward at the weakest point. It was going . . . going . . . "Yes!" Barry stood and threw the torch to the side. He got up and darted back toward the ladder.

"Hurry!" Craig yelled, his voice lost amid the crackle and drone of the field as he resumed his grip on the rungs. Barry was moving, maybe fifteen feet away, but then there was an audible pop, and Barry and the array section fell into the fiery sea.

"Wha . . . " Craig clutched the ladder with both hands. A depression was forming in the field, like an expanding vortex with the falling array at the center, sucking it down as it fell. The structure got smaller as the static receded all around, but then in an instant it was lost from view as the field bounced back. Craig held tight and shut his eyes just as the sky flashed. The ladder shook as the balloon bobbled in the winds, and then all was calm. He opened his eyes and saw the snow falling below him, and then he began to climb.

THURSDAY, JULY 10, 9:07 P.M. MT
Vicinity of Flagstaff Pulliam Airport—Flagstaff, Arizona
Elevation: 7,008 feet

The fuselage of her jet had groaned, and Katherine's ears popped when the sky flashed, and then the winds had buffeted the plane, shaking the floor under her feet. She steadied herself and looked out the window. The snow was falling, just like she'd seen from the bunker, and soon wisps of fog were curling off the first flakes that touched the ground. Maybe this wasn't so bad. She could wait this out and then walk back to the airport to find another plane or perhaps take the helicopter. She would not make the same mistake again. Yes, she would survive this. She was not destined to die here. She was a Morgreed, and the Morgreeds deserved better.

The fog was growing heavy outside, blocking any moonlight from reaching through the windows. Katherine felt for a reading light and turned it on, then looked around and froze. Tendrils of fog were seeping through the floor in the front half of the cabin. The damage to the plane must have been worse than she'd thought. She backed away. It was coming in faster, and she couldn't see through to the cockpit. She turned and scurried to the rear, ducked into the lavatory, and pushed the door shut. She flipped on the light and looked in the mirror, scowling at the purple bump on her scalp.

Something cold and dry touched Katherine's ankles, and she looked down to see fog creeping along the floor. It was coming from the door or the floor or both—she couldn't tell. "Go away!" she screamed, stepping onto the toilet, but it payed her no heed. "Stop!" She waved her hands to try to push it back. It swirled from the disturbance, and a few strands circled her head.

Katherine breathed one of them and coughed. It was cold, but it burned all through her chest. She coughed again and took a painful breath, watching in panic as the fog continued to build. She tried to wave it away, but it kept advancing. It was getting thicker. It was everywhere. She couldn't avoid it. She breathed it in. Freezing fire poured down her throat, forcing her to cough and suck in more. She was drowning in a blazing inferno. Spasms racked her body. She tumbled off the toilet and landed on the floor, gasping until she could gasp no more.

CHAPTER 20

THURSDAY, JULY 10, 9:30 P.M. MT
Main control base—the desert south of Phoenix, Arizona
Elevation: 1,100 feet

"Amazing. Simply amazing," Milford muttered, pacing back and forth in the bunker. He'd been walking aimlessly, eating a chocolate bar and talking to himself ever since getting to see the process up close. "The possibilities . . . "

Laura had moved to the couch and was sitting in silence with Ashley, praying and waiting, when she heard the beat of the helicopter approaching.

"They're back!" she said, running to the window. Was he okay? Was it really him?

"Can you see it?" Ashley asked.

"No, it sounds like it's coming from another direction."

"It should be safe to go outside by now."

"Yes," Milford said, joining them. "I'm anxious to hear what they have to report."

Laura opened the door and ran with Ashley to the parking area, where they watched the Huey come in for a landing. She could see Craig in the cockpit concentrating on shutting down the machine, and her heart swelled. He was alive. He'd made it. She wanted nothing more than to hold him and never let go, but she waited until he got out and it was safe to approach, then sprinted to the helicopter and leaped into his open arms.

"My goodness, Laura," Craig said, spinning her around. "You haven't done that since we were in college. You nearly knocked me over."

"I was so worried," she said, hugging him, then dropping to her feet. "I was afraid you might not come back."

"I wasn't so sure about it either."

"Where's Barry?" Ashley asked.

Craig's smile faltered. "He didn't make it. Let's go inside and we'll fill you in."

They entered the bunker. "Thank goodness you're back, but what happened?" Milford asked as they walked in the door.

"A lot," Craig said, taking a seat. "Obviously we found a helicopter. We landed on the balloon, and I climbed down with Barry to cut off the array."

"You what?" Laura asked. All she could envision was Craig hanging one-handed over empty space with a hacksaw like some crazy mountain climber. What was he thinking?

"It wasn't as dangerous as it sounds, really. They must have designed them for in-air inspection or maintenance. Anyway, I'll spare you the details, but Barry died finishing the job. He got the array off and went down with it seconds before the flash."

Laura shuddered. That didn't help her mental picture.

"So it was too late," Milford said.

"I don't know," Craig said. "I was on the ladder and I watched it fall. You know how you can see the top surface of the field by where the sparkling stops?"

"Yes," Milford said.

"Well, as the array fell, it pulled the field down with it for a while. It looked like I was above the eye of a hurricane, but then it bounced back all of a sudden right before the flash."

"When the reflector fell, it should have taken down the whole thing," Milford said. "The field can't bridge a gap like that."

"I think we need to assume that it can," Laura said, forcing the images from her mind and catching up with the conversation. "Remember, the reactors are feeding far more power into it than we ever accounted for in our models."

Milford smacked his forehead. "Why didn't I consider that? The reflector distribution was based on the power levels we anticipated. More powerful reactors would have much greater range. Thus, fewer reflectors would be needed. We could probably take down a hundred balloons and it wouldn't matter!"

"You mean we risked our lives—and Barry died—for nothing?" Holly asked.

"Yes," Milford said. "Well, no. You did prove that this won't work."

"So what do we do?" Craig asked.

"I've been thinking about the possibilities while you were away, and in case I forget, Craig, I should remark that your wife has once again been responsible for pulling me out of a place of despair that has always followed me. She's been an invaluable friend and colleague. I'm not sure I could say the same of myself. But, anyway, I considered that you might procure another helicopter, and I thought of what we would do if the balloon mission failed. Based on the success of our journey here, I think we should fly to another control base and shut it down from there."

"Where are the other bases?" Ashley asked.

"Come," Milford said, hobbling over to a map on the wall. "This shows the base locations around the globe. The red dot is us here at main control. The black dots are the secondary installations. As you can clearly see, the closest ones to us are in Argentina, Hawaii, and Alaska."

"Hawaii is out," Holly said. "We can't fly that far over water without refueling."

"So is Argentina," Craig said. "It's too far, and I have aviation maps of only North America. We'd be in completely unknown territory."

"Your maps were in the other helicopter," Holly said.

"Oh, you're right."

"Barter Island," Laura read, looking at the dot on the map in Alaska. "Could they have put it any farther north?" She turned to Milford. It was good to have him back.

"They were located to service the system," Milford said, "not for convenience. If I recall correctly, Barter Island was one of the DEW Line sites during the Cold War. They already had a radar installation and support facilities, so it was easy to convert it."

"How do we know the terminal will be working there?" Ashley asked.

"We don't, but we know it's not working here, so I say we go for it."

"What do you think, Holly?" Craig asked.

"Okay, but I'm exhausted. This isn't going to be easy."

Craig thought for a moment. "Me, too. We really need some rest if we're going to try it."

"How about we sleep here tonight?" Laura suggested. "We can wait out the next run at two o'clock and maybe get in the air before the following one at seven."

Holly winced. "That's a long delay. People are dying every time the system runs."

"Oh," Laura said. It was true. She knew it, but the reality was hard to fathom.

"Yeah . . . " Craig drew out the word in a somber tone. "I don't know what to say, but we won't help anyone if we're too tired to stay in the air. I don't think we have a choice."

"Will the helicopter be okay on the ground?" Ashley asked.

"It was before we found it," Craig said, "so it should be."

"If we're all agreed," Milford said, "then let's go to sleep."

THURSDAY, JULY 10, 9:41 P.M. MT
Flagstaff Pulliam Airport—Flagstaff, Arizona
Elevation: 7,014 feet

Valentina pulled her mask aside and tested the air in her basement refuge. After sealing herself in, she'd waited only a few minutes before hearing an explosion of shattering glass in the terminal. That sound was replaced in an instant by the total silence of the atmosphere turning to vacuum, and she heard nothing aside from her hammering heartbeat until the winds from above came ripping through the building.

The door to the closet had pressed in against its frame, sucked outward by the lack of pressure on the other side, but it held firm, and so did her duct tape. Fortunately there was a flashlight in the closet, since the lights went out in the room, and she watched for any fog coming through the door until she was certain enough time had passed for it to have gone.

Valentina set her air mask on the floor and pulled off the sweat-shirt, then tried massaging her right arm to coax some feeling to re-turn, but it was to no avail. This was something more serious than it falling asleep from lack of circulation. Her thoughts went back to the control bunker. She'd grabbed Barry's arm after regaining conscious-ness, and that was with her right hand. It had hurt terribly, and she'd let go. She got up after that when Barry took her out of the room but kept her arm pressed against her side and didn't use it. She could feel it then, and keeping it in place was not an issue.

Then it hit her. When Katherine discovered she was awake, she made Barry cuff her. She'd screamed from the pain. It had felt like something was tearing through her chest. Is that what caused it? Probably, but she didn't know how. So many other things were on her mind at the time, and her left arm had been mostly numb, too, until she got the cuffs off, so she hadn't given much thought to the lack of feeling aside from wishing the pain would go away.

Now the nauseous buzz of anxiety was filling her body. What if it didn't get better? What if it was stuck like this forever? The worry was making her sick. She would have to put off these thoughts until later. She took the sweatshirt and tied it again, taking more time to make it a sort of sling to keep her arm in place across her stomach.

Valentina took a few deep breaths of musty janitorial air scented heavily with cleaning products. The odor was reminiscent of her training gym, and she focused on it, willing her body to calm down. She imagined herself in the boxing ring, blocking out every thought that was not relevant to her present circumstances. Her headache was slowly subsiding, and she knew she needed to come up with a better plan than staying in the closet.

She was in Flagstaff, Arizona. The geography of the American states had never been a subject of much concern to her, but she'd been working with maps and charts enough in the last few years to picture where she was fairly well. Flagstaff was north of Phoenix. The surrounding states were California, something, something, Colorado, and New Mexico. Colorado sounded important. Why? She'd heard something about that state recently. No, she'd read something. The letter . . . He would be in Colorado . . . Leadville . . . Camp Hale . . . She'd read it over and over before burning it. Camp Hale was high up in the mountains. The system probably hadn't reached it yet. Could he still be there? Was he still alive? Could she even get there?

It took a few minutes, but Valentina worked at the duct tape until it was all peeled off the door. She gathered up the air tank and flashlight, then ventured out into the corridor. Everything looked about the same until she ascended the stairs to ground level, where the impact of the system was evident.

The terminal was a mess, but she found a magazine and news shop and browsed the selections until finding a road atlas and some maps of the surrounding states. She spread one out on the counter and estimated the distance to Leadville from Flagstaff. It looked like five hundred to six hundred miles. Maybe it could be done with a car and basements spaced along the route to provide shelter, but where could she get a car? She looked up and saw a sign advertising the obvious answer—the car rental area of the airport.

Valentina walked to the rental office and collected some keys from a cabinet, then went out to the lot to find the vehicles. She tried several, but none of them would start, or if they did, the engine wouldn't run for more than a couple of seconds. She remembered

Katherine and Barry talking about the cars not working outside the bunker. The system field was probably shorting out all the circuit boards. None of these new cars were going to do the job. It had to be an older vehicle, probably with a carburetor and other archaic technology. The old Ladas some people still drove back in Russia would fit the bill, but finding one here would be highly unlikely.

The passenger parking lot was her next stop. There were not many cars present, but her hopes lifted when she saw an antique Chevy pickup jacked up on mud tires. She tried the door. It opened. Climbing up was a bit of a challenge, but she managed, and fortune smiled her way again when a key dropped into her palm from the sun visor. She held her breath and reached around the steering wheel with her left hand to try the ignition. The engine sputtered for several seconds and then roared to life.

This plan was showing some promise. Valentina reached over again to put the truck in drive, grateful that it had an automatic transmission, and then pulled out of the lot. She stopped by the fire trucks to load up with as many air tanks as she could find, then collected provisions, duct tape, and headache medicine from the terminal. Finally she was ready to go. She pointed the headlights toward the airport exit and drove off into the night.

THURSDAY, JULY 10, 10:18 P.M. MT
Main control base—the desert south of Phoenix, Arizona
Elevation: 1,100 feet

Craig was having a hard time falling asleep. He lay on a blanket in the bunker with Laura cuddled by his side, but memories of the day were keeping him wide awake and thinking. "Laura, are you awake?" he whispered in the darkened room.

"Yes," Laura replied softly, her head resting on Craig's shoulder.

"How are you holding up?" Craig asked. "We haven't had much time to talk since this all started." And for a while before, now that he thought of it. With Laura staying at the observatory and his work taking him all over New England, they'd spent few nights together since the beginning of the summer.

"I'm doing all right. I have you, and there's still hope that Autumn and Summer are alive. I'm trying to take it one day at a time and trust that God is watching over them—and over all of us."

Craig couldn't stop thinking about Barry. The look on his face when the platform dropped. Panic. Fear. Acceptance. Would it ever stop haunting him? "I need to tell you what happened on the balloon."

"There was more to the story?"

"Yes. I said Barry died finishing the job, but that's not the whole picture. We were working together, and it was risky. My torch ran out of gas, and he told me there was another one up in the helicopter. I climbed all the way up there and looked, but there was no other torch, and when I made it back to him, he said he knew. It didn't hit me until later, but he sent me away so I'd be off that platform when it fell. I think he realized there would be no surviving it, and he gave his life for me—for all of us."

"Wow," Laura whispered.

"If I hadn't run out of gas, we would have made that cut together. I—" He paused, unable to speak as emotion gripped his throat. He pictured Barry falling. He would have been right there next to him. Down, down, down. What would that have felt like? Would he have survived until hitting the desert sand, or would the vacuum have killed him in the air? Either way, he wouldn't have been here. He would never have felt Laura by his side again. He held her tighter as his eyes welled. "I-I was willing to finish it no matter what. I guess . . . I would have lost you . . . I don't know how I feel about it."

"Feel grateful," Laura said, taking his hand in hers. "Sending you away like that was his decision. We may not know why he did it, but he wanted you to live, and we can be thankful for that. He was very brave."

Craig's lips trembled. "I know. You're right, but it bugs me wondering if I could have done the same for him."

"You would have. I know it, and maybe he did, too."

Craig sighed. Laura always knew what to say to help him feel better. Having her with him now . . . He needed her. He couldn't do this without her. He wiped a sleeve across his eyes. "Barry mentioned on the way that he had no one left. I told him about the twins and all of you . . . "

"Then we all have him to thank for returning you to us. Don't feel guilty, Craig. He gave you a gift. Be thankful."

"I love you so much," Craig whispered, then kissed Laura's forehead and drew her closer.

THURSDAY, JULY 10, 10:30 P.M. MT
Camp Hale—Leadville, Colorado
Elevation: 9,200 feet

Autumn lay in her sleeping bag, nestled in the back of the station wagon they'd been given for the night. She had a lot on her mind.

"Summer," she said, "do you think Roman is right? Could everyone really be dead?"

"No," Summer answered, "I can't imagine it. How could God let something like that happen?"

"I've been wondering about that," Autumn said. "I don't believe He could. All those people . . . It's too Old Testament, like the Flood or Sodom and Gomorrah."

"Yeah, and He promised that wouldn't happen again."

"But God did those things," Autumn said. "He didn't promise that people wouldn't cause death and suffering, like in wars or the Holocaust. God didn't create the climate system; we did."

"That's true." Summer unzipped her bag several inches and rolled back the top.

"Do you think he's lying?" Autumn asked.

"Who? God?"

Autumn chuckled. "No. Roman."

"I don't see why he would, so I have to assume he's just wrong about what's happening out there."

"That's what I'm thinking," Autumn said, hoping Summer was right. "All we have to go on is what people said they saw from a distance. How can they know what's happened everywhere else? For all we know, everything could be fine back home. Maybe Mom and Dad are watching the news right now and praying that we're okay." It was a comforting thought. The alternative was . . . She didn't want to think about the alternative.

"I hope so," Summer said, "although it's a lot later in their time zone. They'd probably be asleep. I wish we could be there right now to see."

"Yeah . . ." Autumn gazed at the roof of the car, picturing the stars twinkling above. "The trail was fun before this all started, but I want to go home."

Summer turned on her side to face her. "Maybe we could. We're not far from Leadville. I bet we could get a bus or airplane out of there."

"How would we get out of camp? They have guards all over."

"They're only watching the roads and trails. We could wake up early and head through the forest, then move down to the highway once we're out of sight. We could make good time walking on the road."

"But Roman is expecting us to meet him for breakfast. What if they look for us?"

"I doubt anyone will care, and he seemed too busy to worry about what happens to us."

"Hmm," Autumn said. "Okay. Why not? It's not like we were planning to stay here anyway."

CHAPTER 21

Valentina was feeling a little better as she drove the old Chevy through the desert north of Flagstaff. Her headache was gone, thanks to some pain pills, caffeine, and the refreshing night air blowing in the window. Her heart was heavy with sadness and loss, but she also felt free for the first time in many years. She didn't know where Katherine had gone or what had become of her, but they were through. There was nothing more for that woman to demand of her, and she was finally released from her unyielding oppression.

Bracing a knee against the steering wheel, Valentina unhooked her necklace's clasp and threw it out the window. It was the first time she'd removed it since Katherine made her put it on. Katherine had explained how the tracking device worked and how it would send an alert if it lost contact with her skin. It felt liberating to be rid of it. She'd had almost no privacy. Her office, home, and car were all bugged. Her mail was screened, as were her phones and computers.

Katherine listened in on her conversations at will and would often send text messages ordering her to do things immediately. She grudgingly complied, and most of Katherine's demands were work

253

related, but acting the part of the adulteress had been the most difficult and demeaning role she'd been forced to play. Katherine seemed
to revel in making her toy with Barry and other men, then slap them
down just as aggressively. Valentina hated it, and she was sure that
was why Katherine pushed it so much. It was all about power, control,
and constantly reminding her that her will was not her own if she
wanted her child to live.

A chill swept through Valentina's body as she thought back to the
one time she tried to reach out for help. She'd made careful plans, but
Katherine's surveillance system proved to be more elaborate than she
thought, and she'd paid a heavy price for her efforts. The police detec-
tive she'd arranged to meet was murdered by Katherine's men right
in front of her, and the same men had then taken her to "Mr. Smith's"
basement gym and beaten her senseless. The Society kept her locked
up for several weeks as she recovered, with Katherine explaining to
Barry that she was out of the country on an unplanned assignment.

Though that lesson had been painful, what had really broken her
was the meeting Katherine planned in order to make her position
clear. Her baby was a little over a year old at that point, and the Society
made arrangements for his caretakers to bring him to Washington on
vacation. Valentina was strapped to a chair when they brought him
into the room. He was adorable, even more so than the photos had
conveyed, and they held him mere inches away from her. He looked
at her inquisitively and reached out his little hands to touch her face.
She longed to hold him, but they took him away, and Katherine explained that there would be no further warnings.

Valentina's thoughts wandered back to the present. What would
Barry and Dr. Pennychuck do back at the bunker? They were stranded

and it was a dismal prospect. Was there any way she could help them? Maybe. Trying to drive to the base had come to mind, but she didn't know the way, and the chances of finding it in the desert were next to zero. Maybe once she reached Leadville, she could figure something out. She owed it to Barry. He was the only reason she was still alive, and she couldn't leave him there.

She owed it to Dr. Pennychuck, too. His work and his life were ruined. The things she'd done were not of her own free will, but that thought did little to ease the guilt she felt. Calling in the hit on his car and then visiting him in the hospital had been some of the hardest things she was forced to do. She'd kept up the daughter act until leaving his room, but anyone that saw her walking out of the building would have seen tears that were genuine. Yes, she would not rest until she found a way to save them. There was still time.

All these thoughts aside, it had been an interesting drive. There were no other cars on the roads, except for those crashed off the sides of the highway—people who'd been traveling when the system hit. On several occasions Valentina had to slow down and navigate around larger accidents or debris, and she was glad to have a vehicle with good off-road capabilities.

She'd made one stop so far at a gas station in Cameron off Highway 89, where the realization hit that she had no way to pay. Her pocketbook was probably still on the terminal desk back at the bunker, but it hardly mattered since the pumps were showing all kinds of errors on the screens. Unsure how to get them to operate, Valentina had rummaged around the building and found a length of clear flexible hose, which she used to siphon gasoline from a nearby pickup until her tank was full. That was a tool to hang on to, she'd realized, as the powerful V8 in her truck was thirsty and would likely need to be filled again.

Valentina turned off Route 160 in Tuba City and spotted a hotel. The next system run at two o'clock was close enough that it was time to find shelter, and she was not going to take any chances attempting to reach the next town. She parked the truck and headed for the lobby, carrying an air tank and a backpack stuffed with rolls of duct tape. She found the basement stairs and descended into the darkness with her flashlight.

FRIDAY, JULY 11, 6:00 A.M. MT
Main control base—the desert south of Phoenix, Arizona
Elevation: 1,100 feet

Craig woke to the beeping of his watch and sat up. He must have fallen asleep not long after talking with Laura since he didn't remember thinking about anything following their conversation.

"Good morning." Milford was standing at the window, eating a bag of cheese puffs. "Did you sleep well?"

"I guess so," Craig said, feeling Laura stirring next to him. "Did the system run during the night?"

"It did," Milford said. "It woke me a few minutes after two o'clock, right on schedule."

"Hey." Laura sat up next to Craig and leaned against his shoulder. "How did you sleep?"

"All right. I was out, though I sure miss our bed."

"Me, too. I had a rough night. I kept dreaming about Summer and Autumn and all the . . . people we've seen."

"We'll find them, Laura. I know we will."

"Is it time?" Holly asked from across the room.

"Yes," Milford answered. "We should get going. I'm going to stop in the restroom."

Craig stood and stretched. "Could one of you give me a hand? This helicopter doesn't have much for passenger seats, but we could strap that couch in."

"Sure," Ashley said, moving to assist him.

"We'll need to find supplies on our way," Laura said, yawning. "There's very little left here, and all our extra clothing and food was in the other helicopter."

"What's the temperature in Alaska at this time of year?" Holly asked.

"I don't know," Laura said, "so we'll need to prepare. Craig, does the helicopter have heat?"

"We'll see." Craig picked up one end of the sofa and carried it toward the door.

"Craig," Ashley said, holding the other end, "if we make it to Alaska, will we get to see the northern lights?"

"Um," Craig said, "I'm not sure. Laura, do you know?"

"Probably not, Ashley," Laura said. "It's not likely to see them during the summer months. Plus, we're going through a full moon. This is about the worst time to go."

Ashley sighed. "That's too bad. It would have been neat."

"It would," Laura said. "The aurora is fascinating. The colors are breathtaking if you see them firsthand. It feels like you're getting a glimpse into heaven."

"Autumn could probably paint it," Holly said. "I've seen some of her works of the night sky."

Laura smiled. "Actually she has. I took her to see the aurora several years ago when she was getting really serious about art. She made some marvelous paintings. I have one in my office at the college. I know I'm biased, but honestly I've seen very few painters that can match her ability to capture light the way it glows in the aurora."

"I know it's not the same thing," Craig said, "but when I was standing on the balloon platform and the field was intensifying, it was one of the most awe-inspiring sights I've ever seen. I could feel the energy of it. Being so close was much different than viewing it from the helicopter. If we get a chance, maybe we can land on another balloon so the rest of you can see what it's like."

"Ha," Holly said. "No thanks. Doing that once was enough for me, and we need to focus on flying to the control base safely."

"Holly is right," Ashley said, "but it was a nice thought, Craig."

FRIDAY, JULY 11, 7:30 A.M. MT
Camp Hale–Leadville, Colorado
Elevation: 9,200 feet

Roman sat at a picnic table, eating his breakfast. The twin hikers had been gone when he checked for them earlier, and they hadn't been seen by anyone around camp. He wasn't overly surprised. He would have liked to speak with them further, but he could understand if they weren't willing to stay. Being marched at gunpoint could have that effect on people. Hopefully wherever they went, they would consider his warning about returning to the trail, but that was out of his hands.

"Sir," an officer said, approaching, "a representative from Leadville was at the barricade. He asked for a meeting with you."

"Why?"

"He said the town is starting to panic, and they've had a lot of people come up from elsewhere seeking refuge. He thought we might be able to help."

"I don't know what we can do, but I can talk to them."

"He asked if you could come to the fire station at nine?"

"Okay. I'll do that. Thanks."

FRIDAY, JULY 11, 7:34 A.M. PT (8:34 A.M. MT)
McCarran International Airport—Paradise, Nevada
Elevation: 2,181 feet

Holly set the Huey down at the airport just south of Las Vegas. Craig had flown high up over the last run of the system and then to Kingman, Arizona, for a fuel stop and had been going over the operation of the antique machine with her. She found the flight controls intuitive, but the buttons and switches for other aspects of operation required some explanation. Craig didn't remember every detail, but they were getting by. Holly liked the way it flew and the way it sounded, and Craig agreed that adding one to the fleet would bring a vintage appeal that many customers would enjoy, if they were to ever continue the business. They agreed that seemed unlikely.

"We're going to find a baggage cart to pull into the terminal," Laura said, leaning in between Craig and Holly. "We need supplies and food, and they should have most of it in there. Do you want to catch up after you fuel, or should we wait and all go together?"

"Let's go together," Craig said. "We don't want to get separated. I know we've done this a few times, but it doesn't get any easier, and things are starting to smell."

"Yeah," Holly agreed. "Let's go together." Craig was right. It didn't get easier. If not for necessity, she would never agree to step foot inside another airport.

"Is everything okay in the back?" Craig asked. "Do you need anything?"

"We're okay," Laura said. "The couch is great, although it would be nice to have seat belts. I'd hate to see Milford get knocked around if we encounter any rough spots."

"We'll see if we can come up with something."

"Are we ready to shut down?" Holly asked. If they were going to do this, there was no use in delaying the inevitable.

"Yes," Craig said.

FRIDAY, JULY 11, 8:43 A.M. MT
Lake County Fire Station—Leadville, Colorado
Elevation: 10,152 feet

Roman parked in front of the fire station in Leadville and turned to face the rear seat. "I suppose you could come in with me," he said to Summer and Autumn. He'd been a few miles into his drive when he spotted a couple of hikers on the road ahead and pulled over to investigate. The twins had been surprised to see him, and after a brief discussion, he offered them a ride to the town and accepted their apologies for running off.

"You want us to come to your meeting?" Autumn asked.

"I don't see why not," Roman said. "You know the scientists that developed this system. I doubt anyone else here can say the same."

"All right," Summer said, opening her door.

Roman stepped out and gazed at the tall mountain peaks surrounding the former mining town. "This is nice. I like the historic buildings."

"It's like living on top of the world," Autumn said.

Roman nodded. "Not a bad place to be right now. Come on. Let's go." He led them into the station, where they were introduced to the mayor and the chief of police.

"Thank you for coming," the mayor said. "We have a number of things to discuss. May I ask who you are, and who are these lovely young ladies you've brought with you?"

"Roman Muscovite," Roman said, "commander of the Colorado division of the Climate Freedom Militia. With me are Summer and Autumn Pottersmith. Their mother is Dr. Laura Pottersmith, who worked with Dr. Pennychuck on the design of the climate system."

"You've joined the militia?" the mayor asked, looking at the twins with surprise.

"No," Autumn said, "we were hiking the Colorado Trail and came across the camp yesterday."

"They may have useful insight," Roman said, "so I thought it would be a good idea to bring them along."

"Oh," the mayor said. "Well, welcome. Um, Roman, can I ask what your militia is doing at Camp Hale?"

Roman nodded. "We chose that location as an assembly point due to its isolation and elevation. The militia was expecting an invasion by the UN, and we wanted our base to be well above the initial altitude of the climate system, which we believed was meant for other purposes. We were expecting to either defend our position or use it as a staging point to go on the offensive in coordination with the other state divisions."

"Have you been in contact with the other divisions?" the chief of police asked.

"No. We lost all communication when the system started."

"As did we," the mayor said. "We've had a lot of people arrive in town, and they're all describing the system as a 'field of death.' Many of them have seen it hit nearby towns, but so far no one has made it here that was actually in the field."

"Our scouts have described the same thing," Roman said. "It seems anyone caught under the field does not survive, and the system altitude is rising each time. It won't be long until Camp Hale is hit, and it will reach Leadville soon after."

"Which brings us to the question of what to do," the chief said. "The people here have remained mostly calm so far, but we fear panic and mayhem are not far off if we don't find a solution."

"So we were wondering," the mayor said, "if the militia would be able to assist in keeping order."

Roman was wary of the prospect. "We're not law enforcement."

"I know," the mayor said, "and many of my colleagues are not comfortable with the idea, but for the good of the town, we need to do something."

"If the system isn't stopped, it won't matter."

"True," the chief said. "It may be inevitable, but we don't want to see the town destroyed if there's any chance this can be stopped."

The mayor nodded. "And that's another thing we wanted to ask you. "Do you have any idea how to stop it?"

Roman shook his head. "If the UN is behind this, for whatever reason . . . they're choosing to keep it running despite what's happening. Personally, I have real doubts that there was ever any intent for it to do what we're witnessing, and I'm not sure anyone is even alive at the controls."

"So you're saying it's hopeless," the chief said.

"I don't know."

"Excuse me," Summer said. "Mom told us about how the reflector balloons had to be positioned to keep the field intact, and if you took any of them away, the whole thing wouldn't work. I don't remember the explanation, but it was something about boundaries and infinite power. You guys have all kinds of guns. Maybe you could try shooting down a balloon."

"No," the mayor said. "The UN instituted the death penalty for anyone attempting to harm the system. I couldn't approve of that."

"But with no communication," the chief said, "and with what we are seeing, I don't think that's a concern. There may not be a UN anymore."

"Good point," the mayor said.

"Summer," Roman said, "you're saying one balloon can take down the whole thing?"

"I think so, yeah. Mom said that was classified. They didn't want people to know."

"She did say that," Autumn agreed.

"There are plenty of balloons surrounding the mountains," the chief said. "Can your militia take one down?"

Roman stood. "We can try. I'll go back to camp. The next run is at noon. We'll move out immediately afterwards and take a shot at it."

The mayor stood and shook his hand. "Thank you, and good luck. Please come back once you've finished to let us know how it went."

"I will."

"And thank you, Miss Pottersmith," the mayor said, turning to Summer, "for sharing that detail. You've given me some real hope."

"Sure," Summer said, shaking his hand, "but don't tell anyone you heard it from us. I don't want Mom to get in any trouble."

The mayor nodded. "Understood."

CHAPTER 22

FRIDAY, JULY 11, 10:20 A.M. MT
US Highway 160–South Fork, Colorado
Elevation: 8,209 feet

Valentina was tired. She'd had a long drive along Highway 160, passing through a number of small towns and staying in the basement of a casino for the last event. That was a few hours ago, and she knew she'd need to find a place to rest soon. Leadville was still too far away to make it without getting some sleep. She was yawning and struggling to keep her eyes open as she approached the town of South Fork, so she hoped there would be a suitable basement that would work as a shelter.

She was jolted wide awake and almost jammed her foot on the brakes when she saw another car on the road, moving in the other direction. It passed by and she drove on. Had she seen that, or was it a hallucination? Her question was soon answered as she drove into town and spotted a few people loitering outside a diner. The system must not have reached them yet. Did they know? She had to warn them.

A road sign caught her attention as she was looking for a promising refuge. It was for a hospital. The pain in her shoulder seemed to flare up at the thought. Would anyone be there? Could they help her? Did she have time? She checked her watch. She had about an hour and a half to find shelter, assuming the field would hit here next, though she wasn't sure of that based on the balloons she'd seen from the road. It was worth checking, and they would probably have a basement she could use.

Valentina followed the signs and parked in front of the clinic. *Hospital* would be an overstatement for the small facility. She locked the truck and headed for the door, then paused. What would she tell them? They would certainly ask how she got shot and why she drove here from Arizona to seek treatment. She would think of something. She pushed through the door and entered a small waiting room, which was empty. There was no one at the reception desk either. "Hello?" she called out.

"Just a second," someone answered from another room.

Valentina waited, looking about, until a middle-aged woman in a white coat came to the desk.

"Can I help—" The woman looked up from some paperwork and saw Valentina. Her expression was a mix of alarm and concern. "Aren't you that scientist from the press conference? What happened to you?"

So much for coming up with a story. "Yes," she said, "I've been shot. Can you help me?"

"Oh my. Yes, of course. It's a good thing you caught me now. I was preparing to leave. Nearly everyone in town has cleared out because of the climate system. Quick. Come with me and let's take a look."

"Thank you." Valentina stepped through the door that the doctor held open and then followed her into an exam room.

"I'm Doctor Russet, by the way, but please call me Leah. Here. Take a seat and tell me what happened."

"It's a long story," Valentina said, sitting up on the table and tugging at the knot she'd tied in the sweatshirt.

"Relax. I'll get that," Leah said.

"Be careful. I can't feel my arm or hold it up."

"Understood." Leah undid the knot and supported Valentina's arm as she pulled the sweatshirt away. "Is it here in your shoulder under the bandage?"

"Yes."

"Okay. Let's take this shirt off. It's soaked with blood. I'll get you something clean once we're finished."

"We need to be quick," Valentina said as Leah unbuttoned her shirt and removed it. "The system will be running soon, and I think this town will be hit."

"I know. I've heard some stories from folks passing through on the highway. My husband and I are heading up to the mountains as soon as I'm done here. We have a little cabin. Hopefully this will all be sorted out soon. Now I'm going to slowly let your arm down to your side. Tell me if anything hurts."

"No, that feels okay."

"Good. Next I'll need to take the bandage off. How long has it been in place?"

Valentina thought for a moment. "It was about forty-eight hours ago, and Barry changed it a few times."

"You've waited that long without getting to a hospital?"

"Yes, I had no choice."

"Oh dear. I want to hear your story, but let's keep focused. Here we go . . . Okay. It's off."

"Ouch."

"Sorry," Leah said, then began cleaning the area with disinfectant. "It looks good overall. I don't see any immediate signs of infection. Would you mind if I take a couple X-rays?"

"No, go ahead."

Leah helped her off the table and into an adjoining room. A minute later, they returned, and she brought up the images on a computer. "It's still in there, right under your collarbone," she said, studying the screen. "There are a lot of nerves in that area, and the bullet is right in the midst of them. Fortunately it's not too deep and I can remove it."

"Yes, please. Will my arm work once you get it out?"

"I can't say," Leah said, uncapping a small needle. "This will sting a bit, but it will ease the pain."

Valentina grimaced as the needle pricked her skin.

"Okay. Lie down and we'll give that a few seconds. Nerve injuries are not my area of expertise, but I can tell you that sometimes people recover fully, and sometimes they don't at all, with results everywhere in between. Bullet wounds can inflict a lot of trauma, so you'll need to see a specialist for a more accurate diagnosis. Are you ready?"

Valentina nodded, then looked away and closed her eyes as Leah positioned a bright light over her shoulder and leaned in. She expected serious pain, but the sensation was more like a dull tugging.

"Got it." Leah dropped something onto a metal tray with a clink. "Small caliber, hollow point. You're lucky it didn't penetrate deeper or hit a bone or major artery."

"Barry said it took him a long time to stop the bleeding. I was unconscious."

"Do you mean the EPA director?"

"Yes."

"Well, you should be grateful to him. As I said, I don't think it hit a major artery, but without proper attention, you likely wouldn't have survived this."

"I have no doubt about that," Valentina said, feeling more tugging as Leah stitched the wound closed.

"All right. That's done," Leah said as she applied gauze and a dressing. "The stitches can come out in a week."

"Thank you." Valentina sat up and attempted to raise her arm.

Leah took her hand and guided it into the sleeve of a clean shirt. She buttoned it and then secured the arm in a cloth sling. "Give it time," she said, wiping a tear from Valentina's cheek. "Your body needs to heal. It's not going to be better right away. Take it easy, and try not to move your shoulder very much. These," she said, procuring a bottle of pills from a cabinet, "will help with the pain, but take them only if you really need to. Otherwise, stick with Tylenol or ibuprofen, whichever you find works best."

"I had a fever for a while. Should I be concerned about that?"

"If it passed, you're probably fine. Everything looked really good to me. Your friend Barry must have taken good care of you."

"He did . . . We need to get to a basement room with a sturdy door and with no windows or vents. I've been driving almost nonstop from Flagstaff and waiting through the storms that way. If the system doesn't hit here at noon, then it probably will by the next run."

"Is it true that people are being killed?"

"Yes, I've seen it firsthand. We need to warn the rest of the town."

"Oh, there's no need. Everyone else already left."

"But I saw a few people when I drove through."

Leah shook her head. "They've been warned, but they wouldn't leave if God Himself came down and told them to go. They think the whole climate thing is a scam. You'll never convince them."

"All right, but is there a basement here?"

"Yes, I think it fits your description. Jansen, my husband, will arrive any minute. We can sit it out together."

"Good. I need to get some things from my truck. Would you be able to help me?"

Leah smiled. "Yes. What do you need?"

FRIDAY, JULY 11, 11:00 A.M. PT (12:00 P.M. MT)
Reno-Tahoe International Airport—Reno, Nevada
Altitude: 13,000 feet

Holly held the Huey stationary high over the Reno airport in anticipation of the event that would soon run below. Following their supply mission in Las Vegas, they'd installed some rudimentary seat belts in the rear, and then Craig flew to Tonopah, Nevada, for a fuel stop.

"Holly," Craig said, "take us up a little higher."

"Okay. Why?"

"I was thinking. When the balloons rise to a higher altitude, the vacuum they create covers more airspace. The atmosphere remaining above will consist of thinner and thinner air each time. I'm not sure what that would mean for the winds, but we should probably stay progressively higher above it."

Holly nodded. "That makes sense. What's our service ceiling?"

"I'm not sure exactly. Probably seventeen thousand feet. Maybe a little more."

"I hope we get to Alaska before we can't fly above these things."

"No kidding."

FRIDAY, JULY 11, 12:02 P.M. MT
Russet Medical Clinic—South Fork, Colorado
Elevation: 8,209 feet

Valentina, Leah, and Jansen sat in a basement room of the clinic, waiting for the noon event to pass. They'd brought in air tanks and masks, and Jansen taped them in as Valentina instructed. She'd been concerned upon realizing the basement was exposed to ground level on one end with a sliding glass door. They were in a separate utility room at the far end, but it had only a hollow wooden interior door, nothing like the commercial steel units Valentina encountered at her previous stops. There was no time to find alternate arrangements, so she hoped it would suffice.

"Do you hear anything?" Valentina asked. "It makes a crackling staticky sound that gets louder."

"I'm not sure," Leah said.

"Maybe," Jansen said.

"Keep listening. If it's going to hit here, we'll know very soon."

"Hmm," Jansen said, "I'm definitely hearing something."

"Get ready." Valentina put her mask on and started the flow of air.

Leah and Jansen did the same, and soon they all heard the unmistakable drone of the field building outside.

"Any minute now," Valentina said, looking at her watch.

Seconds later, a boom echoed through the basement. The door to their room cracked down the center and buckled outward from its frame. The winds blew in and sent a section of the door flying inches from Valentina's head. It smashed into the rear wall of the room, then fell to the floor once the gust subsided and all was quiet.

Valentina put her left hand to her chest, breathing heavily until she realized that her lungs were working properly. The short time it took for the door to give way must have prevented their little room from losing pressure completely before it returned with the wind, but the partial depressurization had been enough to make her chest ache.

"Well, wasn't that something!" Leah said, removing her mask.

"No!" Valentina shouted. "Put that back on!"

"Is that snow?" Jansen asked, pointing to the white flakes that were falling outside and drifting into the basement through the missing slider.

"No," Valentina said, noticing that it had stopped already, which was odd. It had come down for only a few seconds, but when she'd seen it from the bunker, it lasted much longer. She watched it turn to fog and wondered whether it caused any skin reactions as it rolled into the room. It was cold and dry, and the hairs on her arm prickled as it enveloped her. Soon she could barely see her hand just a few inches from the glass of her face mask.

"What is it?" Leah asked.

"Nitrogen and oxygen," Valentina replied, waving the mist around with her hand as the scientist in her perked up with curiosity. "They were solidified by the reaction. I can't begin to imagine the compounds that were produced, but they're highly unstable. The gas is lethal if you breathe it, so don't take off your masks until it's all gone."

"How long will that take?" Jansen asked.

"A few minutes. I've watched it before, but this is the first time I've felt it."

"I'm sorry," Leah said. "I suppose our basement wasn't up to the task."

"We survived," Valentina replied. The fog was already thinning.

"Where are you headed?" Leah asked.

"Leadville. I'm hoping to find someone there."

"Oh, what a coincidence. That's where we're going."

Valentina rose to her feet, and they cautiously walked outside as the last wisps of fog were trailing off into the sky. She looked up and saw a couple of balloons in the distance. They had already initiated their ascent to the next altitude, and she understood why the snowfall had been so brief. They'd been right near the upper edge of the field.

"My car!" Jansen shouted from behind her.

Valentina turned to see a BMW sedan crumpled under a fallen tree.

"I just bought that!"

"It likely wouldn't work now anyway," Valentina said, removing her mask. "The electrical field destroys the computers in newer vehicles. We can take my truck."

"Are you sure?" Leah asked. "We wouldn't want to impose."

Valentina dug in her pocket and held out the key. "Actually I was hoping one of you wouldn't mind driving. I was falling asleep at the wheel when I arrived here. I need to rest."

CHAPTER 23

Roman turned his Subaru off Highway 70 in Wolcott and pulled into a large open field where one of the reflector balloons was stationed. Several militia trucks followed behind, towing a flak cannon, surface-to-air missile launcher, and heavy-caliber mounted machine guns. Most of the equipment was decades old, and most of it had been obtained through questionable means, but none of that mattered in their current situation.

"That's huge," Autumn said, stepping out of the car after they parked.

"Yeah, wow," Summer agreed. "Thanks for letting us come. This should be interesting."

"Of course," Roman said. "It was your idea. Here. I have a box of earplugs. You're going to need them."

"Thanks." Autumn took a pair and stuffed them in her ears as she watched the trucks position the artillery in the field.

Roman gazed up at the balloon as he walked over to the men. It was floating roughly 1,500 feet above them and cast a large shadow on the ground.

"Sir," one of the men said, "we're thinking targeting the reflector array is our best option. There's no need to bring down the entire balloon."

274

"You're probably right," Roman agreed. "Try not to use more ammunition than is necessary. I'll radio the other squads to hold position until we see how this goes. Wait for my signal."

"Yes, sir," the soldier said. Roman jogged back to his car and radioed instructions to the groups that had traveled to other balloons in proximity to the camp.

"Are we ready?" Autumn asked.

"Yes," Roman said. "Take shelter behind the car just in case, though we should be out of range of the debris field."

When the signal was given, the militiamen opened fire on the array with a salvo of missiles and several rounds from the flak cannon. The ground shook as explosions burst from the underside of the balloon and bits of twisted metal rained on the ground. Once the smoke cleared, they could see the mangled reflector structure hanging lopsided from its mount, so they sent up another volley aimed at the connection. The array fell and smashed into the earth, setting off the alarm in Roman's car.

"Wow!" Summer exclaimed, taking her hands off her ears.

Roman silenced the alarm. "Good. I'll instruct the other groups to do the same thing. Hopefully that will be enough. Let's get back to camp."

FRIDAY, JULY 11, 3:05 P.M. MT
St. Vincent Hospital—Leadville, Colorado
Elevation: 10,152 feet

"What now?" Jansen Russet asked, parking Valentina's Chevy in front of the hospital in Leadville.

"See if they can send someone out with a stretcher," Leah said, "and hopefully they'll have a room available where she can rest."

"Okay. I'll be right back," Jansen said, then got out of the truck.

Leah sat in the middle of the bench seat with her arm around Valentina, who was leaning against her shoulder, sound asleep. Valentina had shared some of her story as they began the drive from South Fork but quickly dozed off. Leah tried to wake her gently when they arrived but gave up, figuring they should let her rest and recover. The poor woman had been through so much—Leah couldn't imagine it, and she'd been astounded to hear of the treachery behind the scenes of the climate project. What a day it had been.

Jansen returned to the truck with an orderly. They opened the passenger door and lowered Valentina onto a stretcher. She moaned and shifted but remained asleep. Leah jumped down and followed them inside, where she explained the situation to one of the doctors on duty.

"So," the doctor said, "she's been shot, she has no identification, and you want us to look after her until you return?"

"I know I'm asking a lot," Leah said, "but my credentials are on file in your system, and I'll take responsibility for her. She needs a safe place to rest for a little while, and she is technically my patient."

"What should we tell her if she wakes up before you're back?"

"Tell her we borrowed her truck to go to our cabin, but we'll return soon, and we'll bring our Jeep so we can go our separate ways. Please ask her not to leave. We'll be only a couple hours."

"All right," the doctor said. "We have some rooms open. She can stay."

"Thank you," Leah said, turning to follow Jansen and the orderly down the hall, where she made sure Valentina was safely deposited into a bed. "Sleep well," she whispered, pulling a blanket over her. "We'll be back soon."

"Ready?" Jansen asked.

"Yes, let's go."

FRIDAY, JULY 11, 5:10 P.M. MT
Camp Hale–Leadville, Colorado
Elevation: 9,200 feet

"I don't understand," Summer said, leaning against Roman's Subaru, in which they'd taken shelter from the winds. "Mom said it would take only one balloon."

"And we destroyed four," Roman said, "so that should have been plenty."

"But the system also wasn't supposed to kill anyone," Autumn said, "so maybe she was wrong."

"I guess," Summer agreed.

"So what do we do now?" one of the officers asked. "Should we try for more?"

Roman thought. "Yes, we'll send out additional groups and shoot down as many as we can, but make sure everyone leaves enough time to make it back here before ten o'clock tonight in case it doesn't work. We don't want anyone to get caught at lower elevations. Also, send someone to Leadville to inform the mayor of our plans."

"Yes, sir," the officer said.

"Can we come with you again?" Autumn asked.

Roman nodded. "Grab some food from the mess area, and meet me back here in five minutes. We're going to have a long evening."

FRIDAY, JULY 11, 6:30 P.M. PT (7:30 P.M. MT)
Huey helicopter—British Columbia airspace
Altitude: 3,000 feet

Laura sat on the couch in the rear of the Huey, watching the lengthening shadows of the setting sun pass by on the ground below. They'd left Vancouver, British Columbia, after stopping previously in Ashland and Portland, Oregon, and Seattle, Washington, and they'd all been absorbed in their own thoughts for a while.

"Milford," Laura said, breaking the silence, "you said the Barter Island base was an old DEW Line site. What did you mean?"

Milford took a moment to finish chewing a mouthful of smoked-salmon-flavored potato chips he'd found in Seattle. "You've never heard of it?"

"No."

"Me neither," Ashley chimed in.

"Well, I suppose you're both much too young to remember the Cold War."

Laura laughed. "Yes, I was just a kid when that ended."

Milford sighed. "I would say you've never lived under the fear of the world being destroyed by nuclear war, but given the present circumstances, that's kind of a moot point."

"You could say that," Ashley said.

Milford nodded. "Well, back in the fifties, everyone was concerned about the Soviets sending aircraft over the arctic with nuclear bombs. The United States and Canada constructed a line of radar bases across the far north called the Distant Early Warning Line. It was still in operation when I learned about it in school. We watched government film reels that showed all about the hardships of construction during the arctic summers. It was quite the project, and I guess in some ways it was a similar type of undertaking to our climate system."

"What happened to it?" Laura asked.

"Oh, it was modified and updated over several decades until they finally closed everything down. Some of the sites were eventually converted to other purposes, like the one we're going to, and I suppose others were decommissioned or abandoned."

"It's kind of sobering," Laura said, "to think that they built that whole thing and the bomber attack never came. I can understand why people would think the climate system was a waste of money if they didn't believe in the problem."

"Yes, but it's one of those situations where we'll never know what would have happened if it was done differently. Perhaps the Soviets never attacked because the line was constructed, and maybe they would have if it was not. If we hadn't built the climate system, we have a pretty good idea what we'd be facing."

"But," Laura said, "if we hadn't built it, this wouldn't have happened." She didn't want to prompt that conversation again with Milford, but it was true. None of the climate models had predicted planetary impacts even close to the scale of this tragedy. The cost in lives. If they had somehow known . . .

"But what about Morgreed, though?" Ashley asked. "She and her cohorts might have done something else if the system was never built."

"You're right," Milford said. "We'll never know, because we can't go back and try another route. For all we know, something worse would have taken place."

"That's hard to imagine," Laura said.

"What were the other options?" Ashley asked. "I mean, what were the other proposals the UN was considering before they chose yours?"

"There were quite a few," Milford said, "and a lot of them had merit, which is why it took so long to make a final decision. There were a bunch of plans to reduce carbon emissions, but they were turned down. That had been tried for years with only limited success since too many countries were failing to make meaningful change."

"And many were still increasing emissions," Laura added.

"Correct," Milford said. "There were also various proposals to increase the reflectivity of the planet to prevent it from warming up so much from the sun. They had ideas for seeding the atmosphere with reflective particles and doing extensive terrain modification. The problem with those methods is they might mask the symptoms, but they don't fix the cause. They don't do anything to reduce greenhouse gases."

"Were there any ideas similar to yours?" Ashley asked.

"Certainly. My plan fits into the category of sequestration. That is, removing carbon from the atmosphere and preventing it from returning. I had a lot of competition, and honestly there were some very good proposals. I was worried that the high potential cost of my plan and the reliance on unproven nuclear technology would sink it. It was surprising how so many of the committee members simply brushed aside those concerns."

"Maybe they were paid off by Morgreed?" Ashley said.

Milford took on a grave expression. "If that was the case, then Katherine's influence must have been extensive."

"It would make sense," Laura said. "Your plan was the only one to make use of her reactor technology. If she could steer the selection committee in your favor, that would benefit her company and her interests."

Milford sighed. "It would also mean that my plan wasn't necessarily the best choice."

FRIDAY, JULY 11, 8:12 P.M. MT
St. Vincent Hospital—Leadville, Colorado
Elevation: 10,152 feet

Valentina watched as Katherine snatched her baby and backed away. She couldn't move, and she could barely speak.

"You will never see him again," Katherine said, pulling a gun from her pocketbook and firing it at Valentina's chest.

"No!" Valentina tried to scream, but she couldn't make a sound. She couldn't see Katherine or her baby. A dense fog was filling the room. It was cold. She couldn't breathe.

"Valentina?"

"No!"

"Valentina?"

"Give him back!" Valentina shouted, reaching for her child and attempting to sit up.

"It's okay," someone said as a gentle hand pressed her down.

Valentina opened her eyes. Leah, the doctor, was leaning over her.

"It's okay," Leah repeated. "It was just a nightmare."

"No," Valentina said, shivering, "he's gone. I'll never see him again . . . Where am I?"

"We're in Leadville." Leah held a damp washcloth to her forehead. "We brought you to the hospital to get some rest."

"We made it?"

"Yes. You've been asleep for several hours. I hope you don't mind. Jansen and I borrowed your truck to drive to our cabin and pick up our Jeep."

Valentina collapsed back into the pillow as the tension in her body eased. They'd arrived. She was close. "That's fine. What time is it?"

"Just after eight."

"Thanks. I'm sorry. I was confused. Thanks for everything you've done."

"You're welcome, and we wanted to thank you as well. If you hadn't stopped at my clinic when you did, Jansen and I wouldn't have made it here. We're very grateful. Now, I found you a clean change of clothes. I hope they're about the right size, and you can take a shower here if you'd like."

Valentina gave a weak smile. If she would like? "I would love to. I feel awful."

"Okay. I'll let Jansen know you're up. You're welcome to stay the night at our cabin."

"That's kind of you," Valentina said, slowly sitting up on the bed, "but I need to get on the road and find the camp as soon as possible." She tried her arm—still nothing. At least it had been taken care of.

"Be patient," Leah said.

"I know." She gazed at the sling. *This* was not a welcome change, but she would manage. Her days in the ring were over. It would be okay. She just needed to find him.

Leah gave her a brief hug. "Good luck. We'll be praying for you."

CHAPTER 24

FRIDAY, JULY 11, 9:42 P.M. MT
Camp Hale—Leadville, Colorado
Elevation: 9,200 feet

"What an evening," Roman said, navigating his Subaru through the militia camp. "That's eight more balloons. Hopefully this time we've done it."

"We'll know soon," Summer said.

"Yeah," Autumn agreed. "It will be so nice to sleep all night without those winds."

"We'll see." Roman shut off the engine. "Have a good night."

"Bye." The twins got out.

Roman stepped out of the car and opened the back door to fold the seats down, then spread out his sleeping bag.

"Commander Muscovite," his radio squawked.

"Yes."

"We have a visitor from Leadville at the command truck who wants to see you."

"Now?" He'd already sent someone to give them an update. This had better be important.

"Yes, sir. She's been waiting for you to return."

"All right," Roman said, shutting the car doors. "I'm on my way." He walked toward the box truck. Who would come so late at night, and for what purpose? It wouldn't be the mayor or the police chief. Command said "she." He hadn't spoken to any women in the city, so it was likely someone he hadn't met yet. Maybe she'd come with some important news. Hopefully it would be something quick. He was tired and wanted to go to sleep.

"Sir," an officer addressed him as he reached the truck.

"Who is it?" Roman asked.

"I don't know. She's waiting inside."

Roman walked to the rear and climbed up the bumper, then stood frozen at the back of the truck.

"Roman." She got up from a chair.

"Valentina?" He blinked. Were his eyes deceiving him? Was he that tired?

She took a step forward. "Is there somewhere we can talk?"

He blinked again. She was still there, and that was her voice. "Um," he said, checking his watch, "of course. We can go to my car."

"Sir," an officer asked, "is everything okay?"

Roman looked at Valentina and then back at the officer. "I don't know." What was she doing here? Where was the person from Leadville? Was it really her? It had been so long . . . He jumped to the ground and turned back.

Valentina took his hand and stepped off the bumper, then followed him into the night. Roman had waited for this moment for so long and imagined countless versions of how their conversation would play out, but he was also worried. What would she tell him? Would he under-stand? "I have so many questions," he said, opening the passenger door.

Valentina waited until Roman joined her in the car before speaking. "I . . . " Her throat closed up as the emotions of too many years came flooding to the surface.

Roman looked at her as the interior lights faded. "Are you okay?"

"No," she whispered as the horizon exploded in a brilliant flash of white.

Roman gripped her hand and waited as the gusts rocked the car. "What's going on? What brings you here now? Can you tell me what happened? Why did you leave me? Why all the secrecy?"

Valentina wiped her eyes and forced out the words in a whisper. "Our baby didn't die."

"What? But you said—"

"I know," she cut him off, her voice trembling. "Everything in that letter was a lie. I had a gun to my head when I wrote that."

"What?" Roman asked. Lie? A gun to her head? "Why would—"

"Please, just listen. I . . . This is so hard to talk about."

He leaned back but kept a gentle hold on her hand. He was rushing her. He needed to slow down. She'd come to him. He wanted answers, but he needed to be patient. "Okay. Take your time."

"Do you remember Katherine Morgreed?"

"Yes, your academic sponsor." He would never forget that demanding tyrant.

Valentina shivered. "I thought we could move to America, like you planned, but I never imagined what she wanted from me. You were away when the baby came. She took him. She stole him right out of my arms. There was nothing I could do. She was watching everything I did. She knew everything. She—she forced me to do things, horrible things. If I didn't, she would kill our son, and she would kill you. I'm sorry. I couldn't tell you. The baby didn't die in the hospital. I didn't leave you out of grief, Roman. I had to do it if I ever wanted us to be together again. I wanted to tell you. I wanted to write to you, but I couldn't. She would know. I tried to get help once, and there were . . . consequences."

Roman stared. His muscles tightened and he clenched his jaw. Katherine Morgreed would pay for this. But what was Valentina saying? Their plans had fallen apart. She'd written the letter. He'd never understood, but . . . "You mean, all this time, you still . . . "

"Yes, Roman. I love you. I never meant to hurt you, but there was nothing I could do."

"But the divorce papers?" They'd had her handwriting, her signature. The lawyer said she wouldn't even agree to meet him to discuss it. He'd been stunned, shocked, crushed. She'd ripped herself out of his life and out of his heart with no warning.

"She forced me to sign those."

"I had no idea," Roman said, pulling her close as she cried. These were answers, but it was too much all at once. "I never understood. I've been so worried. But how—"

She gasped. "Ouch!"

He let go. "What?" Had he hurt her?

"My shoulder. Katherine shot me."

"Oh," he said, looking down at the sling on her right arm. Katherine wouldn't just pay for this. She would die. How could she do those things? If only he'd known. He would have stopped it. "I'm sorry. I didn't realize . . . "

"No, it's okay, but it hurts. I have so much I need to tell you, but I'm exhausted. I can hardly think straight."

"Why are you here now? Is our son with you?" He hadn't seen anyone with her, but perhaps—

"No," Valentina said, choking up on the word. "He's dead, just like everyone else that was caught in the system."

"Oh . . ."

"I'm sorry. I'm so sorry."

Roman took her hand again. He closed his eyes, pausing to think. She'd said so much. It would take time to process it all, but the important thing was that she was here, now. Katherine would have to wait. "No, don't be sorry. You had no choice. It's not your fault. I've been hoping for so long that you would come back to me, and here you are. This is a wonderful surprise."

Valentina's hand softened in his. "So you didn't . . . find anyone?"

"Valentina, no," Roman said, brushing away her tears and looking into her eyes. "I haven't even come to terms with you leaving me. I couldn't . . . Look. I've kept this picture of you in my wallet. Do you remember?" He dug the wallet from his pocket and pulled out the photo.

Valentina sniffled and focused on the image of her younger self laughing at the river. "That was the day we went for a walk along the Dvina. I was pregnant. I had no idea then . . . "

"I've looked at this every day, and I've wept over it too often. I've missed you terribly. You were my life. I've been lost and so worried about you. I can't believe you're here. How did you get here?"

She handed the photo back. "Katherine left me for dead in Flagstaff. I drove here. I sealed myself in basements when the system was running, and I had some help. I remembered your letter and I had to find you."

"You survived the events?"

"Yes. I tried to replicate our bunker at the control base. With a good enough basement room, it's possible."

"And you've been working on the climate system, right? What happened?" He'd seen her on the television just the other day. She'd looked unhappy. Clearly there had been good reason.

"It's a long story, and I have a lot to explain, but the important thing is that we have to stop it."

"We've tried. We destroyed the reflectors on twelve balloons around camp, but obviously that wasn't effective. Summer and Autumn said it would take only one."

"Summer and Autumn?"

"Dr. Pottersmith's girls. She's an associate of Dr. Pennychuck. They hiked into camp yesterday."

Valentina paused. "When Dr. Pennychuck arrived at the bunker, there were people with him. There was one I've met on occasion while visiting the institute at Dartmouth. Pottersmith . . . Laura?"

"Yes."

"Are they still here?"

"Yes."

"I have to see them. They would have been right about taking down a balloon, but Katherine had her own agenda for the whole system. She's responsible for this mess. It's putting out far more power than any of us anticipated. I've been thinking about it as I drove here, and I believe the reactors are powerful enough to maintain the field with a fraction of the balloons we have. Based on what you're saying, that must be the case."

He knew it. This wasn't the plan. "So what can we do?"

"We don't have much time. The field will hit camp soon. If it doesn't reach here on the next run, it will be the one after. You need to move everyone to Leadville and prepare basements for shelter. They need to be sealed up tight, or the fog will kill everyone if the vacuum doesn't. Then we need to go take out a reactor. It's the only way to trigger the system to stop."

"Valentina, that's a suicide mission. Haven't you seen the news footage?" Certainly he wanted to stop it, but throwing themselves against a hail of bullets was not a good plan. An hour ago, perhaps, but now that she'd come back into his life? No.

"Yes, I've seen it, but that was before. There are no guards now. Does your militia have weaponry to destroy the autocannons from a safe distance?"

"I suppose."

"Then we can do it."

"You're sure that's the only way?" It was still too risky. What did they know about nuclear reactors? They couldn't just walk in and blow it up. One wrong move . . .

"Positive. The control system is stuck on override with a patch I uploaded, and the terminal was destroyed. Dr. Pennychuck and Dr. Pottersmith are at main control, but there's nothing they can do. I'm hoping we can get to them once we stop this, but it's up to us. We need to move everyone now."

"All right," Roman said, picking up his radio. "Command, come in."

"Yes?"

"This is Commander Muscovite. Call in the officers for an emergency meeting right away. I have important news."

"Thank you," Valentina said when he put down the radio.

"You know," Roman said, opening the car door, "I prayed for a miracle the other day. I never expected I might get two."

"What do you mean?"

"You've been returned to me, and you've brought the answers we need." He'd offered that prayer in case some heavenly being was listening. Maybe there was something to it after all.

She got out and took his arm to walk back to the command truck. "If what I know about your militia is correct, I don't think they'll trust anything I say. I'm pretty much the face of the UN as far as they're concerned. They'll certainly recognize me."

"No," Roman said, stopping to face her. "They're coming around to thinking something else is going on, and you have the explanation that makes sense of all that's happened. And I don't care what those divorce papers say. If you'll still have me, you're . . . I mean . . . " How could he put this? "Will you still be my wife?"

Valentina's gaze met his, and something changed, deep inside. "Yes," she said, her reply barely audible. "Yes." She spoke a little louder, her voice quivering amid fresh tears. He reached out as his own came, and as he took her into his arms and kissed her, the iron prison he'd constructed around his heart to survive without her began to crack. His tears as he held her were for all she'd lost—for all they'd lost—but tears of joy were also mixed in, and he hadn't felt those in a long time.

CHAPTER 25

"Are we ready?" Craig asked, climbing into the Huey after their stop at the airport in Ketchikan.

"Yes, I think so," Laura replied from behind him, leaning in and massaging his shoulders. "How are you two holding up?"

"We're all right, I think."

"Yeah," Holly agreed.

"Okay," Laura said, taking her seat. "Hopefully we can get some sleep back here."

Craig turned to Holly. "Juneau is next, right?"

"Yes, it should be about 230 miles."

"Good," Craig said, switching on the battery power and the fuel pump. Their stop at Port Hardy had gone well, but he'd been concerned when they left Prince Rupert, British Columbia. Something had seemed off with the way the rotor spun up. The flight went smoothly, so he attributed it to tiredness or random variation in the machine, but he made a mental note to pay attention next time to see whether it happened again.

"Huh," Craig said.

291

"What?" Holly asked.

"It's not starting," he said, trying again. This was not good. Not good at all. "I think the battery may be dead."

Holly looked at the overhead control panel. "Did we have the generator switched to charge it? I don't remember."

"I'm not sure. I thought so. Hmm, the voltage is reading low."

"Is something wrong?" Laura asked.

"Yes," Craig said, "I think we have a dead battery. We can't start the helicopter."

"You mean we're stuck here?" Ashley asked.

Were they? He didn't know anything about this airport or have any friends in the area like he had near the control base. "I don't know."

"There must be something we can do," Milford said. "We're at an airport. Don't they have spares?"

"I don't know," Craig said, shutting the switches off. "How long do we have until the next event?"

"Just under two hours," Laura said.

"Okay. It's a small airport. Laura and Ashley, can you check around the terminal? See if there are some flashlights and anything like a maintenance building. Holly, we can split up and search the hangars and aircraft for suitable batteries. Dr. Pennychuck, do you have any ideas?"

"I'm not up for too much walking yet," Milford replied, "but I'll take a look around and see if they have any food."

"Okay." Craig got out and opened the battery compartment.

Holly joined him. "The connections look good."

He stepped back. "I sure hope it's not a problem with something else. We can't exactly take it in for repairs."

"If we can't get it working . . . "

"Let's not think about that. Maybe there will be another battery we can swap in." He read the tag on the dead one. It was brand new. Not a good sign.

He and Holly headed off to search for a replacement, while Ashley and Laura walked to the terminal building. A few minutes later, he had checked all the aircraft he could find, and he met up with Holly as she came out of a hangar.

"I haven't found anything," she said. "Have you?"

"No," he replied. "There are some small propeller planes, but nothing with the right size or voltage to get us going."

"Craig, Holly!" Someone was shouting from the direction of the terminal.

"Coming!" Craig took off at a run. He reached a maintenance building, which Laura and Ashley had opened. The power was out, but their flashlights were illuminating a small trailer parked along the wall.

"Is this useful?" Laura asked, pointing at the trailer. "It looks like the one you have."

"Yes!" Craig said, relief washing over him at the sight of the machine. "That's a portable starting generator. Give me a hand and we'll pull it over to the Huey."

"Will it start?" Holly asked.

"I sure hope so."

They pulled and pushed the trailer across the airfield to where the helicopter sat. Milford was waiting for them with several bags of food.

"Will that thing help us?" Milford asked as Craig studied the controls.

"It should," Holly said, "assuming it works."

"Holly," Craig called over, "get in the cockpit, and we'll try this. You know how to start off of ground power, right?"

"Yes," Holly said, then climbed into her seat.

Craig pressed the starter on the generator, and the engine cranked several times, then turned over. He pulled a cord bundle over to the helicopter and connected it, then gave Holly a thumbs-up before stepping away. "Please," he prayed, crossing his fingers as Holly flipped the switch. The rotor began to turn, then picked up speed, going faster until reaching full RPMs.

Craig climbed into the cockpit after disconnecting and shutting down the generator. "Let's give it a few minutes to make sure we can run on our own power."

"Can we take that starter with us?" Holly asked.

"I wish, but it's too big to fit. Juneau is larger. We might find a new battery there."

"You know," Ashley said, "I've wanted to visit Alaska for a long time. It's always seemed so distant and mysterious."

"It's beautiful," Laura said. "Craig and I came here for our honeymoon."

"Did you take a cruise?"

Craig laughed.

Laura chuckled. "Are you kidding? Can you picture Craig on one of those tourist boats? No, he planned a whole wilderness adventure. We went hiking and canoeing, we took flights to see the mountains, and we even stayed a couple nights at a cabin on a little lake where the only transportation was the seaplane that dropped us off at the dock. It was wonderful."

Craig grinned. "It was."

Ashley smiled. "That sounds really nice. I wish I could do something like that, but . . . "

"I know," Laura said. "I don't think any of us have really taken the time to consider what life will be like if we make it through this. But there will be people left if we can stop the system in time. I'm counting on it because I have to believe that we'll find Summer and Autumn."

"You're right. Wow, I just realized that I'm still worried about missing work."

"Technically you're still doing your job," Milford mumbled through the food in his mouth. "You're taking good care of me."

"There are a lot of things we'll need to let go of," Laura said.

"Are we ready?" Holly asked.

Craig looked over the gauges. "I hope so." So many things could go wrong, but he took the helicopter into the air and prayed they would make it.

SATURDAY, JULY 12, 3:15 A.M. MT
Camp Hale—Leadville, Colorado
Elevation: 9,200 feet

"Commander Muscovite," a voice said over Roman's radio.

He pulled it from his belt. "Yes."

"Sir, we're moving the barricade aside, but the event that just passed covered Red Cliff. That's right down the highway."

"That close?" His heart raced. They were lucky it hadn't reached them.

"Yes, sir. We could see it from here."

"Thank you. We're almost ready to move out. Come join the convoy as soon as you're finished there."

"Yes, sir."

Roman put down the radio and turned to Valentina. "That was close, too close. We should have left already. It doesn't usually take so long to pack up."

"I doubt your militia usually has their family members along," Valentina said. "Getting all those kids up and ready in the middle of the night can't be easy."

"True. That's a good point."

"Thank you for doing this."

"For doing what?" He hadn't helped with the kids.

"For listening to me. For taking action right away. We might be able to save the lives of all these people."

He wrapped his hands around her shoulders, taking care not to hurt her injured side. "Valentina, you make it sound like this was a hard decision. It's Leadville or death. No one here would think twice about that. Plus, you were very convincing speaking to the officers."

"True, but I don't know if they had a harder time believing my story or that you were married."

Roman laughed. "Yeah, you'd think that would have come up at some point before now."

"Sir," an officer said, approaching them, "the convoy is lined up and ready. We'll follow after you."

"Good. We'll leave in a moment. Is there someone available to drive my wife's truck? She'll be riding with me."

"Yes, sir. We can take care of it."

"Excellent."

"That sounds so nice," Valentina said.

"What does?"

"You saying 'my wife.' It's been too long since I heard those words."

"It's been too long since I've been able to say them."

"Roman, we're ready," Summer said as she and Autumn ran up to the Subaru.

"Where have you two been?"

"Helping here and there," Autumn said.

"Wow!" Valentina looked them over. "You look just like your mother."

"Dr. Severnaya?" Summer asked.

"Yes."

"Sorry," Roman said. "Autumn, Summer, this is Valentina, my wife." The words did feel good to say.

"What?" the twins asked in unison.

Roman chuckled. "Get in the car. We can talk on the way. We've got to go."

"You're married?" Summer asked as soon as they closed the doors.

"To her?" Autumn added. Her tone was . . . incredulous.

"Yes," Roman replied. "I'm almost as surprised as you are." He paused, and his smile faded. How many people would respond the same way? If only they knew what she was really like . . .

"Girls," Valentina said, turning to face them, "I believe we've met only a few times—and indirectly at that—but I'm sure you've heard a good deal about me from Dr. Pennychuck, and I doubt he had anything pleasant to say."

Summer and Autumn shared a quick glance, but Roman caught it in the mirror.

"You don't have to comment," Valentina continued. "I know what you must think of me, but there's an explanation, and I'll share it with you when we have more time."

"Okay," Autumn said.

Roman started the engine. Valentina likely had more stories to share, and she would do so eventually, though maybe some things were better left unsaid. He didn't need to know everything. He didn't want to.

"By the way," Valentina said, "your mother is at the control base near Phoenix. I saw her briefly."

"She is?" Autumn asked.

"Why? How?" Summer asked.

"I was with them for only a few moments, and we hardly spoke, but she traveled from New Hampshire on a helicopter with Dr. Pennychuck and your father and two women I don't know."

"They're alive?" Autumn asked.

"Yes, but they'll need our help to get out of there. We'll figure something out if we can get this system stopped."

"But," Summer said, "if you just saw them, then how did you get here?"

"That's another story I'll need to tell you."

"We have some time," Roman said, taking her hand in his. "Maybe you could give them the quick version."

"All right. Are you two familiar with Katherine Morgreed?"

SATURDAY, JULY 12, 1:25 A.M. AKDT (3:25 A.M. MT)
Juneau International Airport—Juneau, Alaska
Elevation: 25 feet

Craig brought the Huey down after the fog cleared and flew slowly over the Juneau airport. Their flight from Ketchikan had been a nerve-racking experience with everyone worried about the state of the battery, especially when they went to high altitude to ride out the event.

"There's the heliport," Holly said, pointing at a collection of machines sitting on the tarmac.

"That's a good sign," Craig said. "Those might not fly, but hopefully at least one of them has a good battery."

"I can get out and check if they have power before you shut down."

"Yes, let's do that."

Holly was out the door and running as soon as the skids touched the ground. She checked a few of the nearest helicopters and gave Craig a thumbs-up.

"Did she find a battery?" Ashley asked from the rear.

"It looks like it," Craig said. "Hopefully they're compatible."

Holly climbed back into the cockpit. "They have power, but the computers are out. We're definitely better off in this if we can fix it."

"Okay," Craig said, shutting down.

Holly watched the blades until they came to rest. "Is there any power?"

"My thoughts exactly," Craig said, then switched on the battery. "Nope. It's dead."

"Then let's get to work."

SATURDAY, JULY 12, 3:43 A.M. MT
Lake County Fire Station—Leadville, Colorado
Elevation: 10,152 feet

"And then I drove to the camp and waited for Roman," Valentina said, finishing her story as they pulled up to the fire station. Sharing it—even with many parts left out—felt surprisingly good. She'd bottled it up for too long.

"We had no idea," Autumn said, "and I don't think Mom or Dr. Pennychuck did either."

Valentina paused. "They know at least some of the details now. I'm sure Barry filled them in after Katherine and I left the base."

"That certainly helps explain why everything went wrong," Summer said.

"Yes." Roman shut off the engine. "Now let's go meet the mayor."

They entered the fire station and found several officials and emergency personnel discussing the situation. One of them left the room and returned shortly with the mayor, who had been sleeping.

"What's going on?" the mayor asked, yawning as he joined them. He showed obvious signs of stress, not unlike the countless other politicians Valentina had met. Fortunately for him, though, his stress didn't stem from Katherine's harassment and blackmail.

"We've had a development," Roman said. "Taking down the balloons proved to be ineffective, and we don't have time to hunt down enough of them to crash the system."

"So your mother was wrong?" the mayor asked, looking at the twins.

"No," Valentina said. "It would have worked if we hadn't changed everything."

"And you are?"

"She's my wife," Roman said. "Dr. Valentina Severnaya, Pennychuck System director with the EPA."

"Um," the mayor said, obviously surprised, "why didn't you mention her before?"

"It's a long story," Roman and Valentina said in unison.

"Mr. Mayor," Valentina said, "there was a conspiracy to ruin the climate system headed up by Katherine Morgreed and her associates. Because of their actions, shooting down balloons is not an option open to us anymore. We'll need to disable a reactor."

The mayor stared at her. "You're joking."

"No, but it will take some planning, and in the meantime, we need to prepare for the system hitting the town."

"It will reach Leadville this afternoon," Roman said. "We've abandoned Camp Hale."

"What can we do?" the police chief asked, joining the conversation.

"We need to prepare underground bunkers," Valentina said, "strong enough to withstand depressurization outside, and they must be airtight."

"Depressurization?" the mayor asked.

"Yes." The broken door in the clinic basement flew through her mind. "The system is solidifying nitrogen and oxygen within the field, which drops the pressure to near vacuum almost instantaneously. The wind results from air filling in from above, and then the snow-like solids sublimate into toxic gases, but they dissipate back to normal atmosphere."

"Why would anyone want to do this?" the chief asked.

Why indeed . . . "It wasn't the intent and I can explain that later. We need to get started right away. Do you have any suitable basements in town?"

"What about the schools?" the mayor asked. "We had bomb drills when I was a kid. Are those bunkers still there?"

"Yes," said the fire chief, who'd been listening. "We inspect them periodically, but they've been used as storage space for a long time. We'll have to move a lot of stuff out."

"Why would your schools have bomb shelters?" Roman asked.

"Because of the Soviets," the mayor said. "They built them that way or added them during the Cold War, you know, in case the Russians bombed us."

"Are they airtight?" Valentina asked, conscious of her accent. It was mild but discernible.

"I'm not sure," the fire chief said. "We'll have to take a look, but we have three schools in town. There should be plenty of room for everyone."

"Even with all the refugees?" the police chief asked.

"And we have at least a few thousand people," Roman added.

"Umm," the fire chief said, "no. I don't think they'll handle that."

"Fit everyone you can into those," Valentina said, "and we'll need to find more room for the rest. We should have time to reinforce and seal up other basements. I did it on my way here with duct tape and sturdy rooms with no openings."

"All right," the mayor said. "It looks like we'll need to dust off the town emergency binder and get started."

CHAPTER 26

SATURDAY, JULY 12, 8:00 A.M. PT (9:00 A.M. MT)
Haines Junction Airport—Haines Junction, Yukon
Elevation: 2,150 feet

After they replaced the battery in the Huey and spent some time testing to ensure that it would start the helicopter and accept a charge during flight, Holly flew them from Juneau to the tiny airport at Haines Junction.

"Do you need any help?" Holly asked as Craig dragged a fuel hose over to the helicopter.

"No, I've got this if you want to walk around awhile."

"Okay, thanks," she said, heading toward the small terminal to find a restroom. When she came out, she found Ashley sitting in the parking lot and staring off at the mountains. She was a picture of loneliness.

"I like this airport," Ashley said as Holly sat down next to her.

"Why?" Holly glanced at the facilities. There wasn't much to like.

"Because I don't see any bodies. I hate it every time we land, especially at the big ones. The bodies are everywhere."

"I know what you mean," Holly said, putting an arm around Ashley and pulling her close. "I try not to look, but sometimes it can't be avoided."

"Yeah . . . You know, I've seen people die at the hospital. It's always sad. You think about their family and how hard it must be for them.

303

I've cried sometimes. I get to know them when they're there for a while. But this is all so different. It doesn't make sense. These people weren't sick. They were just going about their day."

"Hmm." Holly looked across the lot to where Craig and Laura held each other in a tight embrace as Craig filled the tanks. How were they holding up? This had to be hard for them, not knowing whether the girls were okay. "Seeing them makes me think about our parents, and in a way I'm kind of glad they died before this happened."

"How can you say that?"

"Because I know they're gone. I don't have to wonder if they're still alive."

"Oh."

Holly sighed. "I've been thinking. We don't talk anymore like we used to, like before they died."

"We've been busy."

"No, it's more than that." Busy was an excuse, not a reason. "I feel like we've drifted apart."

"But we see each other all the time. We live in the same apartment."

"Well, yes, but I don't know what your thoughts are anymore. We're more like roommates than sisters. Even on this trip—or whatever you'd call it—we've barely spoken. I would have lost you if you hadn't run into Dr. Pennychuck, but we've kind of gone ahead on autopilot like it's not a big deal. It's been bothering me."

"I've thought about that," Ashley said, "but I guess I've taken it for granted that you're here with me. You always are, although I think I understand what you're saying. But I'm also scared. I don't know what's going to happen. What if they can't stop this thing? You've been busy flying and talking to Craig, but I've listened to Laura and

Dr. Pennychuck for hours. They're really worried. I think they try to keep most of it from us, but our time is running out."

Guilt hit Holly. She *had* been bothered by the coincidence that brought them together. Ashley *would* have been lost if circumstances had been different, and she'd thanked God that they were not, but in the midst of all those thoughts and emotions, she'd neglected her sister—her only family—and she'd been too preoccupied to see it. "I'm sorry," she said, holding Ashley a little tighter. "I didn't realize. You're right—my thoughts are mostly on the helicopter and reaching the next fuel stop and my own worries. I didn't think about your experience. Maybe . . . Do you want a break?"

"What do you mean?"

"Craig is flying the next leg, and we'll reach Chicken well before the next event."

"Chicken?"

"Alaska. It's a little town."

"Oh."

"So he shouldn't need me up front. How would you like to sit in as copilot?"

"Are you sure?"

"Yes, we can switch places if there's an emergency. I think you'd enjoy it."

"I think so. Thanks."

"Hey, I've got to watch out for my little sister."

Ashley laughed. "Being one year older hardly qualifies you for that role."

"Maybe not," Holly said, getting to her feet and extending a hand, "but I can try. Come on. It looks like Craig is ready to go."

SATURDAY, JULY 12, 2:16 P.M. MT
Lake County High School—Leadville, Colorado
Elevation: 10,152 feet

If the residents of Leadville had been annoyed or confused by the air raid sirens sounding in the middle of the night, those feelings quickly gave way to a determined sense of community once the news spread of the plans to prepare shelters. With the aid of the militia, the townspeople had got to work identifying suitable basements and converting them into bunkers to withstand the coming storm.

Roman was occupied coordinating with the mayor and volunteer citizen leaders over the radios, while Summer and Autumn drove Valentina around to inspect work on the various sites. They'd then returned to the high school, which was assigned to the militia. Years' worth of records, old furniture, and other items had been cleared from the bunker, and the troops were busy sealing and reinforcing any possible weak points as well as parts of the ground floor above.

"I need to rest," Valentina said, taking a seat on a bench outside the school.

"Here's some water." Summer handed her a bottle. "How are you feeling?"

"Well enough, but I'm tired, and my shoulder still hurts. If you want my advice, try to avoid getting shot. It's nothing like in the movies, where the hero just brushes it off and continues the fight. It drains you."

"That must be hard," Autumn said. She'd seen plenty of those movies. "I hope it gets better."

"Thanks. I do, too. It's frustrating. So many things are suddenly impossible without two hands. Like, I can't even put my hair up."

"I didn't think of that," Autumn said. "Would you let me braid it?"

"Autumn loves hair," Summer said.

"Be my guest. Oh and by the way, Autumn, I like the colors in your ponytail."

Autumn flipped it forward over her shoulder. The brilliance had faded, but the color was holding up. "Thanks. It's fun, and it helps everyone tell us apart."

Valentina sat back and closed her eyes as Autumn brushed out her hair and began separating it. "That's so relaxing. I haven't had anyone do that since I was little."

"It must have been so stressful," Summer said, "all those years you had to work for Katherine."

"*Stressful* doesn't even begin to describe it. It will take me time to recover, if I ever do. I have to be careful how I act and speak around all of you. My 'other self' is always ready to pounce, and I don't like her. I hope Roman still sees some semblance of who I once was, because I don't."

Autumn began braiding. "How did you meet him?"

"I was in school in Russia. He was recruiting for the government, and I was on his list to interview. He was so nervous, and I could tell he liked me. He was stationed not too far from my university, and we met several times. I told him that Katherine was sponsoring my education with the agreement that I would work where she directed afterwards, so I wouldn't be a candidate for his government positions. He said he'd still like to see me, so we began to meet socially, and he was such a gentleman. It wasn't long until we were discussing marriage."

"He's really glad you're here," Summer said. "He was so serious before you arrived—and kind of depressing. I wish you could see the difference."

"Thanks. That's nice to hear, but it pains me to think of all the hurt he's gone through because of me."

"Now you're together again," Autumn said, "and hopefully you can find a way to start over."

"Maybe, but there are things that will always haunt me. I have nightmares. I can't make that all go away. I don't know if anything could."

Summer sat on the bench next to her. "Are they about your baby?"

"Yes. There's hardly a night that goes by when I don't dream about him. I can't let it go."

Autumn paused. Everything Valentina had shared was so far outside her own experience. What should she say? "Valentina," she said, "I'm so sorry for everything you've been through." Her fingers resumed their work. "I know this might sound trite, but when I struggled with nightmares after Summer nearly died, I finally prayed, and that made a world of difference."

Valentina sighed. "I wish it was that simple, but you still have your sister. Your family loves you. It turned out okay, and you were able to move on. It's different for me. Every day I've had to pretend that nothing is wrong. I've had no one to talk to, and Katherine was unrelenting with the pressure to do what she demanded. I was all alone and consumed by hate. Every time I saw her, I fantasized about killing her, and I could have done it. My hands would start shaking, and I'd be tempted to forget about the consequences and just do it. If it wasn't for my son, I would have, and Katherine knew it. Now she's probably gone, and so is my son. I never got to say goodbye to him. How can I move on from that?"

Autumn wrapped a hair tie around the braid and took a seat on the bench. "I can't imagine going through what you did, but you're not alone. We're here, and you have Roman, but you need peace in your heart that none of us can give you. Only God can heal those wounds. I know He did it for me, and He will for you if you let Him."

Valentina's eyes were watery as she looked at her. "I can't. Your God is all about forgiveness, but that's too much to ask. I hate Katherine so much. She ruined my life. I can never forgive her."

"I know it seems impossible," Summer said, resting a hand on Valentina's shoulder, "and you're not ready to forgive, but God doesn't require us to do impossible things on our own strength. He'll help you more than you can imagine. Jesus said, 'Come to me, all you who are weary and burdened, and I will give you rest.' Start with that. Just ask Him to help you, and take it one step at a time."

"Can we pray for you?" Autumn asked.

"You can try."

SATURDAY, JULY 12, 1:10 P.M. AKDT (3:10 P.M. MT)
Barter Island Long Range Radar Service Airport—Barter Island, Alaska
Elevation: 2 feet

After taking off from Haines Junction, Craig chatted with Ashley in the cockpit and showed her how the helicopter worked while Holly caught up with Laura in the rear and Milford took a nap. Then Holly took the controls for the flight to Fort Yukon, and Ashley stayed up front with her. Laura thought that the sisters seemed happier since they'd talked in the parking lot, and after riding out the system and stopping for fuel, they were more than willing to remain in the cockpit for the last leg to Barter Island.

"We're here," Holly said, landing the Huey near the fuel depot.

"The building looks okay," Laura said, though she wasn't sure how she'd know otherwise. It was a long complex of connected rectangular structures that were raised off the ground.

"There were people here," Ashley said, pointing to some bodies.

"Yes, let me go in first," Craig said, "in case anyone needs to be, um, moved out of the way."

"Thanks." Laura shivered as Craig opened the sliding door and a cold wind blew into the cabin. He ran over to the building and examined the entrance, then went to one of the bodies and rummaged through the dead scientist's jacket until finding a key card. He swiped it in the reader on the door and disappeared inside, then returned after a minute.

"It's empty," he said, "and fortunately the staff were outside. Otherwise, I don't know how we'd get the door unlocked."

"That is fortunate," Milford said. "They probably went out for a better view of the sky. There would be a security garrison nearby with access cards, but they're probably stationed in the town, and we don't have time to search. Let's go in."

Ashley joined the others walking toward the building and pointed at a small town in the distance. "This place is desolate. Do people really live here?"

"Yes," Holly said. "That town is called Kaktovik."

"Brrr." Ashley crossed her arms. "If it's this cold in the middle of the summer, I wouldn't want to be here in wintertime."

Laura shivered at the thought. Milford had explained the DEW Line operations on the last leg of their flight. Back in the sixties, people had worked shifts of nine months or more at these remote outposts with little contact with the outside world. She'd barely stepped foot on the ground and was already feeling overwhelmed by the isolation of the place.

"We can all be thankful that the building is heated," Craig said, holding the door open for the others to enter.

Milford shuffled to the control terminal and studied the screen. "Odd," he said. "This seems to be showing the current status, but these are my settings for the reaction. Whatever Dr. Severnaya did must not be reflected on the displays."

"Some of it is correct," Laura said. "Look. It shows the countdown to the next run, which will be at 3.1 kilometers."

"That's a bit over ten thousand feet," Craig said.

Milford grabbed the mouse. "Let's turn it off." He clicked on the box for system power, but an error message popped up. "Locked by user V_Severnaya."

"Try it again," Laura said, though it was likely futile. They'd come thousands of miles. Was it all for nothing?

Milford hit Cancel and tried to bring up the settings again but got the same error. "It figures," he said. "Trillions of dollars spent on this, and we couldn't even program for simultaneous user access."

"What do you mean?" Ashley asked.

"Dr. Severnaya had this screen open at main control," Milford explained. "She would have to exit it for someone else to access that function. The system allows only one user at a time. There's good reason for it, but it's a real annoyance when someone leaves a screen up and forgets."

"We can't exactly call her," Craig said.

"No, and that terminal is unusable anyway. We'll need to go about this another way. Hmm, let's see if we can bring up altitude control." He clicked on the box. It displayed "3.1 kilometers" and a check mark next to "Automatic control." He clicked on the check mark to disable it, and a log-in prompt appeared. "This is better," he said, typing in his username and password with one finger. Another error message popped up. "Unauthorized user."

"Unauthorized?" Laura asked. "How can that be?"

"Dr. Severnaya," Milford said. "She must have had my access removed." He clicked to cancel, but the message was replaced by a status bar, which was progressing toward one hundred percent.

"What's that?"

"I don't know," Milford said as the bar reached the end. A message displayed saying something about initializing, and then the altitude and reactor power boxes changed to maximum and grayed out.

"The altitude setting went to forty kilometers," Laura said. Could it do that? Why so high?

"And one hundred percent reactor power," Milford added, trying to click on the controls. "They aren't responding. It doesn't even ask for a log-in."

Laura stared at the screen. Something was wrong. "What's happening?"

"I don't know. Perhaps Katherine or Valentina added a fail-safe."

"Look!" Ashley called from where she stood by a window. "They're going up."

Everyone joined her as several balloons visible out over the sea to the north made steady progress upward.

"If they go to forty kilometers," Craig said, "we can't fly over that. That's, like . . . 130,000 feet."

"Just over 131,000," Milford said. "That's maximum altitude for the system. We designed it to reach most of the way into the stratosphere and cover the ozone layer."

"Milford," Laura said, "that will turn over ninety percent of atmospheric mass to vacuum. Will it even recover?" She pictured the atmosphere vanishing in an instant and the earth's surface morphing into the barren rockscape of the moon.

Milford shut his eyes and frowned. "I don't know. Maybe, if gravitational forces remain steady, but there's too much to consider, and that's not our only problem. Reactor power is at one hundred percent."

"Is that bad?" Holly asked.

"Yes," Milford said. "I had numerous conversations with the engineers at Morgreed Industries. The oscillating burst reactors become highly unstable at peak output. They could fail in numerous ways, and the radiation exposure to the environment could be catastrophic . . . Eighty percent was supposed to be the highest setting allowed at max altitude—and less as we go lower."

"If Morgreed lied about the power output," Laura said, "perhaps she lied about the stability problems, too."

"I doubt it. Not if her intent was to ruin the system."

"Don't the reactors have safety systems?" Craig asked.

"The control program *is* the safety system," Milford said. "One hundred percent shouldn't be allowed. They must have altered the program."

Laura watched one of the balloons. It gained altitude with each second, and she pictured it as a tiny dot in one of her terrain models. As the reflector network rose, more and more balloons would activate until the sky was blanketed. No point on earth would remain out of their reach. Nowhere would be safe. There would be nowhere left to run to. "So," she said, "if the reactors fail, we're dead from radiation, and if they work, we're dead from the field. This is not good."

Milford returned to the terminal. "I wonder," he said, clicking on the field calibration box. "It works! They didn't lock this one. Look. These are Dr. Severnaya's actual settings."

"Can you change them?" Laura asked. It seemed unlikely, but they had to try.

"Yes," Milford said, moving a frequency slider.

"So we can't turn it off," Laura said, "or change the altitude or power, but we can adjust the calibration."

"That appears to be the case. Maybe they figured this didn't matter, or it was simply an oversight."

If they could change that . . . Laura's skin prickled. They would be in the field, but would they be okay? "Can you change it back to target carbon? If the field doesn't react with the oxygen and nitrogen, we might avoid the vacuum."

"Good idea," Milford said, adjusting the numbers. "There. That's what I intended for us to use, but who knows what will happen with this much power?"

"Is there anything else we can do?" Craig asked.

"You may as well fuel up the helicopter, but otherwise find a comfortable chair and wait. We might not be making any more flights."

SATURDAY, JULY 12, 4:43 P.M. MT
Lake County High School—Leadville, Colorado
Elevation: 10,152 feet

"Valentina!" Roman yelled, running through the basement bunker until he found her. "They spotted some balloons in the distance, past the mountains."

"So?" That was nothing new. Why was he so excited?

"We can hardly see them."

Were there clouds? She didn't understand. "Roman, calm down. What are you saying?"

"The balloons went up."

"Yes, they do after each run."

"No, I mean way up. They're still ascending. We can hardly see them now."

Valentina frowned. He couldn't mean . . . "I need to see," she said, heading for the exit.

Roman, Summer, and Autumn followed her outside. The massive balloons were visible in every direction, high up in the atmosphere.

"What does it mean?" Roman asked.

"I'm not certain," Valentina said, though it couldn't be a good sign. She recalled the conversation in the bunker and froze, her fingers searching for the necklace that now lay on the side of the highway. *She* was still coming after her, even here. She would never give up, and if she couldn't win, no one would. "This is Katherine's doing."

"You mean she's alive out there somewhere?"

Valentina shuddered. "I hope not, but I don't know. Katherine had a fail-safe added to the patch I installed. She didn't explain it, but that's the only thing I can think of."

"What should we do?"

What else *could* they do? "Make sure the bunkers are finished, and get everyone inside. If the settings have changed, all bets are off on when the system will run next. If we survive it, then we have to get to a reactor without delay."

CHAPTER 27

"It's time," Milford announced an hour later, watching the system status change to active on the control terminal.

Laura and Craig rose from where they'd been sitting against the wall, as did Holly and Ashley, and they all gathered in front of the windows.

"Is this going to hurt?" Ashley asked. "I mean, if the reactors fail."

"I can't say," Milford said. "It's all theoretical, but this building is not protected like main control. The walls will probably block the field from charging inside, but otherwise we're exposed."

"I can see it," Craig said, pointing as sparks began lighting up the air.

Laura took Craig's hand. "I hope our girls are somewhere safe."

"Me, too."

"I would not advise watching this," Milford said, leaving the terminal to join them. "If it flashes, the timing could be different than we've seen previously."

"There's only one thing we can do now," Holly said, joining hands with Ashley and Laura.

"What's that?" Milford asked as he was pulled into a circle with the others.

"We can pray," Craig said, closing his eyes.

SATURDAY, JULY 12, 6:10 P.M. MT
Lake County High School—Leadville, Colorado
Elevation: 10,152 feet

After the event passed, Valentina withdrew from Roman's arms and checked the time. Everyone that was packed into the basement had been waiting silently since the process started. They heard the same droning buildup of static as during previous events, but it was much louder than before. They couldn't see whether there was a flash, but as the sound of the field hit its peak, an incredible crack like a million bolts of lightning split the air and shook the foundation of the building. And then there was nothing. No shattering glass, no wind—only silence.

"Where are you going?" Roman asked as Valentina walked toward the door.

"This was different," she said. "I have to see outside."

The militiaman at the exit opened the heavy bunker hatch for them, and they ascended the stairs to the ground floor of the school. Valentina was almost running as she headed down the hallway and pushed open a door to the parking lot, and then she stopped.

"What is it?" Roman asked, coming up behind her.

Valentina put her hand out into the air and then stepped outside. Tiny flakes of ash-gray snow were falling softly and building up on the ground, but there were no wisps of fog, and the air felt fresh and clean. She laughed as she walked through it, then stopped and turned in place with her arm outstretched, watching the little flakes bounce off her clothing. They were warm to the touch and crumbled to powder when she closed her fist over them.

"Is it safe?" Roman asked from the doorway.

"Yes," she said, "come and see."

Roman joined her, taking her hand as they stood face to face.

"It's carbon," Valentina said. "Dr. Pennychuck's plan—it worked!"

"How?"

"The field calibration must have changed. I don't know how, but it did."

"So we're safe?"

Her smile faltered. "No, I don't think so."

"Wow," Summer said as she and Autumn ran out, "this is neat."

"What's wrong?" Autumn asked.

Valentina took a moment before she spoke as the snow continued to fall. "The system brought the carbon out of the atmosphere, all at once. If it runs again on the same calibration, there won't be any carbon left to react."

"What would that mean?" Roman asked.

"With this much power and no reaction, it's likely the field will cause feedback. That energy has to go somewhere, and we might be looking at a nuclear accident the likes of which we've never seen."

"How bad?" Roman asked.

"Anyone still alive now on earth would be dead. We have to stop it. Get your troops ready. We need to get to that reactor."

Milford stepped out of the control building after the last flakes of gray snow had fallen and trudged across the field to join his companions.

"It worked," Laura said, turning a radiant smile his way. "Could you have ever imagined your reaction would produce carbon snow?"

"It's astonishing," Milford said, "although not entirely unexpected after what we've seen it do already. Would you mind handing me some? I'm not quite up to bending down yet."

Laura scooped up a handful. "It's warm," she said, placing it on his palm.

"That makes sense. It took a lot of energy to do this . . . " He froze. It was an enormous amount of energy. It was a wonder the reactors had remained stable, but he was holding the product of the reaction.

"What?" Laura asked.

"This is a problem," Milford said. "This stuff turns to powder at the slightest touch. It will stay that way. It's not going back into the atmosphere."

"Isn't that good?" Craig asked.

"Environmentally, yes, but otherwise, no. We can't turn off the system, and it will run again on schedule. Without the carbon in the air, those reactors will build up a full power field with nowhere for it to go."

"So the reactors get damaged, right?" Craig said. "Doesn't that put an end to this?"

"It puts an end to us," Laura said.

Milford let the carbon fall through his fingers. "Kaboom."

SATURDAY, JULY 12, 6:45 P.M. MT
Lake County High School—Leadville, Colorado
Elevation: 10,152 feet

"Commander," an officer said over the radio, "we're ready to go."

"Excellent," Roman said. "I'll take the lead."

"Yes, sir. We'll follow you."

"Hop in," Roman said to Valentina and the twins. "It should be about three hours to Grand Junction if this carbon stuff doesn't slow us down."

The convoy of trucks was lining up in the parking lot. "It looks like we're going to war," Autumn said.

Roman turned to face her. "We are."

SATURDAY, JULY 12, 5:06 P.M. AKDT (7:06 P.M. MT)
Barter Island control base—Barter Island, Alaska
Elevation: 36 feet

Milford sat at the control terminal, staring through the screen as he tried to think of a way out of their predicament. Something caught his attention, and he focused on the display in front of him. One of the status boxes was flashing, so he enlarged it.

"Laura," Milford called, "this is interesting."

"What?" she said, coming over to see.

"The carbon sensors are registering a change."

"That makes sense, but I'm surprised that they show only a small drop. I would think it would be zero."

"No, they don't respond that quickly. Remember, we were expecting extremely small changes. The sensors on the balloon tethers are very precise, but that comes at the price of speed. It wouldn't have ever mattered for how we planned this to work."

"Does this help us?"

"I don't know."

CHAPTER 28

"There it is," Roman said a few hours later, parking in front of the security fence encircling the reactor complex. "Any farther and we become targets for the autocannons."

"Those signs on the fence make that pretty clear," Summer said.

Valentina unbuckled her seat belt. "We have to hurry. We have only a little over an hour if it's still on schedule."

"I know," Roman said, picking up his radio. "This is Commander Muscovite. We need to work quickly. Fire up some flares to locate the defenses; then take them out."

"Yes, sir," came the reply from the artillery leader. A couple of minutes later, flares burst in the night sky above the protected range between the fence and the complex. Radar-targeting autocannons lit up the sky with thousands of rounds per minute, shooting at the flares and revealing their locations. The militia artillery thundered with deadly accuracy, and when they sent up another salvo of flares, there was no response from the complex.

"Let's go," Roman ordered.

A semitruck accelerated down the road toward the gate and crashed through, leaving a path for the others to follow. Roman sped after the truck until they reached the reactor building. Then some of the men who'd done demolitions work with the army moved in and blasted the doors open.

"You girls might want to stay here," Roman said, opening his door.

Summer was already getting out of the car. "No way! This is cool."

"All right, but keep at a safe distance."

The four of them headed for the building. Security alarms were blaring all over the complex, though no one was coming to halt their advance.

"This way," Valentina said, leading the troops into the interior. "I've visited these sites before and they're all the same. There's a security door ahead. You'll need to destroy it."

The demolitions men blasted the door and several others as they worked their way through the facility, finally reaching the entry room for the reactor dome. Valentina punched a few numbers into the keypad, and the door unlocked.

"You have access to this?" Roman asked.

"Yes, I needed it for my work. Katherine had them all set with the year the Arctic Circle Society was founded."

Roman and the others followed Valentina into the room. There were lockers and benches, and radiation suits were hanging on the wall. At the other end, an air lock opened to a decontamination chamber.

"The reactor dome is through there," Valentina explained. "Autumn, Summer, will you please help me put on one of these radiation suits?"

"Sure," the twins said.

"You're going in there?" Roman asked. Surely that wasn't her plan. She was injured. It was too much. Someone else could do it. Someone . . . Someone besides her. He couldn't lose her again. Not like this.

"I have to," Valentina said. "I'm the only one here who knows anything about how those reactors work. I've seen them up close."

"But . . ." Roman said, then resigned himself to her decision. There would be no arguing with her, and she was right. She was the expert. If he couldn't stop her, then he would help her no matter the risk. He pulled the other suit off the rack. "I'm going with you. I can't let you do this alone."

"Can we help?" one of the demolitions men asked.

"No," Valentina said. "There are no more suits, and we don't have time to go to another access point. You'd be dead in minutes going in there unprotected. Give Roman a bag of explosives. We might need them."

"I can't get your arm in the sleeve with the sling on," Autumn said.

Valentina pointed to a backpack she'd brought. "There's duct tape in my bag. You'll have to tape it to my side."

"Are you sure about this?" Roman asked. Was there no other way? "You're injured. Can't you give someone else instructions on what to do? Can't I go without you?"

"No, we don't have time. I have to do this."

Roman was stalling, but there was no time to delay. If it were a question of ordering his troops into certain danger, he would do it. It would grieve him, but the mission was more important than the lives of a few men. But this . . . He couldn't bear it. He could never ask her to do this. Tears came to his eyes. "Please . . ."

Valentina gasped. Roman reached for her.

"Sorry," Summer said, pausing from tightening the shoulder straps of the air tank. "Should I take it off?"

Valentina's expression was pained. "No, it can't be helped. We have to go. Roman, hurry up."

Roman fastened his helmet and flexed his fingers in the heavy gloves. "I'm ready." He tried to sound confident. She needed him, and he had to check his emotions.

Autumn tucked Valentina's braid out of the way and lowered the helmet over her head; then Summer connected the air.

"Okay," Valentina said. "Please hand me my bag. Roman, these devices on our chests are radiation exposure indicators. Once they reach the red, it's time to get out."

"Got it." He followed Valentina into the air lock and closed the door. They entered the decontamination chamber and closed another door, then opened a thick hatch to the reactor dome.

"It's huge," Roman said as they stepped over the threshold into a corridor that ran around the outside of the lower reflector.

"This way," Valentina said, stepping onto a staircase that ascended roughly 150 feet up the side of the reflector housing, much like those on the storage tanks at fuel distribution facilities. When they reached the top, the stairs opened onto a catwalk that ran around the rim of the reflector, which was bathed in a dull red glow from the lighting in the dome.

"How do we get to the reactor?" Roman asked, looking at the structure in the center of the dish. "There aren't any stairs."

"It's not really built for access. They take the reactors out by crane for maintenance. The only way to get there is to slide down the reflector."

Roman watched as Valentina took a seat on the rim and pushed off. She slid down the smooth metal surface until coming to rest where it leveled out at the bottom.

"Come on," she yelled.

Roman followed her and arrived at the base, where Valentina was already beginning to climb a ladder up the side of the reactor tower. He judged it to be one hundred feet—maybe more—and was only a few rungs up when a siren echoed through the dome in concert with the security alarm. He looked up and saw the massive doors of the dome beginning to slide apart, revealing the stars in the sky above.

"We're running out of time," Valentina shouted, climbing as fast as she could with only her left hand able to grasp the rungs.

"Reactor start in five minutes," an automated voice rang out.

Roman caught up to Valentina on the ladder. How was she doing this? She had to be going on pure determination. "What's your plan?"

"We have to get to the pistons and disable the drive mechanism. If they don't move, it will cause an error and stop the system."

"Can we blow it up?"

"I think so, as long as we have time to get down."

The dome was nearly halfway open as they pulled themselves onto the oscillator platform. Twelve large pistons were arranged in a circle connected by a drive mechanism above, and under each piston was a corresponding cylinder set into the platform.

"They fire in a pattern like an engine," Valentina said. "We need to destroy that linkage so the pistons don't move. When they plunge into the cylinders, the fuel rods inside them react with a burst of radiation, and we can't be here."

"Reactor start in four minutes," the voice announced.

"I can get up there," Roman said. He began climbing up an access ladder to the top of the pistons.

"Hurry!" Valentina shouted.

He stopped at the top of the ladder. The linkage was only a few feet away, though he would need to reach through a narrow gap to place an explosive. He hooked an elbow onto the ladder and shrugged off the backpack, then tried to switch arms to bring it around in front of him, but a loud clunk emanated from the reactor. He dropped the pack as he nearly lost his balance.

"No!" The backpack fell to the floor of the reflector far below. "I'll go get it," he yelled, racing down the ladder as fast as he could. He knew there was no time. The dome doors were nearly at full open, and the oscillator drive was humming as it warmed up. He glanced up. Valentina ducked between two of the pistons, disappearing from his view. What was she doing? They had to get out of here. She'd mentioned something about dismantling the drive mechanism with a wrench, but that would require minutes she didn't have.

"Reactor start in three minutes," the voice announced as the dome doors retracted completely with a loud thud.

SATURDAY, JULY 12, 8:57 P.M. AKDT (10:57 P.M. MT)
Barter Island control base—Barter Island, Alaska
Elevation: 36 feet

The mood had been somber among the group at Barter Island. Having no further ideas on how to stop the system, they'd retreated to quiet conversation, Laura with Craig and Holly with Ashley. Only

Milford remained at the control terminal, watching the carbon count fall and clinging to the hope that a solution would present itself.

At three minutes to initialization, the carbon reading dropped another digit, and then a window popped onto the display. Lines of computer code appeared, following a scripted protocol he'd forgotten about:

‹CARBON TARGET ACHIEVED›

‹AUTOMATIC CONTROL DEACTIVATED›

‹RETURN TO MAIN?›

‹Y/N›:_|

Milford looked at the time. It was almost at two minutes to activation. He dropped the bag of roasted peanuts he'd been eating and hit *Y* on the keyboard, then the enter key.

"Milford, what are you doing over there?" Laura asked.

"Hold on." The scripted lines continued until the window vanished and the display screen returned.

SATURDAY, JULY 12, 10:58 P.M. MT

Morgreed Industries reactor complex–Grand Junction, Colorado

Elevation: 4,583 feet

"Reactor start in two minutes," Valentina heard over the loudspeakers. She grasped a wrench in her left hand and, in the low light, strained to read the identification plates on the cylinders until she found number 01. That would be the first to fire, she hoped. It seemed futile, but she started hitting the underside of the piston with the wrench as hard as she could, trying to flare out the soft lead of the sheathing so it wouldn't fit into the cylinder.

SATURDAY, JULY 12, 8:59 P.M. AKDT (10:59 P.M. MT)
Barter Island control base—Barter Island, Alaska
Elevation: 36 feet

"What's going on?" Laura asked, coming over to stand by Milford.

"Please work," Milford muttered, typing into a log-in prompt as fast as he could with his right index finger.

"Are you logging in as Barry?"

"Yes!" Milford exclaimed as the prompt cleared and brought up the system-power selection screen. He clicked the button for system shutdown and then hit "Okay" on the confirmation box that popped up.

SATURDAY, JULY 12, 10:59:27 P.M. MT
Morgreed Industries reactor complex—Grand Junction, Colorado
Elevation: 4,583 feet

Roman had heard the one-minute announcement along with a repetitive banging as he scrambled up the last rungs of the ladder and reached the oscillator platform.

"Valentina!" She was wielding the wrench inside the circle of pistons.

"Reactor start in thirty seconds."

"I have to stop it!" Valentina hammered at the piston with feeble blows as her strength waned.

"Get out of there!"

"No, I . . ."

"Twenty-five."

"Stop." Roman ducked inside the circle and took hold of the wrench, then pulled Valentina into as close of an embrace as their cumbersome suits allowed.

"Twenty."

"We failed." She collapsed against him.

SATURDAY, JULY 12, 8:59:45 P.M. AKDT (10:59:45 P.M. MT)
Barter Island control base–Barter Island, Alaska
Elevation: 36 feet

Laura watched the screen, astonishment on her face. "Did you just . . ."

"Yes," Milford said, leaning back in his chair.

SATURDAY, JULY 12, 10:59:50 P.M. MT
Morgreed Industries reactor complex–Grand Junction, Colorado
Elevation: 4,583 feet

"What happened?" Valentina looked around as the humming of the oscillator drive ceased and the dome doors began closing.

"It stopped," Roman said. "Twenty seconds must have passed by now."

"I don't understand."

"Valentina," Roman said, "your radiation indicator is red. We have to get out of here."

SATURDAY, JULY 12, 9:01 P.M. AKDT (11:01 P.M. MT)
Barter Island control base–Barter Island, Alaska
Elevation: 36 feet

"How did you do that?" Laura asked.

Milford let out a long breath and pressed a hand to his forehead. "It was the sensors. They finally triggered the system to come off of auto. The override code likely didn't account for that possibility, and it was deactivated, so I was able to shut it down."

"How were you able to log in? Those were the director's credentials."

"I remembered a conversation we had a while ago. He was complaining about how annoying it was to have to change his password every month, and he told me his strategy of updating it to the six-digit month and year format each time so he'd always be able to remember the current one. Fortunately it seems he kept that up."

"Is it actually stopped?" Holly asked.

"Yes. It won't run again."

"Are you sure?"

"Positive." Unless . . . Did Katherine have other surprises in store?

"Can you make the balloons come down?" Craig asked. "I'd feel better if they were all moored at ground level. Those tethers would make flying dangerous."

"Yes," Milford said, bringing up the altitude box and setting it to "Docked." "I'm also disabling automatic control from engaging on its own."

"So there's no chance of this ever starting again?" Ashley asked.

Milford shook his head. But was he forgetting anything? Was there any way? "No, not without access to the control system. I would have to purposefully initialize it."

"Could anyone else do that?" Craig asked. "We don't know who may be alive at or near the other bases."

"Maybe." That was a good point. Milford tried another window on the display. "Yes, Director Calavari had administrative access. I can disable all other users."

"Do it," Laura said. "We need to be absolutely sure."

"Is that wise?" Holly asked. "What if you need to change something later?"

Milford thought. "I've turned off everything. There's no conceivable reason to change that. I don't want to take the risk of someone hacking in. This is the only way to be sure that won't happen."

Holly nodded. "I guess that makes sense."

"There," Milford said, selecting all and disabling access. "I'll change Barry's password, too. Once that expires at the end of the month, no one but him would have the information necessary to reset it."

"We know that won't be happening," Craig said.

"What do we do now?" Ashley asked. "Can we go home?"

"I don't know if there's even a home to go to," Laura said, "but my first priority now is to find our girls."

SATURDAY, JULY 12, 11:12 P.M. MT
Morgreed Industries reactor complex—Grand Junction, Colorado
Elevation: 4,583 feet

"They're back!" Autumn yelled as Roman and Valentina rushed into the decontamination chamber and quickly closed the hatch to the reactor dome.

"I guess they were successful," Summer said. "I can't wait to hear what happened."

They watched through the air lock doors as Roman and Valentina were blasted with chemicals and soaps, rinsed with water, and then blown dry until no traces of moisture remained on their radiation suits. Then they entered the air lock and waited a few moments until the door to the changing room opened.

"You did it!" Summer removed Valentina's helmet.

"No," Valentina said. "Something made it stop at the last moment. I don't know what happened."

"But it stopped," Roman said, working on removing his suit. "There must be a good reason."

Valentina gave him a worried look. "I'll feel better if we can figure that out."

"Is there a control room here that could give us a clue?" Roman asked.

Valentina paused. "Yes, perhaps. They're all linked to the system."

"Your radiation indicator is red," Autumn said, helping remove Valentina's suit. "Will you be okay?"

"Considering we should all be dead, I'll be fine."

"How's your shoulder?" Summer asked as she pulled off the straps for the air tank.

Valentina winced but then smirked. "I don't think this is what Dr. Leah had in mind when she said to take it easy."

"You are amazing." Roman leaned in to give her a kiss. "You were so brave in there. I don't know how you do it."

One of the militiamen cleared his throat. "Sir, is there anything you'd like us to do next?"

"Yes, we'll need to get to the reactor control room as soon as my wife is ready. You may need to open more doors."

"There," Autumn said, placing the strap of the sling over Valentina's shoulder. "Is that good?"

Valentina nodded. "Yes, let's go."

SATURDAY, JULY 12, 9:47 P.M. AKDT (11:47 P.M. MT)
Barter Island control base—Barter Island, Alaska
Elevation: 36 feet

"I took anything that might freeze," Craig said, entering the control building with an armload of supplies from the helicopter. "I don't know what the temperature is out there, but it is not warm."

"Thanks." Laura laid out their sleeping bags on the floor.

Everyone jumped at the sound of a phone ringing.

"What's that?" Holly asked.

Milford was closest to the phone and picked it up. "Hello?"

"Who is this?" a distinctly Russian female voice asked.

"Dr. Severnaya?"

"Dr. Pennychuck?"

"How . . ." they said at the same time.

"Where are you?" Milford asked, putting the phone on speaker as the others gathered around. For once, he was glad to hear from her.

"We're in the control room of the reactor in Grand Junction, Colorado. I've been calling the system control bases over the satellite link."

A chill ran through him. "Is Katherine with you?" Was there really no way to access the system? Had he thought of everything?

"No. I assume she's dead. What are you doing in Alaska? How did you even get there?"

No. She said no. What a relief. "We flew here. Craig found another helicopter. We stopped the system."

"Thank God. We were attempting to disable the reactor, but it shut down on its own."

"It's off for good. I've made sure of it."

"Milford, who is with you?"

"Laura and Craig Pottersmith, Holly, and Ashley." There was something different in Dr. Severnaya's voice, but he couldn't identify it.

"What about Barry?"

"No, he died."

"Oh . . . " She sounded like she was drifting away.

"Dr. Severnaya?" Milford asked.

"Hello?" another woman said.

"Summer?" Laura asked.

"Mom!"

"Honey, are you okay? Is Autumn with you?"

"Yes, we're fine. We're with Roman and Valentina."

"We've been so worried about you."

"So have we. Where are you guys?"

"Alaska. Dad's here—and Holly and Ashley and Milford. Can you put us on speaker phone?"

"No, this doesn't have it."

"Hi, Summer," Milford said. "Can you put Dr. Severnaya back on?"

"Not now. She's really upset about something."

"Oh," Milford said. "Well, who else is there?"

"Autumn and me, Roman, and a bunch of militia guys."

"Summer," Laura said, "how did you get there?"

"We ran into the militia during our hike, and Roman had lots of questions, and then his wife, Valentina, showed up, and we all moved to Leadville. We're heading back tonight."

"Dr. Severnaya is married?" Milford asked. Her? What kind of man could possibly—

"She is."

Although Barry did say there was more to her . . .

"Are there survivors there?" Craig asked.

"Yes, Dad. Thousands. Valentina had us make bomb shelters, and then carbon snow came down from the sky. Everyone's okay. Can you guys come?"

"Yes," Craig replied, "but it will take a while. We're staying here overnight, and it's slow going by helicopter."

"Great! We can't wait to see you. Hang on. I think Valentina wants to talk again."

"We love you," Laura said.

"You, too. Bye."

"Dr. Pennychuck?" Dr. Severnaya said, her voice shaky.

"Yes." What was she so upset about?

"How did it happen?"

"What?"

"Barry. How did he die?"

"Dr. Severnaya," Craig said, "I can answer that. We went onto a balloon together and cut off the reflector. He wouldn't leave until the job was done, and he saved my life in the process."

"That makes two of us . . . We need to leave soon. It's a long drive back to Leadville. Dr. Pennychuck, are you sure the system can't be run again? I don't want to worry about Katherine's people causing any more trouble."

"Yes," Milford said. "I grounded the balloons, turned off autocontrol, and disabled all log-in profiles."

"How? Barry removed your access."

"Yes, but fortunately he shared his password with me once. The system is dead." There. He'd actually said it. He never could have imagined saying those words so soon after starting the system. It was over. All those years . . . all the planning . . . the anticipation. And after all that, seeing it end brought such relief.

"That's good," Dr. Severnaya said. "I need to say goodbye for now. We have to go, but we'll meet when you reach Leadville. We have a lot to talk about."

"We certainly do." Milford paused. "Goodbye."

"Goodbye, Milford."

He waited a moment and then pressed the button to hang up. It finally came to him. Dr. Severnaya sounded . . . nice.

Laura put a hand on his shoulder. "Is everything okay?"

He turned to her as a tear rolled down his cheek. "Yes, Laura. It is."

EPILOGUE

"Summer, Autumn," Laura called from the kitchen, "can you set the table?"

"Sure, Mom." Autumn came in from the next room and took some plates from a cabinet.

"That smells good," Summer said. "How many place settings do we need?"

"Ten—and the high chairs," Laura replied after counting through the guest list in her head.

"We're going to have a full house," Craig said, looking up from chopping vegetables.

A knock sounded from the front door. "I'll get that." Summer walked down the hall and returned with Holly and Ashley and their husbands.

"We brought dessert," Holly said. "Sorry we're a little early."

"Nonsense," Laura said, giving her a hug. "How's life across the street treating you?"

"Good, and thanks for your help with the garden yesterday. I think it will be a good year."

"Sure. I think so, too. And how are you, Ashley?"

"I'm still feeling pretty good," she said, taking a seat at the counter, "but tomorrow is my last day at the hospital before the baby comes. Dr. Russet wouldn't budge on that."

"I can't wait," Laura said. "You're going to be a great mom."

"Thanks."

"I think I hear the door again," Summer said.

"Auntie Summer!" a pair of toddlers shouted as they rushed into the kitchen.

"Hey, kids!" she said, kneeling to give them a hug. "I hope you're hungry."

"Yes!" They squirmed away.

"They're so cute," Laura said as they darted between her legs and giggled.

Valentina entered the kitchen and smiled. "And they're quite a handful. They've learned how to climb, and now nothing in our house is safe."

"We made some bread," Roman said, placing a basket on the counter. "We had a salad, too, but they got to it and dumped it on the floor."

Laura grinned. "Twins . . . At least you have a boy and a girl. I don't know if you could handle sisters."

Valentina laughed. "I don't know either. Speaking of handling . . . Summer, can you and Autumn watch them next Saturday? Roman and I would like to go hiking."

"Yeah, I think so."

"What are you signing me up for?" Autumn asked from the dining room, struggling to walk around the table with Valentina's children clinging to her legs and laughing.

Summer chuckled. "She means yes."

"Valentina, Roman," Laura said, "take a seat. We're just about ready to eat."

"Thanks," Roman said. "I'm very hungry. I was helping to build housing today."

"How's that going?" Craig asked.

"Good. We should have a home for every family by next year."

"We don't mind sharing," Holly said. "It's nice to be together."

Ashley raised an eyebrow. "You might not think so once I ask you for help changing diapers."

"No, that will be great," Holly said. "You'll need to return the favor soon enough."

"Holly? Are you . . . "

"Oh," she said, putting a hand over her mouth. "We weren't quite ready to announce that."

Ashley pushed herself off the chair to give her sister a hug. "Congratulations!"

Roman laughed. "This is why we need to build more houses. We won't all fit in Leadville if it keeps up."

"That would be wonderful," Laura said, moving everyone to the dining room. "It's a sign that we have hope. Please take your seats. Thanks for coming. I would like to share a few thoughts. Today marks three years since we stopped the climate system. Our time since then hasn't been easy, but we've pressed on and faced the challenges together. It's so exciting to see life beginning anew, even around our little table, and I wish Milford was still alive to see it. He would have enjoyed being an honorary grandpa."

She paused, allowing a moment of silence. "I want all of you to know how grateful I am for you. I feel so blessed to have you all right here on our little street. Craig, thanks for being such a wonderful husband and father. You've been our steady rock. Summer and Autumn, I love you with all of my heart. Every day I give thanks to God that you were returned to us safely. Holly and Ashley, I'm so happy for you both. I can't imagine our family without you. Roman, I can never thank you enough for watching over our girls and convincing them to stay at the camp with you instead of continuing on the trail. You've also done outstanding work bringing unity to this town."

"It's easier than selling cars," Roman said, sharing a wink with Summer and Autumn.

"And, Valentina," Laura continued, "I still can't fathom the hardships you endured, but it's been amazing to see you use your story to help others. You truly inspire me, and you've become my dearest friend and colleague. It brings me such joy to see the happiness you've found and the peace God has given you."

Valentina stood, tears welling in her eyes, and wrapped her arms around Laura. "Thank you," she said as she hugged her. "Thank you all. You've been so wonderful to me, which reminds me of something. A long time ago I was asked a question by someone I'd rather not mention. She wanted to know about my dreams for the future. Looking around this table now, I realize I have a hope and a purpose beyond anything I could have imagined. I have the best friends in the world and a family that . . . " Valentina paused, turning to her toddler son, who was yanking on her arm from his high chair.

"Hold you, Mommy!" He reached for her with pudgy little hands.

"Of course," she said, scooping him up.

"Me, too!" her daughter demanded.

Valentina picked her up as well. "I have a—"

"Family hug!" her son shouted, eliciting a laugh from everyone.

Roman stood and embraced them, and one by one the others around the table circled around and joined in.

"I have a family that loves me," Valentina said, her face radiant with joy, "and a place I can call home."

THE END

"He heals the heartbroken
and bandages their wounds.
He counts the stars
and assigns each a name.
Our Lord is great, with limitless strength;
we'll never comprehend what he knows and does.
God puts the fallen on their feet again."
PSALM 147:3–6 MSG

AUTHOR'S NOTE

CLIMATE CHANGE CONTINUES TO BE one of the most politically divisive issues in our world. My intent in writing this story was not to address that debate but to explore the problems that can be created when the people trusted to provide solutions bring other priorities into the mix. As Dr. Pennychuck would say, politics and profit are some of the biggest obstacles preventing us from coming to consensus on this issue.

Regarding the science and physics of "the system," one doesn't have to think too hard to envision the many devastating effects that the process as described would have in reality. I've intentionally left some things vague or inconsistent, as otherwise I fear the situation would be so grim for the survivors that humanity would have no hope of continued existence. I will leave it to the reader to imagine what life in Leadville would be like for our protagonists following the events of the book, but I like to envision them living happily in close community. There would likely be other survivors around the world, but only a very small percentage of the population lives at high enough elevation to have escaped the field.

I would like to touch on one aspect of the story that I struggled with. As a Christian and an author, it's important to me to share my faith in Jesus. I worked that in explicitly in my first novel, *You Bring the Coffee, I'll Save the World,* in which a few of the characters have very frank discussions on faith as one of the minor plot lines. Some of the characters in this book do express their faith and offer prayer, which would be a very real response to what they faced; however, I decided it should be subtle. Craig, Laura, Summer, Autumn, Holly, and Ashley draw their strength from their belief that God is in control. They trust that He will see them through and bring their family back together. It's a wonderful thought, but it brings up many hard questions. As Summer and Autumn discussed, would God allow the actions of humans to wipe out nearly the entire population of earth? I think not, assuming that would not be in line with His plans. Thus, I view this story as a sort of alternate theological reality where the questions may not have answers aligning with the world we know but nevertheless the light of Jesus shines through. I'll leave it at that.

Finally, a few words about Valentina. My original concept for her was to be an associate of Katherine Morgreed with similar goals and aspirations to those of the Society. The character evolved into an unwilling henchman pressured to do Katherine's bidding. However, as I filled in her story to explain her relationship to Katherine, she quickly became my favorite character to write about and took a leading role. She served to illustrate just how wicked and heartless Katherine was, and as I wrote her story, the image of her in my head cried out for help, much as Barry saw the plea in her eyes as she collapsed at the control terminal.

Writing is an intriguing process. Imagining these scenes and interactions brings on real emotions, and tears came to my eyes many times as I wrote Valentina's experience. In a way, she embodies the suffering that so many women endure. Whether it's the loss of a baby, an abusive relationship, or the struggle to cope with the demands of career and family, so many women face difficult situations that apply disproportionately to their gender. They are vulnerable, but at the same time, like Valentina, the strength they exhibit can be extraordinary. Mother's Day passed as I was working on this novel, and I was struck with a deep appreciation for the mothers (and women in general) that I know and for what they go through day to day. They are amazing, and that sentiment clearly added some color to the ending of my story. Valentina will never get back the child that was taken from her or the years that she lost, but she finally came to a place where she is loved and cherished, and with God's help, her heart has been made whole. I pray all who are hurting will find that as well.

Now, go outside, take a deep breath, and be thankful that the system will never run again.

ACKNOWLEDGMENTS

I AM DEEPLY GRATEFUL TO the many people who provided inspiration, encouragement, and assistance throughout the writing of this novel.

Melissa—my loving wife, number one fan, and hardest critic. You know when the story is working and when I've gone off track. I can always trust your judgment. Thank you so much for all your support and excitement as I've pursued this journey. I love you!

Calista—my daughter. This is all above your head for now, but the joy and love you've added to our family have brought new meaning to our lives and provided countless quotable moments of cuteness and laughter. I would not have been prepared to write this book before God blessed us with you.

Mom and Dad—thank you for the many things you do for us and for your assistance with the scientific premise and other suggestions for improvement. You've provided love and support, and I'm so thankful for our family.

"Milford"—though your portrayal in the book bears little resemblance to you, it was your involvement with environmental science that spurred my train of thought leading up to the Pennychuck plan. I've greatly appreciated your enthusiasm and helpful critique.

Laura—you inspired this whole adventure with one little clay mug so lovingly made. You have a kind and gentle heart that shines through your smile, and thinking of you as a potential character when I was brainstorming my next novel opened the door to prominent themes of family and relationship that made this the story it is.

Craig—I hope you like you in the book! Give your wife a hug, take care of her, and never let her go. Also, consider helicopter lessons.

"Katherine"—it's probably best you never know who you are.

Leah and Jansen—your hospitality has been so generous. Thank you for being such good friends.

Jocelyn—my first test reader. Your quick feedback and positive response gave me great encouragement, and I value the friendship we've built since. Thanks for putting up with all my questions, and stay safe on those snowy summits.

Erin, Kelly, and the other members of Seek the Peak Group—thank you for reading this novel in its early form and sharing your thoughts.

Ryan—thank you for your detailed input about operations and facilities on Mount Washington. I've attempted to keep things as accurate as possible where fictional integrity allows. I do apologize for locating the helipad by the main parking lot, but that makes it so much more convenient for Craig.

Rachel—your critiques as a fellow writer were most welcome, and I can't thank you enough for the care you put into your notes. You helped me craft a better story.

Katelyn—thank you for your assistance as I queried this novel. Your insights and recommendations were invaluable to drafting a good pitch.

Holly—it was because of you that I joined Twitter and found the writing community on there. Thank you! I'll never know what would have happened otherwise.

Bethany—your challenge to do what we do for God's glory came at just the right time as I was contemplating whether and how to include my faith in this story. You are truly unstoppable.

Avril—you have brought tears to my eyes and tugged at my heart. I tried my best to pour that feeling into several scenes where I needed it. Thank you for sharing your story so honestly.

The Mount Washington Observatory—thank you for your tireless efforts to provide summit forecasts to aid us hikers in planning our trips safely. Your little fortress on the rock pile was an easy choice for one of the main locations in this book.

#FaithPitch—thank you for providing the platform that connected me with my publisher.

The team at Ambassador International—thank you for believing in my book and giving me this opportunity to reach the world with my story! I humbly offer all praise to God.

Kayla—my editor. You showed me where improvement was needed after I thought the novel was finished, and it's a stronger book because of it. I've learned so much from your comments and corrections. You understood the minds of my characters (and everything else about the story), and your insight has been invaluable. You're the best. Thank you!

Jesus—You have made all this possible. Thank You for the certainty of hope that we have in You, regardless of what happens around us.

Finally, to all the Valentinas that I know and the many more that I don't—in one way or another, your stories and strengths contributed to the heart of this novel. Keep up the fight. You are loved.

For more information about
Michael James Emberger
and
Silent Altitudes
please visit:

www.michaeljamesemberger.com
www.facebook.com/MichaelJamesEmberger
@MEmbergerAuthor

For more information about
AMBASSADOR INTERNATIONAL
please visit:

www.ambassador-international.com
@AmbassadorIntl
www.facebook.com/AmbassadorIntl

Thank you for reading this book. Please consider leaving us a
review on your social media, favorite retailer's website,
Goodreads or Bookbub, or our website.

More from Ambassador International

Akhan and Tarpi, two prisoners from Africa, are being trafficked to Europe when an attack forces them into a life-altering journey. As they try to stay one step ahead, the two friends meet someone who unexpectedly turns their life around.

Meanwhile, the secret society behind the world government is making their move. Through science, assassinations, and religion they are posed to set the ultimate ruler into place.

Former Navy SEAL Doyle has been prowling the broken remnants of a devastated America for years. Alone in an armored bus loaded with weapons and supplies, he's grateful for his solitude. Being alone makes it easier to survive, as others can become a liability in the end of the world. But when a particularly brutal attack leaves Doyle in need of fuel and repair, he has no choice but to venture into the nearest settlement . . .

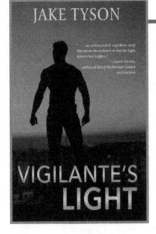

After being captured in Venezuela by guerrillas and used as a genetic engineering experiment, Gideon finds himself with strange super-abilities.

When he is rescued and returns home to Sojourn City, it is in shambles. The police are understaffed and the poorest area, the Brooks, is torn apart by crime.

Gideon decides the city needs a vigilante protector, but at what price?

9 781649 600509